Mandy Magro lives in Cairns, Far North Queensland, with her husband, Billy, and her daughter, Chloe Rose. With pristine aqua-blue coastline in one direction and sweeping rural landscapes in the other, she describes her home as heaven on earth. A passionate woman and a romantic at heart, she loves writing about soul-deep love, the Australian rural way of life and all the wonderful characters who live there.

www.facebook.com/mandymagroauthor

www.mandymagro.com

MANDY MAGRO

Flame Tree Hill

mira

This edition published by Mira 2019
First published by Penguin Group (Australia) 2013
ISBN 9781489263575

Published by
Mira
An imprint of Harlequin Enterprises (Australia) Pty Limited (ABN 47 001 180 918), a subsidiary
of HarperCollins Publishers Australia Pty Limited (ABN 36 009 913 517)
Level 13, 201 Elizabeth St
SYDNEY NSW 2000
AUSTRALIA

® and TM (apart from those relating to FSC ®) are trademarks of Harlequin Enterprises Limited
or its corporate affiliates. Trademarks indicated with ® are registered in Australia, New Zealand
and in other countries.

A catalogue record for this book is available from the National Library of Australia
www.librariesaustralia.nla.gov.au

Printed and bound in Australia by McPherson's Printing Group

For my beautiful mate, Katie

Prologue

LOUD country music blared from the speakers of the Commodore as it roared down the darkened road. The four teenagers within were in high spirits, bantering as they drove home. The paddock party to celebrate the end of high school had been massive. A night to remember, full of excited conversations of what the future would hold now that their school years were behind them, be it uni, jobs in the city or a more permanent role helping run the family properties around Hidden Valley. At four in the morning the country roads were deserted, apart from the occasional kangaroo. One bounced across the road ahead, causing the driver to swerve a little. The dangers of drink driving had been drummed into everyone at school, and by their parents, but what could go wrong on a long dirt road with no other traffic for miles?

'Fucking hell, look out!' someone yelled from the back seat.

An enormous bull stood metres away from the speeding car, its eyes wide in the headlights. The panicked driver swerved to avoid a collision and the Commodore spun wildly out of control on the dirt road. The passengers screamed in terror while the driver fought to regain control. Within seconds their lives were hanging by a thread.

An earth-shuddering crash was instantly followed by the crunching of metal as the car flipped onto its roof and slammed into a massive gum tree. Then, just as abruptly, everything fell silent, the pungent smell of leaking fuel filling the air. Slowly the driver's eyes opened on the horrific scene. Was it possible they had all miraculously made it through alive? And how long was it going to take for someone to find them?

Chapter 1

KIRSTY Mitchell tidied up her paperwork and switched off the desk lamp, groaning with fatigue as she pulled on her bulky woollen jacket. She glanced out of her fifteenth-floor office window, dismayed that there wasn't even a flicker of sunlight left to brighten her monotonous day. It was five-thirty in the afternoon but the sun had clocked off hours ago, leaving night to fall like a thick shroud. The darkness made her feel as though she were suffocating at times; she would have given her right arm to see at least an hour of sunshine a day. But her demanding job as a secretary at a solicitor's firm meant she was in the office before daybreak, and when she finally walked out the doors at the end of the day, there were only shadows cast by the streetlamps lining Fleet Street to greet her.

Even though Kirsty had lived in the UK for over a year, she still wasn't used to the lack of vitamin D and was beginning to understand how people could suffer from seasonal affective disorder, otherwise known as SAD. Not that she was overly depressed – just sick and tired of the dreary, bleak winter. It wasn't in her nature to be stuck in an office all day long, or wearing a posh suit, high heels, pantyhose and make-up. But here she was, in the big smoke, doing just that. As her mother always used to say, you can take the girl out of the country but you can't take the country out of the girl. But her working visa was almost finished, and soon she would be back on home soil with plenty of sunshine to enjoy. On the one hand, she couldn't wait to get back to the tropics of North Queensland, but on the other . . . she had left for a good reason. How was she going to cope being back among the people she had held the truth from for all these years? Would she arrive home only to run away again?

The lift seemed to take forever to get to the ground floor. Kirsty tucked her scarf into her thick jacket and stepped out into the foyer. She glided easily through the revolving doors, a feat that had taken her days to master when she first started working in the building. Now she shuddered as she stepped out into the icy wind, her eyes instantly watering, the ache to feel sunshine upon her skin almost overwhelming her. Pulling her scarf up and over her mouth, she tugged her beanie down as far as it would go, briefly glancing towards the night sky. The absence of sparkling stars was still so strange after living beneath glimmering country skies for most of her life. To Kirsty's surprise, white fluffy snow covered everything in sight, cheering her up a little. The forecast had said it was going to snow, but in London snow often turned to slush within minutes. She adored the way the snowflakes fell so effortlessly from the sky, floating down, before coming to rest. It was blissful to watch.

Shoving her gloved hands into her pockets, she moved briskly towards home, her high-heeled shoes tapping the pavement with each stride. Only three more weeks and she would be basking in a glorious Aussie summer, surrounded by her loved ones. But after three years away would everything still feel the same? Would the haunting memories of the accident plague her relentlessly if she were living back near where it had all happened? She thought briefly of her camera and photography stuff, stored in a dusty cupboard at her parents' house. After high school she had received her acceptance letter from Griffith University, a Bachelor's degree in photography within her grasp. But the accident had changed everything. Kirsty hoped her love of photographing the rural landscape could be rekindled.

Photography had been her passion ever since her parents had given her a Polaroid camera for her seventh birthday. She would photograph absolutely anything, watch with amazement as the photo slid out, then stand and shake it gently until the picture emerged. She still found it enchanting, the way a photo could capture a moment forever. Her friends and family had kept encouraging her, telling her she had a gift. A university degree would have established her worth, given her the confidence to follow her dream.

Kirsty's bag vibrated as Jimmy Barnes's husky voice sang 'Khe Sanh' from its confines. She quickly rifled through the bottomless pit, moving aside her purse, keys, lipstick, perfume and packets of chewy until she found her mobile phone. She flicked it open just before it went to voicemail.

'Hello?'

'Hey, sis! Happy birthday!'

'Robbie! Oh my goodness! It's so good to hear your voice.'

Her brother's Aussie drawl gave Kirsty a rush of homesickness.

'I tried to ring you at home but obviously you're not there. Have you had a good day? Any plans for tonight?'

'I'm off to the Velvet Club with Jo and Calvin – it's a great place in Soho. We're meeting a few mates there for drinks then hopefully I'm going to dance till dawn. Well, that's the plan anyway – not too sure if I can pull an all-nighter . . . Getting a bit old for it.'

'Ah, the lovely Jo . . . Say hi to her for me. Sounds like you two are up for a big one. Wish I was there with you.' Robbie had had a sweet spot for Kirsty's best friend Jo for years. Not that anything had happened between them – at least not that Kirsty knew about. 'And you're not that bloody old, sis – twenty-four is a spring chicken in my book. Try being twenty-seven. I'm going to need false teeth and a walking stick soon, I reckon.'

Kirsty heard her dad mumble something in the background and Robbie replied with an 'Oi, fair go, Dad.' She rolled her eyes, smirking, missing their repartee and Robbie's dry humour. 'Come on, twenty-seven is hardly old either. Anyway, how are things back home?' she asked while walking as fast as she could, dodging the bigger snowdrifts.

'All's good here. Dad's got me working from dusk till dawn, as usual. There never seems to be enough hours in the day to get everything done. I miss having you around to keep us blokes on our toes, Kirsty. I'm counting down the weeks till you come home. Not long now, hey?'

'I know, only three weeks to go. I'm disappointed I won't be back for Christmas, but I couldn't get any flights. We'll have to have a belated Christmas dinner in January.'

'Sounds like a plan. Any excuse for a roast dinner is a winner with me. Anyway, Mum and Dad want to talk too so I'll pass you over.'

'Okay, Robbie. Love you and miss you loads.'

'Love you and miss you too, sis. Have fun tonight, and if you can't be good, be good at it!'

Dancing on her tiptoes in the bathroom, Kirsty stripped off three layers of clothing, almost hanging herself with her scarf in her haste, goosebumps covering her body. It had been difficult talking to her parents, especially her mum. Lynette often got a bit teary on the phone, and it made Kirsty realise that it was definitely time to go home – at least for a visit. From her position in front of the old-fashioned handbasin, she stared back at her reflection, amazed at how pale her skin was. It was almost translucent; she was sure she could have quite easily passed as an albino with her long blonde hair and pale blue eyes. She gently traced her finger over the thick red scar that ran from her hipbone to her navel, and she swallowed hard. Six years later and the emotions were still so raw, the nightmares of that fateful night still haunting her sleep. Why had her life been spared when three of her good mates had lost theirs?

She made a mad dash for the shower, hurriedly turning the brass taps, hearing the all too familiar sound of the old copper pipes clanking and banging as they struggled to carry water up from three floors below. She groaned, watching her breath mist in front of her. The central heating had kicked the bucket that morning – not the best thing to happen in the middle of December in England. Upon awaking at six that morning she'd felt as though she were suffering mild hypothermia and frostbitten toes. Wrapping her doona around her, she had pulled on her fluffy white slippers that looked like a pair of lambs and even bleated like them too – a gift from her mother – and shuffled to the phone. Her landlord had listened half-heartedly as she pleaded with him to fix it as soon as he could, her teeth chattering uncontrollably over the phone, his five children creating havoc in the background. Mr Fix-It-Tomorrow had promised he would call by while she was at work but from previous experience Kirsty knew that could mean next week, if she was lucky. She huffed. What an inconsiderate man, leaving her and Jo living in a freaking igloo!

Kirsty's skin tingled as the water spilled from the shower and trickled over her body, leaving trails of scarlet on her skin from the heat. She liked it that way, often emerging from the shower with her body looking as if it had severe burns to its every inch. Maybe it was her unconscious way of feeling like she was back in the baking heat on her family's cattle farm, Flame Tree Hill. Her boyfriend, Calvin, who was a solicitor at her office, refused to bathe with her because of it, although he did try once. His balls were almost fried to a crisp as he attempted to submerge beneath the bubbles of the bathtub, discovering the scalding water when it was too late. Kirsty had had to stifle a laugh as he scurried from the tub, slipped on the wet tiled floor and landed flat on his backside, screaming that his knackers were well and truly knackered, his cockney humour shining through. They'd been together for almost a year and Calvin made Kirsty laugh until her sides ached. She loved his company, but she had to admit that there wasn't much sexual chemistry between them. She loved him for who he was but she wasn't *in* love with him . . . and she was pretty certain he felt the same way, both of them knowing full well that the relationship would end when she headed back to Australia. It was a shame they hadn't fallen madly in love, true love being something she had wished for for years. Was she ever going to be lucky enough to find 'the one' and experience a reciprocated, all-encompassing, deep love? She hoped so.

Kirsty had only ever felt deep, all-consuming, take-your-breath-away love once in her life. But the man in question had packed his bags and headed off to the city to gain a veterinary degree, and before he'd finished studying she'd headed overseas. She hadn't seen him for years. She knew he was married now, and she wondered if he was happy with his life. She'd never have thought he was the sort of bloke to like living in the city. But then again, she never would have thought she'd like it either. She adored London in the spring and summer, and the ease of having everything at your fingertips was a nice contrast to the isolation of the country and the standard hour's drive to get your groceries.

As she lathered up her body, the scent of lavender soap wafting pleasantly within the lingering steam, Kirsty found her thoughts wandering back over her time away from Australia. In three years, she had done a lot of travelling, spending two years making her way through Bali, Thailand, Vietnam, Nepal and parts of America and Europe before coming to live in the UK. It had opened her eyes, given her more understanding of the ways of the world. Since she moved to the UK, she'd seen some jaw-dropping castles, stood in awe in front of Bucking-ham Palace, tried to make the Queen's guards crack a smile without success, shopped in Harrods – well, sort of, as she couldn't afford to buy anything – drunk copious amounts of lager, eaten the stinkiest, mouldiest cheeses she had ever seen (*and* loved them), watched countless games of football, driven down country lanes with the smell of spring in the air, chased lambs in lush green fields, mastered the art of making toad in the hole, won a few games of welly wanging and made some fantastic friends.

She knew the demons of her past were there, back in Hidden Valley, but the ache to return to the wide open spaces of her family property was too powerful to ignore any longer. She missed her family, her mates, her horse, her dog and all the things that made Australia home for her. The sun-scorched land, the huge open skies, mustering on the family property in her wide-brimmed hat, Vegemite on toast for breakfast, rodeos, the country music channel and of course the laconic Aussie humour.

Absent-mindedly, Kirsty watched the soap suds do a quick pirouette around the plughole before disappearing down the drain. Life had dealt her a blow, one that would haunt her for the rest of her life. She wished there was some way to erase the past but she knew that wishing was a waste of time. She exhaled slowly, trying to lift her spirits. It was Friday night *and* it was her twenty-fourth birthday. It had been a long, hard week at work and it was time to have some fun. She turned off the taps and bravely leapt from the shower, tugging her towel around her.

Chapter 2

ADEN Maloney swatted the flies from his face then dropped his gear bag on the dusty ground, grinning as he took in his surroundings. The country smells, sounds and sights were like coming home for him, a familiar comfort he hadn't experienced enough while living in Sydney. It felt like forever since he'd been able to attend a rodeo, let alone ride in one. His wife hadn't been keen on them. She was a bona fide city girl who chose to believe that bull riding was cruel to animals, whereas he knew from plenty of firsthand experience that rodeos were nothing of the sort. He was proud of the rich and colourful history of Australian rodeos and had tried to explain this to her but she'd refused to budge on her beliefs, angry he was defending his own. He had snuck off to the odd few, but it had always caused an argument, like so many other things in their marriage.

Watching the goings-on behind the chutes, Aden went through a rigorous stretching routine. Injury was almost certain if he didn't prepare his body for the brutal force of the bucking bull he was about to ride. Cowboys were arriving in droves, paying their fees from wallets or pockets as they joked with fellow riders. They were gladiators in one of the world's most dangerous sports and it was imperative to keep cool, to act tough. It was never about *if* you were going to get hurt, it was more like *when*. Aden knew this all too well, having endured many a broken bone, but it never stopped him wanting to go back for more.

Humming as he rifled through his gear bag, Aden pulled out chaps, spurs, ropes, straps, liniment, resin and his protective vest. His heart was already thudding heavily, his hands clammy. This was the most nerve-racking time. Once he was *on* the bull he'd be right; it was the preparation that made him tense, not knowing what was around the corner: a trophy, a heroic saunter back to the chutes after being tossed off in front of the fans or, heaven forbid, a ride in an ambulance. He'd drawn the short straw today, and was the opening act on one of the most feared bulls in the circuit.

Rodeos were just one of the many things Aden and his wife, Tammy, had discovered they didn't have in common. They'd eloped within months of meeting each other and the novelty of winning a city girl's heart disappeared once reality kicked in. They had given it their best shot – four years, to be exact – and had even gone to marriage counselling, but in the end they had agreed to split. It hadn't been an easy decision but it was the right one, for both of them. Now here he was, on the road, on the way back to his home town of Hidden Valley, making a few pit stops at rodeos along the way to satisfy the desire inside him for bull riding. It was his passion, the ultimate test of courage.

The rodeo grounds were a bustle of activity, a steady stream of people and horses weaving through goosenecks, food vans and trailers; excitement and expectation hung heavily in the electric atmosphere. Families were sprawled on picnic blankets eating and drinking, children were high on fairy floss, and couples sat on the bum-numbing benches in the grandstands while mates caught up with each other at the bar, hats and sunnies donned to ward off the sweltering sunshine. Aden knew some spectators came every year to the event, rain, hail or shine, while others were newcomers, easy to spot by their dazed smiles and the stark newness of their Akubras. Volunteers manned smoking barbecues or dashed around behind the bar, while the Country Women's Association caught up on the town gossip behind the cake and coffee stand. Everyone from the small community of Yarringin pitched in and pulled their weight, providing a perfect day for a family outing. Aden hadn't realised until now just how much he had missed the community spirit that went with country towns.

Back behind the arena, stock contractors unloaded prized livestock into the holding yards, the many hoofs exiting the cattle trucks thundering over the shouts and whistles. It was organised chaos. The cattle and horses stomped and snorted, pranced and whinnied, as they were gathered in the selected yards, some of them displaying their dominance over the others by biting, kicking or bucking. Aden took a deep, controlled breath, psyching himself, silently confirming he could do this. Not long now. Country tunes faded in and out over the PA: Garth Brooks, Waylon Jennings, Adam Brand and Johnny Cash. Cowgirls and cowboys, dressed in glitzy chaps and western clothing, sat along the railing, above the chutes awaiting Aden's entry to the arena.

The water truck did its rounds in the centre ring, attempting to settle the dust that was suspended over everything. The arena's massive speakers crackled to life as the announcer introduced the national anthem. Aden watched as the spectators stood proudly, holding their hats or hands to their chests, some singing and some miming the words. A minute of silence followed, in remembrance of all the rodeo riders who had lost their lives to the sport they loved. And then it was showtime.

Aden nodded to indicate he was ready. The crowd cheered as the rope was pulled and the colourful chute gate flung open. The snorting, belligerent bull exploded into the ring, determined to get Aden off its back. Aden felt his body shudder with every buck. The bull was hell on hoofs, spinning, lunging and belting out high-kicking bucks. With one arm held high in the air to balance himself, Aden kept the other firmly around the bull strap, thankful for his leather glove, using everything he had to stay pinned to the back of the bull. His adrenaline pumped and the roar of the crowd grew as the buzzer announced that he had made it to eight seconds. Aden grinned triumphantly, the taste of dust in his mouth, as he leapt efficiently to the ground and ducked away from the bull's deadly horns with the help of the experienced rodeo clowns. The bull veered back towards him, a glint in its eye. Aden swiftly heaved himself over the fence and out of the bull's direct path, his entire body buzzing. For the first time in years Aden felt truly alive.

The scattered clouds reflected vivid shades of red and orange as dawn broke over the distant horizon. Aden stretched languorously as he raised his head from his pillow, captivated by the beauty of the outback sunrise. Around him people were beginning to wander about in their PJs, towels over their shoulders as they made their way to and from the portable showers. Horses were whinnying and the bellows of cattle travelled pleasantly on the gentle morning breeze. These were sounds Aden had missed. He could quite easily have lain here all morning in the back of his Land Cruiser, his mood relaxed, but with an eight-hour drive ahead of him he had to hit the road. Today he would be arriving at his final destination. The thought made his stomach flip.

After six years away, he knew there would be some tough challenges ahead. So much had happened in his life since he left. He'd been married and was now on his way to divorce; he'd completed a veterinary degree and become used to living in a city. And he'd tried countless times – with everything from counselling to spiritual gurus – to genuinely be able to forgive James for being behind the wheel of the car that had killed his younger sister six years ago.

One of the biggest lessons he'd learnt in this time was that he couldn't alter the past, so instead he was focused on looking towards his future with optimism. That was exactly what he was trying to do by going home to Hidden Valley, to find happiness in the place where his heart longed to be, and to be around all the people he loved dearly once more.

Aden stood and began to roll up his swag, eager to tuck in to some bacon and eggs before he was on his way. With the smell of sizzling bacon making his mouth water, he pulled on his boots and leapt down from the back of his Land Cruiser. Tugging on his wide-brimmed hat, he grabbed his breakfast supplies, billy can and tea leaves and headed over to where a large group stood around a campfire. It was time to gather the reins of his life and take control once again.

Chapter 3

'LADIES and gentlemen, please make sure your seats are in the upright position, your tray tables are secured and your seatbelts are fastened. We are beginning our descent into Cairns airport and will be landing in approximately fifteen minutes. The temperature today is a lovely thirty-two degrees. Thank you for choosing to fly with us, and we hope you enjoyed your flight.'

Kirsty yawned and stretched her cramped legs under the seat in front of her, watching out the window as the lush green mountain tops of Cairns came into view, surrounded by beautiful aqua blue water. It was a relief to finally be home after travelling for close to thirty hours. She could see the dark patches in the ocean below where the Great Barrier Reef swarmed with sea life. She had forgotten just how breathtaking tropical North Queensland really was.

It had been miserable saying goodbye to Jo and Calvin at Heathrow. She and Jo held onto each other for dear life as the final boarding calls were made, while Calvin had been so very quiet. Jo had assured Kirsty that she would be home in six months' time once her working visa had finished, and Kirsty knew that Jo always stuck to her promises. But Kirsty doubted she'd ever see Calvin again. They'd always known the day would come when they had to say goodbye, not getting more serious than either of them was ready for, but it didn't make it any easier.

After disembarking and collecting her luggage, Kirsty was waved through Customs and headed towards the crowd of people waiting for the passengers. She spotted Robbie a mile away, even after three years of not seeing him. He was over six feet tall, towering above most of the waiting crowd, his battered tan hat pulled firmly down over his mop of shaggy blonde hair. She smiled broadly. In his dusty jeans and chequered shirt he looked uniquely Australian.

As she pushed excitedly through the swarm of weary travellers, Kirsty glanced at the person next to Robbie and felt her breath catch in her throat. A similarly dressed man stood beside her brother, his dark chocolate eyes staring at her with a familiar hint of waywardness. She fought for breath, feeling as though someone had punched her in the chest. *Oh my God. It couldn't be. Could it? Oh shit!* She thought about turning around and running back to the plane, but the concern of looking like a complete lunatic stopped her in her tracks. Besides, the man had already spotted her and was smiling broadly in her direction, cheeks dimpling, his jet black hair hanging about his face in a way that gave him a rebellious edge, adding to his already rugged charm. Kirsty took a deep breath as she smiled back. 'Deep breaths, calm thoughts,' she whispered to herself.

'Robbie!' she squealed and ran towards her brother, falling into his warm embrace, breathing in the glorious scent of the country.

'Sis, you're finally home,' Robbie said with a broad grin as he gently pushed her back to look into her eyes. 'My God, you look so grown up! How are you?'

Kirsty nodded as a wobbly smile formed on her lips. 'I'm fine. It was horrible saying goodbye to Jo and Calvin but it's all good now I'm here with you.' She touched him on the arm. 'It's so good to see you!'

'You too,' Robbie replied, as he kissed her on the forehead.

Kirsty finally made eye contact with the man next to her brother. That distinctive scar above his lip – it was unquestionably Aden Maloney. Kirsty could still picture the horse lashing out and kicking Aden's face like it was yesterday, leaving him bloodied and bewildered while Kirsty's father ran to the house to call an ambulance. A few painkillers and fifteen stitches later, Aden had casually shrugged it off, saying that it wasn't the horse's fault, it was his own, and that he would have to be more wary when shoeing a nervous stallion next time. He still had the scar. She couldn't help but admire Aden's love for horses; it was obvious in the way he treated them with such respect, even when they occasionally hurt him. So it was no surprise to her that he'd chosen to become a vet.

Aden had been the one and only guy she'd had a crush on all the way through school. Not that Aden had ever noticed; he only ever seemed to see Kirsty as Robbie's annoying younger sister. The two boys were forever playing pranks on her, like putting GladWrap over the toilet seat or hiding frogs in her boots. They were absolute scallywags, always up to mischief. She had kept her infatuation with him hidden for fear of humiliation if he ever found out. She didn't even tell Robbie or Jo about him. Then, after the accident, Aden had moved down south to do his veterinary degree, swearing he'd never set foot back in Hidden Valley again. But here he was, flesh and blood, looking tall, dark and sexy as hell. She swallowed hard, her belly doing backflips, forward rolls and triple twists.

'Howdy, stranger,' Kirsty said casually, her voice betraying her nerves. 'I heard through the grapevine that you'd shacked up with some city sheila and got married. I thought you would have had three kids, a dog and a house with a white picket fence by now.' She suddenly worried about how bad her hair looked after not brushing it for almost two days, and whether her breath was okay, even though she had brushed her teeth several times on the plane.

Aden grinned. 'Nah, you're not getting rid of me that easily. Couldn't live in the city much longer.'

Kirsty looked at him quizzically, blowing a strand of hair from her eyes before she spoke. 'So what *are* you doing back in the sticks? Are you on holidays?'

Aden looked sideways at Robbie, hesitating slightly, and Robbie jumped in.

Relieved, Aden looked down at his boots as though the timeworn Blundstones were an object of deep fascination.

'Kirst, I meant to tell you on the phone last week. Aden's moved back to Mareeba and into the spare room at our cottage, just till he gets on his feet. He's decided to start a mobile vet service for Dimbulah and Mareeba. Lord knows we really need one in Hidden Valley, with only the one vet all the way over in Atherton.' Robbie ended his spiel by giving Kirsty an award-winning smile.

Aden looked up from the floor and made eye contact with Kirsty. She found it hard to keep the shock from her face. Aden Maloney, living under her own roof? Holy crap! She scratched at an imaginary itch on her head, her mind in a spin. 'Oh, um, well, sure. I s'pose.' Suddenly desperate to get away from Robbie and Aden, she looked around for an excuse, drumming her lips with her fingers. 'Give me a sec, I'm just going to grab a trolley for my bags.' She chortled uncomfortably then went in search of the baggage carousel, tripping over her feet but skilfully rebalancing herself before she fell flat on her face.

Aden watched her walk away, taking all of her in. It had been years since he'd seen Kirsty, and she'd certainly grown up, with curves in all the right places. She was still as beautiful as she'd always been, her powder blue eyes still so captivating. He mentally slapped himself. *She* was off limits and *he* was recently separated. 'You reckon she's all right with me staying with you, mate?' he asked Robbie. 'She seemed a little, well, dazed and confused.'

Robbie chuckled and threw his hands up in the air. 'Women, they're such complex creatures, hey! But don't worry about it, mate. She'll be fine. You're like a brother to her, always have been. She's probably just buggered from all the travelling, that's all. Tomorrow's a new day – let's talk about it some more then if we need to.'

Aden nodded as he and Robbie headed off to help Kirsty load her luggage. Her reaction wasn't what he'd expected. Why did she seem so nervous around him?

Chapter 4

THE stereo in Robbie's bush-beaten Land Cruiser was on full bore, John Williamson's distinctive voice singing 'I'm Fair Dinkum', as they headed up the Kuranda Range and towards Hidden Valley. Kirsty shuffled her feet along the rubber floor mat, kicking empty Red Bull cans, salt-and-vinegar chip packets and old newspapers out of the way. Robbie claimed that the rubbish, combined with the deep-rooted scent of cow manure in the interior and the thick layer of mud on the outside of his Toyota, gave the old girl character. Not everyone agreed. Kirsty was forever grateful he wasn't like that in the cottage they lived in behind their mum and dad's homestead. Everything had been kept spick and span, just how she liked it to be. She hoped Robbie had kept up his good house-cleaning skills while she'd been away.

The crisp, clean scent of the rainforest invigorated Kirsty's senses. In the distance a shawl of mist draped itself casually over the glorious mountain tops, and magnificent blue Ulysses butterflies danced about the dark green foliage at the side of the road. God, how Kirsty had missed these views. She sighed, contented, as she closed her eyes and breathed in deeply. It was so good to be home.

The Cruiser was snug with the three of them packed in, Aden's muscular thigh squashed up against Kirsty's, his tattooed arm draped over the back of her seat. Every now and then he would sing along to the stereo and she couldn't help but join in with him. It reminded her of days gone by when they would all hit the road on the weekends, in search of the next rodeo or B & S ball. She missed those days. It was so surreal having Aden beside her, the man she had pined for, cried over, felt sorrow for, and loved.

Robbie joined in with the singing too, mucking the words up and trying to cover up his mistakes with a few humming noises, causing them all to laugh. Once they reached the outskirts of Hidden Valley, the city of Cairns now far behind them, the roads began to fill with dusty four-wheel drives and utes, some of them with big stickers on the back windows or tailgates asserting a strong love of everything country. Some were of large bull's horns while others had sayings like *Give blood, ride bulls* or *Save a horse, ride a cowboy.*

Out her window Kirsty spotted the familiar colourful road sign advertising the Hidden Valley Bush Races in September. The massive sign had been there for an eternity, the date painted over each year with the new one. She pointed excitedly as they approached it. 'Are you going to be racing this year, Aden? It's months off yet – you've got heaps of time to prepare.'

Aden tipped his hat and peered out at the sign as it flashed past them, shrugging his shoulders casually. 'Dunno. My old boy is getting a bit long in the tooth for it. He's got fat, too, since I've been away. Mum feeds him too much. I'd be lucky to get him into a decent gallop.'

'You can enter Cash, if you like. He'd give the other horses a run for their money,' she replied.

'Great idea,' Robbie said. 'Why the hell not? It'd be a hoot!'

'Cheers, Kirsty, appreciate the offer. I'll have a think about it closer to the time,' Aden said.

Kirsty breathed in the magnificent smell of the country, a mixture of unpolluted air, fruit flowers, livestock and sun-kissed fields. London seemed like another world to her as she gazed out over the green sprawling hills covered with cattle and horses. Off in the distance a windmill turned lazily in the light breeze. Mango trees lined the sides of the road, their plump golden fruit hanging tantalisingly low. What she would give to eat one right now. Beads of sweat rolled down the curve of her back and trickled between her breasts, soaking through her shirt as the ever-deepening embrace of humidity encompassed her, a sensation she was unaccustomed to after so long away.

The Hidden Valley township hadn't changed one bit, other than the fire station having had a new lick of paint. It was strangely comforting to see that all was as it had been before Kirsty left; no big high-rises spoilt the view. There was no need for them here – there was plenty of space at ground level to fit in all that was required to keep the town running smoothly. Beautiful native trees lined the streets with vibrant flowers and the locals casually strolled, as if not really in a rush to do anything. Not like London, where everything and everyone was going a hundred k's an hour.

Two roundabouts and three train crossings later, they finally left the bitumen highway behind as Robbie indicated and turned right down Brooks Road, a trail of red dust and gravel flying out behind the Land Cruiser. The familiar ramshackle building on the corner was still hanging in there, the walls clinging despairingly to the decaying timber support beams. The roof had caved in aeons ago and there was a jungle of vines and creepers crawling over nearly every inch of it. Kirsty shivered at the thought of how many deadly snakes would be slithering among it all. She had never stepped foot near it, even though Robbie had often dared her to when they were growing up, and had no desire to do so in the future.

As the distance to home shortened, Kirsty's eagerness to get there grew. She flung off her seatbelt and manoeuvred herself so she could hang her head out the window, the wind flying through her long blonde hair, sending it across her face. Robbie slowed as he approached a massive iron gate, a set of bull's horns wired to the centre of it.

'I'll jump out and open it!' Kirsty shouted as she leapt from the Land Cruiser only to land smack-bang in a pile of fresh horse dung. 'Shit!'

'Yeah, exactly!' Aden chuckled as he peered out the door at her, his dimples accentuated by his playful grin and the scar above his lip giving him a charismatic bad-boy edge.

Kirsty looked up from her manure-covered heeled shoes and jokingly gave Aden the finger.

Just as she heaved open the heavy gate and latched it to the weathered timber post she spotted Hank running full pelt towards her, his tongue flapping around the side of his mouth like a flag. She squatted down to the ground to meet him and he ran into her outstretched arms, the force sending her flailing back to the earth as he licked her face profusely, smothering her cheeks in doggy saliva.

'Hank, my buddy, it's so good to see you!' she said as she struggled back up to a sitting position while ruffling his oversized ears. Kirsty had no idea what breeds he had in his bloodline, but the ears pointed to a hound somewhere in his ancestry. She had found him abandoned on the side of the highway eight years ago, and he had rapidly become her best mate. It had been hard leaving him behind when she went overseas. He wasn't really a working dog but he tried his best, normally being more of a hindrance than a help. Her dad's kelpies were the qualified working dogs, trained tirelessly by him to muster the cattle, but Hank's only job at Flame Tree Hill had been to keep Kirsty company, and he'd performed that flawlessly.

Robbie pulled inside the gate and Kirsty shut it securely behind him, deciding now to ride up in the back like she always did. With Hank and Kirsty safely on board, Robbie began the slow drive down the two-kilometre driveway. There was no speeding once you entered Flame Tree Hill; you had to watch out for the livestock.

Being in the back gave Kirsty a perfect view of the vast land she called home . . . and also gave her welcome breathing space from Aden. She was still finding it hard to believe he was *really* here. And couldn't help wondering if it was a good or bad thing. Living with him and Robbie was certainly going to be interesting. She gazed out over the fields, focusing on the beauty of the countryside, the warm breeze carrying with it the distant bellowing of cattle and the chattering of galahs perched high in the many flame trees that lined the sides of the drive. The commanding trees were now bare of leaves but swathed in clusters of striking red flowers. Flame trees only flowered for five weeks of the year and Kirsty felt very blessed to be arriving home to witness it. They were absolutely gorgeous. Hank let out a short, sharp bark as a wallaby went bounding past in a scurry to reach the scrub, but he knew better than to chase it. The bougainvilleas that hugged the front fence line were in full flower, while the jacarandas that dotted the paddocks had glorious purple flowers adorning them. Fields of lush green grass sprawled out before Kirsty with hundreds of healthy-looking red Brangus cattle enjoying the endless buffet. This is what Kirsty had missed, being so close to nature, and she sighed contently as Robbie turned left towards the homestead, leaving the paddocks trailing off behind them in the heat-hazed distance.

When Kirsty was eight, her parents Ron and Lynette had decided to quit sugar cane farming for good and expand into the cattle business. The Mitchells had always run cattle on Flame Tree Hill but only for themselves. One day Ron had turned up at the homestead in a shiny new red truck, a proud smile on his face and thirty Brangus cattle huddled in the back. Kirsty loved cattle, and the thought of having hundreds of them living on the property was like a dream come true. To her parents' surprise, Kirsty had taken to mustering like a duck to water. Her mum had found it impossible to keep her home when the men were going out. Kirsty's spirit thrived in the outdoors.

Her dad had chosen the Brangus breed of cattle because of its ability to handle tough grazing conditions, not uncommon in Hidden Valley. January was the wet season, and the feed might be in endless supply for now, but in the winter months the fields could soon become barren land if they had a year where there was little winter rain. Brangus cattle were a no-fad, no-frills breed renowned for its fertility and easy-calving capabilities. The meat's marbling and tender qualities combined with high-yielding carcases and minimum fat content put more money in the Mitchells' pockets. Also, being naturally polled, it eliminated the need to dehorn the calves, making the cattle easier to handle and minimising hide damage. Her dad proudly referred to them as lead on legs. Kirsty had found them to be a very gentle breed, always fairly easy to handle, other than the rare temperamental bull.

The timber homestead finally came into view and it stole Kirsty's breath. Lynette had mentioned that she'd made some improvements to the garden but Kirsty hadn't realised the extent. A new rustic timber fence encircled the home, giving it an even grander appearance than it had previously had. A pretty pebbled pathway snaked its way through a flourishing assortment of flowering native trees, arriving at the bottom of recently varnished timber steps leading to the front screen door. The old timber door had been replaced with a beautiful hardwood with vibrant leadlight flowers in the centre of it. Kirsty wondered if her mum had made it herself, being so clever in the art of leadlighting. The sweeping verandahs were shaded from the sun by two massive golden wattles, which swayed in the gentle breeze. The aged leather lounge chairs and couch were in the same position as always on the verandah, giving a perfect view of the horse paddocks.

Kirsty could just make out Cash in the distance, named after her country music hero, Johnny Cash. The horse was a mass of rippling muscles with an elegant and graceful exterior, his palomino coat stunning; he didn't have socks but did have an adorable snip on his muzzle. God, he was a handsome horse! He was sniffing a patch of wild lavender that was growing by the fence line. Kirsty grinned at his intelligence – horses were always interested in plant aromas, attracted to the essential oils within them. It was as though they knew the oils contained healing qualities.

Turning her gaze back to the flourishing garden, she continued to admire all her mum's hard work. Sprays of water shot out from a rotating sprinkler, the droplets catching the sunlight as they descended onto the dark green lawn, giving the impression of crystals floating in the air. A pair of rainbow lorikeets frolicked in the stone birdbath she'd given her mum a few years back. The panoramic views from the homestead were proof of why the spirit of the land had claimed her heart. After three years away she now saw everything with new eyes. Flame Tree Hill was a truly beautiful place, and she was so blessed to be able to call it home. She would never take it for granted again and she was going to try her damned hardest not to pack her bags and run away from it once more.

Robbie pulled into the drive and Aden leapt out of the passenger side, his boots crunching on the gravel as he held his hand out to help Kirsty down off the back.

Kirsty responded to his outstretched hand with raised eyebrows, heaving herself over the tray with vigour and snapping the small heel off her manure-covered shoe. She bent down to inspect the damage, groaning as she rubbed her throbbing foot.

'You should have let me help you, Kirsty. Still as stubborn as ever, I see.' Aden grinned as he shook his head.

'You betcha I'm still stubborn. Well, I like to call it "independent". I've jumped down from the back a million times on my own without the aid of a man. Just because I've lived in the city for a few years doesn't mean I've forgotten how to be a country girl.' Kirsty picked her shoes up and tossed them in the nearby wheelie bin. 'I don't need these damn shoes any more. They're bloody lethal out here. It'll be a nice change to be living back in my trusty old boots again.'

Aden laughed as she dusted off her hands and hobbled back to the truck, admiring her feistiness. It was a trait he found very attractive. 'Would you like me to grab your luggage, Miss

Determination, or will you clobber me if I try to help you?'

Robbie chuckled. 'You two don't take long to get back into the swing of things, do you? I've missed hearing you stirring each other up.'

Kirsty grinned at Robbie and then turned her attention back to Aden. 'It'd be great if you could take my bags into the cottage, thanks. I'm just going to head in to see Mum and Dad.'

'Just let Mum know we'll be over in a sec, Kirst,' Robbie said as he trudged off towards the cottage with one of her bags slung over his shoulder.

'No wucken furries!' Kirsty replied, smiling with the fact that Aden and Robbie knew the Aussie lingo. She'd once said that to a coworker in London and they'd been absolutely mortified, not understanding it was a good thing.

'Gosh, something smells good!' Kirsty said as she tiptoed into the kitchen, the smell of roast lamb in the air.

'Woo hoo, my darling girl's home, finally! I've missed you so much,' Lynette squealed, dropping the tongs she was holding onto the bench and running to Kirsty, a warm smile filling her round, freckled face. The soft scent of her rose perfume instantly made Kirsty feel safe and secure, like it always had since she was a child. Her mother hadn't changed at all – she was as plump and vivacious as always. The two women stood hugging for what seemed like an eternity, holding each other close, laughing and crying at the same time.

Lynette finally pulled back from Kirsty, wiping happy tears from her eyes with a tea towel. 'I would have met you out the front, love, but I didn't even hear you pull up over the volume of the telly. I reckon your dad's going a bit deaf in his old age. But don't tell him I said that. He's resolute on staying young and full of beans forever.' She chuckled.

'He's always had the telly up too loud . . . the old bugger must have been deaf years ago.' Kirsty giggled.

Lynette kissed Kirsty once again on the cheek, then, holding her at arm's length, looked her up and down. 'You're looking a little thin, dear. What have you been eating, rabbit food and rice crackers?'

Kirsty waved her hand in the air. 'Pffft, I'm not that skinny, Mum. I just haven't been eating all your good home cooking.'

Lynette gently touched Kirsty's face, her cheery mood turning serious. 'I've been worried about you. I'm praying that the time away has helped heal your hurt. I was getting concerned that you were never going to come home.'

Kirsty wrapped her arms around herself, avoiding her mum's eyes, the reason she ran away from Hidden Valley three years ago still taunting her. 'Of course I was going to come home, Mum. My life is here. I could never live anywhere else.'

Lynette raised one eyebrow, assessing Kirsty, trying to read her, before tutting and reluctantly turning to continue with dinner, talking to Kirsty over her shoulder. 'Your dad has missed you loads, too.' She put a tray of vegies in the oven. 'And speaking of your dad, does he know you're home yet?'

'No, not yet. I'll go in and say g'day to him.'

'I'll make us a pannikin of tea, love; we have so much to catch up on. I'm looking forward to hearing all about your travels over dinner. Aden and Robbie are joining us too. It will be so lovely having all the family together again.'

'Oh, a good old-fashioned pannikin of tea. That's music to my ears,' Kirsty said, smiling, memories of sitting on the verandah with her mum at sunset flooding back. These were the simple memories that would bring tears to her eyes in the UK when she suffered awful bouts of homesickness.

Kirsty snuck into the lounge room, where her dad was settled into his reclining lounge chair in front of the telly, the five o'clock news on, a pannikin of coffee in his weather-beaten hands. He obviously hadn't heard Kirsty come in and she stole a few moments to stand in the shadows and take in her father's face. His hair had gone greyer in the last three years although he still had plenty of it, and his eyes were surrounded by the telltale signs of years in the sun. His long legs rested on the coffee table, his socks bunched up around his ankles, one of them hanging halfway off the end of his toes. He had the physique of a hard-working country man, not an ounce of fat on his body.

'Hey, Dad, I'm home!' Kirsty threw her arms over the back of the sofa and wrapped them gently around her father's neck, kissing him on the head. Ron jumped with fright, spilling his coffee all over his jeans.

'Oh Christ, love! You scared the crap outta me. Nearly gave me a heart attack,' he said as he clambered out of the couch and turned to give Kirsty a hug.

'Oh, I missed you so much, Dad. It's fantastic to be home.' Her heart melted as she stood before him, noticing he had tears in his eyes. He quickly wiped them away with the back of his hand, sniffing loudly and wiping ineffectually at the coffee on his jeans. 'How was your flight?'

'All right, I suppose. I couldn't get comfortable at all and the airline food – oh, don't even get me started. It's like eating cardboard. It's been almost two days since I've eaten anything decent. My belly's rumbling just thinking about tucking into Mum's roast dinner.'

Ron rubbed his stomach and sniffed the air. 'Bloody oath, smells great, doesn't it? Mind you, your mother's cooking always does. Anyway, I better head off and have a quick shower, not to mention change my jeans. I smell a bit like a feedlot.'

'I second that notion, Dad,' Kirsty replied, swiping the air in mock disgust.

Ron laughed and winked. 'Don't you worry, love. You're going to look and smell like this tomorrow after I send you out working in the paddocks for the day with Robbie. No rest for the wicked round here.'

'I've been hanging out to do some dirty work, Dad. I'll be up at sparrow fart, raring to go, Scout's honour.'

'That's my girl,' Ron replied, tenderly patting Kirsty's shoulder as he walked past her and into the hallway. 'It's good to have you home,' he called over his shoulder.

Kirsty watched Ron's silhouette disappear down the dim hallway as she took a deep breath and flopped down into his recliner. She was absolutely knackered but the thrill of being home outweighed all of her weariness and reservations. Tomorrow was a new day and she couldn't wait to wake up to it. Her life back in Australia had begun and she was going to make the most of it. To do this she knew she had to try to forget her past, as it was the only way forward. But did she have the courage to do it?

Chapter 5

BREAKFAST was over before sunrise for Kirsty, while the moon still glowed among the hundreds of sparkling stars on the horizon. The moonlight illuminated the morning mist as it snaked its way around the valleys, giving them a ghostly feel. She sat in her favourite spot on the cottage verandah with a pannikin of tea in her hands, gazing out over the paddocks. Even after almost two months of being home she still got up early before work to admire it all.

Autumn was announcing its arrival, the morning crisp, and the gentle breeze carrying with it a hint of the cooler weather to come. Kirsty loved the winter months at Hidden Valley – the days were still sunny and warm but at night and in the early morning it was chilly enough for slippers and her favourite fluffy robe. Sometimes, on rare occasions, it was even cold enough to stoke up the fireplace. In North Queensland that was a treat.

With a wisp of a smile, Kirsty thought back to the morning she had woken up to no central heating in London. It still hadn't been fixed when she left and she wondered if Mr-Fix-It-Tomorrow had done anything about it yet. That brought her thoughts round to Jo – she missed her terribly. Although they'd spoken on the phone a few times and also kept in contact with emails and Facebook, it wasn't the same as spending time together. Jo's job was going great guns and she was making the most of her time left in the UK. Only four more months and Jo would be home.

The tired squeak of the flyscreen door grabbed Kirsty's attention as Aden wandered out onto the verandah. Tousling his wayward bed hair, he stretched his arms high in the air and yawned broadly before he turned around and spotted her. He was dressed only in a pair of well-worn jeans, his bare chest tanned and muscled, a tattoo of a bucking horse adorning his right pec. A soft feathering of black hair sat around his belly button and Kirsty couldn't help but follow its path down to the top of his jeans, which it vanished beneath. She quickly looked away before Aden caught her, feeling a luxurious rush of lust wash over her. *No harm in looking*, she thought. Who could blame her? Aden Maloney oozed sex appeal, and the best thing was, he seemed oblivious to the way women drooled over him. It made him all the more attractive.

Since arriving back at Flame Tree Hill she had found herself more relaxed around Aden than she'd expected. He didn't seem to bait her like he had when they were teenagers. He wasn't at home much with his veterinary work, but when he was he was very helpful, happily doing his share of the cleaning, even cooking dinner a few nights a week for her and Robbie . . . *and* he was a darn good cook. He still had a wicked sense of humour and Kirsty found herself laughing more than she had in years. His time away in the city had obviously done him good. He seemed more grown up and wiser. A bit like her, she hoped.

'Good morning, Kirsty.' His husky morning voice made her heart skitter.

'Morning, Aden. Sleep well?'

'Like a baby, as always. Got a day off today, but do you reckon I could sleep in? Not a bloody chance. I'm too used to getting up before the crack of dawn to get to work.'

'Yeah, it's been really busy for you, which is great news, hey. And it means you'll be hanging around Hidden Valley for a while,' Kirsty replied. The nearest vet was an hour's drive away, and Aden's mobile vet business had filled a real gap in the market. That, combined with the fact he was a local boy, meant he had more work than he knew what to do with.

Aden grinned at her, his mischievous eyes sparkling. He took a sip of his coffee. 'Yep, it sure does, and no complaints here about the long hours. I've always been one to get out of bed before sun-up. I can't believe how my business has taken off. Robbie was right when he said there was a demand for a mobile vet, and the acupuncture side of it is proving really popular for the horses.'

'I'm so happy that it's all working out for you. And it's refreshing to see a bloke who's not afraid to try alternative therapies. The acupuncture side of it *is* fascinating, but I must admit I'm a little surprised that you even offer it as a service. I didn't think you were the type of guy to be into acupuncture.'

'You might be surprised by what I'm into these days, Kirsty. I'm not the reckless lad you grew up with any more. Living in the city opened my mind to a few things. I even meditate sometimes, when I'm really stressed out. Tammy got me into it when she dragged me off to a class one night with a master from India.' He put a finger to his lips. 'But shh, don't let that cat out of the bag – gotta keep up the tough-guy reputation round these parts. Cowboys aren't meant to be softies.'

Kirsty couldn't hide her surprise. 'Well, there you go. Aden

Maloney, the tattooed rebel without a cause, is now in touch with his New Age side. The city has turned you into a snag, my friend!'

Aden chuckled. 'What the hell is a snag? It makes me sound like a frigging sausage.'

'It means a sensitive new age guy,' Kirsty said, laughing.

'I wouldn't go that far. I still like my boxing, bull riding, camping and shooting. I reckon that warrants me a tough-guy image.'

Kirsty ran her hands through her hair before turning back to Aden, who was casually leaning against the railing, his body strong in all the right places. She ignored the yearning to touch him, silently chastising herself for the thought. 'Yeah, I noticed the boxing bag out in the shed. I've been meaning to ask if you were going to go back into competition. There's a fight night at the town hall in a couple of weeks. Maybe you should enter?'

Aden waved the suggestion away. 'Oh, nah, I'm not fit enough to go back into serious competition. It's just a way to keep myself in some sort of shape, that's all. And when the meditation doesn't work a good old bout on the bag gets rid of any pent-up tension.'

Not fit enough? Kirsty thought. *Have you looked in the mirror lately?*

Aden sat down beside her and his leg brushed against her own. 'Beautiful sky, isn't it? I love this time of the day, just before the sun comes up, when the stars are still flickering. It's otherworldly.' He waved his arm towards the picturesque view sprawled out before them, then rested back further into the couch. 'Ah, I've missed this. It was hard living in the city and waking up to the traffic noise and your neighbours basically living on top of you. I'm not cut out for it long-term.'

Kirsty nodded. 'Neither am I. I mean, London was nice for a while but, boy, did it make me appreciate the wide open spaces here. Flame Tree Hill is heaven.'

'Good on you for spreading your wings and travelling a bit, though, Kirsty. I reckon it makes us all grow up when we see how other people live. I'm just sorry that the main reason you left was because you couldn't get over the accident. At least you stuck around Hidden Valley for a few years and *tried* to rebuild your life, unlike me.'

Kirsty's breath caught in her throat. 'Oh, no, um . . . it wasn't because of the, um, accident. It was just, well, I really wanted to travel. That's all.'

Aden caught her gaze, his eyes full of understanding. 'Don't feel embarrassed about needing to get away. Shit, I did. Living in the city helped in a way, but not as much as I thought it would. I'll always have heaviness in my heart when I think about Bec. That's life. I've just learnt to accept she's not coming back. Mum told me you were suffering from anxiety attacks because you felt so guilty about being the only survivor. You should *never* feel guilty for that, Kirsty.'

Kirsty felt like crawling under a rock. She wasn't ready for this conversation; she wasn't sure she'd ever be ready to sit and talk about the accident with Aden. This was the first time he'd ever spoken to her about it and she didn't know how to respond. What was she meant to say to him? *It should have been me who died, not your sister?* She wiped a stray tear, angry at herself. 'I'm so sorry about Bec. I wish I could have done something to save her. She was too young to die.'

Aden shook his head, his eyes burning into hers. 'No, don't you dare say sorry. It's not your fault. And laying blame isn't going to bring anyone back. It must have been very hard for you, losing three mates. I just wish I could have been there for you more after it happened but I was drowning in my own sorrow, but if it's any consolation I'm here for you now, if you ever want to talk about it. Okay?'

A sob escaped from Kirsty and Aden took her into his arms. She tried to speak but it was impossible, so she let her trembling body rest against his. His compassion was heartfelt, and it should have made her feel better, but it didn't. She wrapped her arms tighter around him, enjoying the moment of closeness, allowing herself the pleasure of his embrace.

Aden held her close, his warm breath on her neck. 'I'm so thankful you didn't die, Kirsty. I don't know what I would have done losing *two* women I love dearly. One was bad enough.'

Kirsty felt her stomach do a backflip. What did Aden mean by *love?* She eased herself out of his embrace, suddenly guilty for taking refuge in it, just as Ron's voice came bellowing from the front of the cottage.

'Robbie? Kirsty? You two awake? We got big bloody problems out in the back paddock!'

Ron was not normally one to shout, especially first thing in the morning. Kirsty could hear his spurs clanging on the timber verandah and worry rose in her throat as she jumped from the couch, ripped open the screen door and pelted down the hall towards the front door. Aden's footsteps hurried behind her own. Robbie emerged from his room, dazed and confused, pulling a T-shirt over his head as Kirsty jostled past him, the three of them arriving at the front door to see Ron looking utterly stressed out.

'What's up, Dad? Is everyone okay?' Robbie asked as he pulled on his jeans.

Ron huffed loudly as he threw his hands up in the air.

'Henry Cooper from next door has just rung. Sounds like our back fence has been knocked down by a couple of his unruly bulls overnight and now there are cattle from here to bloody kingdom come. We can't afford to lose any and I don't want his horny scrubber bulls having their way with my prized heifers. It's the last bloody thing we need just before we start the breeding program for the year.'

'Shit! Let's go round them up then,' Robbie said, wiping sleep from the corner of his eye.

'Count me in,' Aden said.

'Great, thanks, Aden. We're going to need all the help we can get. Henry and his boys are going to meet us out there once they've saddled up.' Ron rolled his eyes, huffing. 'Henry's just got to find where they've gotten to on the property first. Knowing his two boys they'll be up to no good somewhere. It could be bloody ages before they get there to help us.'

'I'll just go chuck some clothes on . . . Can't muster in my PJs,' Kirsty said as she ran off down the hall, no time to think further on Aden's words.

The wind almost whipped the saliva from Kirsty's mouth as she galloped across Flame Tree Hill on Cash. A sharp pain pierced her right nipple and she winced. It felt like she'd been stung by a bee. She hastily shoved her free hand down her top to check that there wasn't an unwelcome insect in her bra, grimacing once again at the tenderness of her breast, but there was nothing there. Was she due for her period? She would have to check her calendar. *Oh, the joys of being a woman*, she thought as she pulled her hand free and took stock of the situation in front of her.

A huge cloud of dust hovered above all the action, thrown up by the bellowing cattle's hoofs, the specks of dirt glimmering in the sunlight. Kirsty could feel it entering her lungs each time she inhaled – all she could taste in her mouth was dirt. But this was country life. What a way to start the day: first in Aden's arms and now out in the saddle. If only it were like this every day. Giving Cash a quick flick of the reins, encouraging him to go faster, she felt the horse's muscles ripple under her as he opened his stride, his sweat soaking through her jeans. The flustered bellows of their cattle carried across the paddock as she and the men took positions around the gathering mob and began to successfully push theirs inwards and the neighbours' unwanted bulls outwards, shouting and whistling frantically. Kirsty kept her main focus on the strong-willed bull just in front of her, kicking up clouds of paprika-coloured dust as he thundered along the hard ground, snot and saliva dripping from his nostrils, showing his fury at being pushed away from the huddle of cows as he snorted. This bull was certainly not one of theirs; his poor appearance, rebellious behaviour, sharp horns and lack of desirable bone structure and musculature made it obvious. She motioned for Cash to turn with a slight tug on the reins, edging around the bull at a canter so she could push him out of the mob. The last thing the Mitchells wanted was to end up with calves bred from an old scrub bull. That would most certainly put a huge dent in their profits.

Cash pushed on as Kirsty determinedly directed the bull towards the neighbouring property. She swore under her breath as the bull abruptly changed direction, racing for the thick scrub at the edge of the property in a last-minute dash for freedom. The rest of the cattle tried to follow suit and began to break ranks from the contained mob, running towards the parts of the paddock where they could hide among tall clusters of trees. Aden appeared to Kirsty's left and cracked his roo-hide whip, the loud reverberation demanding the attention of the way-ward cattle *and* the unwelcome bull. Robbie and Ron galloped across the paddock to try to curb the cattle's escape while Aden stayed beside her, helping her drive the bull towards the broken fencing and back onto Henry Cooper's property. Together, they worked on either side of the snorting beast, cutting off its escape routes. They were intensely focused on any sudden movements, acutely aware the bull's horns were deadly to both them and their horses. Then, with one final crack of his whip, Aden forced the bull across the flattened fence line just in time to see Henry and his two young sons heading towards them on their horses. And thank goodness for that, Kirsty thought, because they still had four or five dogged bulls to clear out as well as getting their own cattle into a secure paddock until they could fix the fence in this one.

Aden directed his horse in beside her, smiling. 'You haven't forgotten how to muster, I see. You're still a bloody pro in the saddle, K.'

Kirsty grinned through the dust covering her face, taken aback by the way he'd called her K. That's what he used to call her when they were teenagers. He was obviously becoming very comfortable around her again and that pleased her. 'I adore mustering – so how could I possibly ever forget something I love so much, Aden?'

Aden tugged the brim of his hat down further, casting a long shadow across his features and limiting Kirsty's view of his face, but she could still see his lips and they were smirking. 'That's so very true, K. I know exactly what you mean about never forgetting something you love.' A loud crack of a whip broke their focus on each other and Aden turned his horse and flicked the reins. 'Anyway, better get back to it.'

Kirsty remained stationary for a few brief moments as she watched him gallop away, his simple words having an odd effect on her. But why? Shrugging it off, she gave Cash the okay to join in the organised chaos in front of her, eager to get the job done while enjoying every thrilling second of it.

Chapter 6

HANK barked insistently as the crunch of tyres on gravel pulled Kirsty's attention away from the telly. She shoved the last of the caramel Tim Tam she had been sucking her coffee through into her mouth and wandered out to the verandah, her muscles still a little tender after being in the saddle all day yesterday. Squinting in the afternoon sun, she could just make out her mother's car, another woman's silhouette beside her mum's. Kirsty shaded her eyes and took a closer look as they got out of the car, a smile erupting as she finally made out who it was, the woman's build a lot frailer than she remembered but her beautiful dark brown skin and almond shaped eyes unmistakable.

'Oh my goodness! Aunty Kulsoom!' Kirsty squealed with delight as she bolted down the front steps and towards her aunty with her arms outstretched. She'd known Kulsoom all her life and they shared a very special connection.

Kulsoom smiled warmly at Kirsty and the two women embraced as Lynette stood by her sister-in-law, smiling.

'I can't believe it's been four years since I saw you last,' Kirsty said, blinking back happy tears.

'I know, it's been way too long. How are you, love? Glad to be home from the big smoke, I'll bet. Your mum was getting worried about you never coming back but I told her she was being silly. The country is in your blood.' Kulsoom tenderly brushed a strand of hair from Kirsty's face.

Kirsty swept her arm wide, motioning towards the vast land. 'How could I ever stay away from this?' She gave her aunty another cuddle. 'This is a huge surprise! When did you decide to come and visit? Obviously nobody told me you were arriving today. I'm a bloody mushroom around here – kept in the dark, as they say.'

'I told your parents not to say anything. I wanted to surprise you and Robbie,' Kulsoom said.

Lynette winked at Kirsty. 'Did a good job of keeping it a secret, didn't we?'

'You sure did, Mum.' Kirsty glanced in the back seat. 'I'm gathering Uncle Harry's not visiting with you this time, unless you have him packed away in your suitcase.'

Kulsoom chuckled. 'No, your Uncle Harry had to stay for work. Which is a shame. But after having time off to come to Pakistan with me he didn't have any annual leave left.'

Lynette placed her hand on Kulsoom's arm. 'Yes, we're going to miss having my larrikin of a brother here with you. But not to worry, it can't be helped. It's just good to have you here, Kulsoom.' Lynette shifted her gaze to Kirsty. 'Anyway, love, let's get inside so your aunty can have a pannikin of tea. She's had a long day of travelling from Tasmania and I'm sure she's well and truly buggered.'

'Too right I am. A three-hour drive, two flights – one delayed, I might add – and then the two-hour trip to here from the airport . . . Well, let's just say I'm not as young and vigorous as I used to be.' Kulsoom tipped her head from side to side to ease out the tight muscles in her neck, the wig she wore sliding slightly off-centre. Kirsty reached out and straightened it for her, the lump in her throat growing bigger by the second. She wasn't going to break down in front of Kulsoom – not here, not now.

'I'll grab your luggage and meet you inside in a minute. I can't wait to hear all about your trip back home to Pakistan to see all your brothers and sisters,' Kirsty said as she headed towards the back of her mum's Prado. 'And taste all the wicked curries I'm sure you learnt to cook while you were there!'

'Well, I'm here for five weeks – maybe more if you're all happy to have me – so you might get sick of my Pakistani cooking by then,' Kulsoom replied over her shoulder as she followed Lynette up the path to the front door of the homestead.

'That is never gonna happen!' Kirsty called back.

After dinner the three women sat snugly beside each other on the verandah, each cradling a warm pannikin of Milo, full of the homemade apple pie they'd had after huge helpings of Lynette's famous ox tail stew and creamy mashed potato. Robbie, Ron and Aden had retired early, leaving the women to themselves.

Kirsty thought back to the way she had caught Aden looking at her across the dinner table. And then there was the way his hand had gently brushed her own when he had taken the tea towel off her to help with the drying up. They had been living under the same roof for a little over two months now and the atmosphere between them seemed to be shifting. In what way she wasn't certain, but it worried and excited her at the same time. She let out a sigh and rested her head back against the cushion of the swing chair. There were more important issues to be thinking of. Like when was the right time was to ask her aunty about her breast cancer. Even though Kulsoom was in remission, Kirsty didn't know how to broach the subject; she still felt guilty about not being in the country to support Kulsoom through that traumatic time. She couldn't even begin to imagine what it would be like to be told you had cancer; the pain and fear would be utterly indescribable.

A mild breeze stirred the leaves on the golden wattle trees, sending a sprinkling of flowers down onto the thick grass beneath. Gently swinging their legs in unison, the women relaxed in a companionable silence, the hinges on the swing chair creaking with every sway. Kirsty watched a possum scurry across the front lawn and speedily climb a tall gum tree, its curly tail wrapping around a tree branch as it swung up and out of sight. Green tree frogs were croaking loudly in the downpipes, rejoicing at the heavy downpour that had occurred during dinner. Kirsty smiled, remembering the fright she'd had as a booming crack of thunder made her jump. She'd spilt her glass of merlot all over her mum's good white linen tablecloth. Then the power had been cut and the skies opened as immense droplets pelted the tin roof of the homestead with deafening intensity. In typical North Queensland fashion it had all been over in ten minutes flat as the power returned, leaving the world with an addictive aroma of crispness that her father referred to as heaven's scent.

Kulsoom exhaled noisily beside Kirsty and slowly removed her wig, scratching fiercely at her patchy scalp before dropping the wig in her lap. 'This darn thing makes my head sweat. I'm looking forward to the day I have my own hair back. It seems to grow so slowly.'

'I've been meaning to ask about your, um, breast cancer,' said Kirsty tentatively. 'I'm sorry I haven't until now. It's just, well, I didn't know what to say and I don't want to upset you.' The tightness that had been in her throat earlier returned with full force as she glanced at her aunt's bald scalp then stared off into the distance, waiting for a reply as tears began to sting her eyes.

Kulsoom patted Kirsty's leg, her voice filled with compassion as she began to speak. 'I understand, love. It's not easy to talk to someone about something that has the possibility of causing their death. It's a horrible disease, but it has also taught me to stop and smell the roses, and to tell those who mean the world to you that you love them as often as possible. That's what drove me to finally go home and visit my family in Pakistan. The cancer gave me the kick up the backside that I needed to get my act together and go.'

'How are you feeling after having a break over there?' Kirsty asked.

'I feel *really* good. I truly believe I've beaten the cancer. I feel better now than I have at any time in the last year, and the doctors are saying there's no sign that the cancer has spread anywhere else, which is great news.'

Kirsty took Kulsoom's hand and squeezed it softly, the toll the cancer had taken on Kulsoom evident in the frailness of her aunt's fingers. 'I'm glad to hear that. I'm so sorry you had to go though all this. Life just isn't fair sometimes. You know I love you loads, don't you?'

Kulsoom squeezed Kirsty's hand in response, smiling as she wiped the wetness from Kirsty's cheeks. 'How could I not? You're forever telling me, my dear. I love you too.' Kulsoom replaced her solemn gaze with a smile, her eyes twinkling playfully. 'By the way, I saw the way Aden kept glancing at you across the table tonight, Kirsty. I could be wrong but I think that boy might have a bit of a soft spot for you. Although, who can blame him? You're an attractive girl.'

'Oh get out! He does not!' Kirsty said, feeling her face flush the colour of beetroot. 'Aden and I are like brother and sister. We've basically known each other all our lives.'

Lynette leant forward on the chair and caught Kirsty's gaze. 'You know what, I thought I noticed it too. But then again, maybe us old hens haven't got a clue and we're reading into something that's not there at all.'

Kirsty shuffled uncomfortably in the swing chair, causing the rhythmic sway to falter. 'I *really* reckon you two should lay off the wine over dinner. It's messing with your heads.'

'I must say, he is a hunk – if I was only twenty years younger!' Kulsoom replied with a wink, sending Lynette into chortles beside her.

Kirsty shook her head at the two giggling women. A relationship forming between her and Aden? Pfft. It wasn't possible. Her mum and Kulsoom had no idea what she was hiding. No one did. And with each new day she spent with Aden under her roof, she was finding herself standing dangerously close to the edge. One little shove and she was going to tumble over.

Chapter 7

THE camp fire threw out a fine spray of glowing red embers as Robbie carefully placed another log across the fire. He stood back beside Aden and Kirsty, the three of them cradling cans of beer, mesmerised by the flickers of golden flames. Kirsty pulled her camera from around her neck and snapped a few images of the fire in all its blazing glory. The red, blue and orange flames against the blackness of the night were striking, the perfect elements for a spectacular photograph.

'Ah, this is the life,' Ron said, a satisfied smile on his face as he leant back in his fold-out chair with a pannikin of tea.

'I agree,' said Lynette. 'Great suggestion to have a barbecue, Robbie. It's an ideal night for it. Mind you, I ate way too much, as usual. I feel like a beached whale.' Lynette leant further back into her chair and popped her feet up onto Ron's lap, wriggling her toes to insinuate she wanted a foot rub. Ron obliged, rubbing her feet tenderly.

'I'm full of great ideas,' Robbie replied, his face flushed from the warmth of the fire. 'I also take credit for the camping trip we're going on. Can't believe Dad gave me and Kirsty a few days off work for it. I don't know what's gotten into you, Dad, but I'm gonna take the offer and run with it before you change your mind.'

Ron smiled. 'After a month straight of work I thought you both deserved some time off. I'm not going to change my mind. Glad you can go too, Aden.'

'It'll be great – I need a break from work. I can't wait to get to Lake Tinaroo and have a ski. It's been years since I've been there,' said Aden.

'I'm really looking forward to having a ski too,' said Kirsty. 'It feels like forever since I've been camping. They don't really camp in England. You'd freeze to bloody death if you tried to sleep outside.'

Lynette chuckled. 'Just make sure *you* pack the food, love. Remember last time when all Robbie took was sausages, bread and tomato sauce? You couldn't look at a sausage for months without feeling ill.'

Kirsty laughed. 'Oh yeah! I'd forgotten about that. We had to live on sausages for four days because Robbie didn't catch any fish. Remember that, Aden?'

Aden nodded, smiling.

'Hey, fair go, you lot,' said Robbie. 'I'm a bloke. We go into nature for the fishing, not for gourmet food. And it wasn't my fault that the fish were on holiday that weekend.'

'Good point, Robbie,' Kulsoom replied with a grin. 'Ah, after a week of being waited on hand and foot by my wonderful family I could easily get used to this.' She gave Hank a good scratch behind the ears as she sat down. He stretched his front legs, walked around in a circle and then positioned himself right on top of her feet. 'Oh, thanks, mate, I now have my own personal foot heater too,' she said with a chuckle.

'You know you're welcome as long as you would like to stay,' Lynette said.

Kulsoom yawned contentedly and rubbed her belly. 'Don't

tempt me, Lynny, or I might never leave. Then poor old Harry will have to fend for himself forever. Bless him. I miss having the old bugger around. Although he's probably enjoying having a bachelor pad while I'm away. I can just imagine it, an unmade bed so he doesn't need to pull all the decorative pillows off at night, the sports channel on constantly and his smelly socks strewn about the place. A man's idea of heaven.'

The group chuckled. The image Kulsoom had just painted sounded like Harry down to a T.

A comfortable silence fell over them as the serenity of the country came to the foreground. The only sound to be heard was the chirping of crickets, the call of a curlew and the gentle night breeze blowing through the leaves of the trees.

'So who's up for some toasted marshmallows and sharing a few good ol' camp-fire yarns? The stories don't have to be true, but they *do* have to make us all laugh. That's the only rule. It's up to the rest of the group to decide whether the yarns being told are true *and* the storyteller isn't obliged to reveal whether they are.' Kirsty said, wiggling her eyebrows. She leant over and pulled a packet of marshmallows from the Esky.

'Why the hell not?' Robbie said, his face lighting up. 'I have some beauties!'

Aden clapped his hands in delight. 'That sounds like fun. I've got a few good ones too.'

'My oath! I haven't done this in years,' Ron said as he leant forward in his chair.

'Righto then, let me go hunt for a couple of twigs to put the marshmallows on and we'll be in business,' Aden said as he stood to begin the search.

Kirsty stood too, brushing the dirt from the back of her jeans. 'Wait up, I'll come and help you.'

Aden and Kirsty walked off into the shadows, scouring the ground for twigs that were big enough to hold over the fire without fingers getting burnt. Kirsty's eyes took their sweet time to adjust to the darkness after sitting by the fire and she could barely see. She let out a small squeal as she lost her footing and tripped over.

Aden knelt down beside her to help her up. 'Shit, are you right? You seem to have a habit of falling over lately.'

Kirsty began to laugh as Aden did too. 'Yeah, I don't think I bruised anything except my pride.' She took Aden's outstretched hand, a quiver travelling down her arm at his touch. She could just make out his broad silhouette in the dark. He stood, pulling her up with him, and then he gently wrapped his arms around her waist.

Kirsty felt her knees go weak; this was more than a friendly gesture. She knew she shouldn't let him be so close but she couldn't move, her body refusing to do what her mind was asking it to. She'd fantasised about him doing this for years so how could she stop now? She held her breath, wishing she could see his face and wondering what was going to happen next. They stood there for what seemed an eternity, neither of them pulling away. Kirsty could feel Aden's warm breath on her cheek and hear the thumping of her heart in her ears. She closed her eyes, letting her body press closer into his, the moment intensifying as their breathing got heavier. There was a sudden crackling of dried leaves behind them, and then Robbie's deep voice nearby. 'Kirsty? Aden? Are you two okay out there?'

Aden instantly dropped his arms from Kirsty's waist, then Robbie was upon them. 'There you are. It's so bloody dark out here I thought you might have lost your way. How's the twig hunting going?'

Aden bent down and then abruptly stood again, holding a handful of sticks. 'Yep, mission accomplished, got a few here, should be enough for all of us.'

'Mission accomplished, all right,' Kirsty muttered under her shaky breath.

'Pardon?' Robbie asked.

'Oh, nothing. Just muttering to myself.' Kirsty noticed her voice sounded a notch or two higher.

'You've always had a bad habit of doing that,' Robbie teased as all three headed back in the direction of the camp fire.

What in the hell had just happened?

'Do you want to know where the saying "raining cats and dogs" comes from?' Ron asked. They were settled around the crackling fire, marshmallows melting into gooey heaven.

'Sure do,' said Kulsoom.

Ron edged forward in his chair. 'In the old days, English houses had thatched roofs with thick straw piled high and no wood underneath the straw to separate it from the inside of the house. Amongst this straw was the best spot to get warm, so all the dogs, cats, mice and bugs lived up there. When it rained it became slippery and sometimes the animals would fall from the straw roofing, hence the saying.'

'And whoever said history was boring?' Kirsty smiled. 'Who's got another one?'

'I can explain where the expression "piss poor" came from,' Aden said, licking his marshmallowy fingertips. 'Urine used to be used to tan animal skins, so families who wanted to make an extra buck would pee in a communal pot and then sell it to the tannery. If you had to do this you were considered piss poor. But then again, there were the folk who couldn't even afford to buy a pot, hence the saying, "don't have a pot to piss in".'

Lynette clapped her hands delightedly. 'What a classic! Not that I can figure out if it's true or not. Who's next? Robbie?'

Robbie rubbed his chin. 'Hmm, let me think. This isn't about where a saying comes from but it's a bloody funny story. I was reading in the paper the other day that a man in Croatia got a nasty surprise when he went to get out of his deckchair and found his testicles had become stuck between the slats of wood on the seat. He'd been sunbaking naked on the beach the whole day, and in the cool morning his shrunken testicles had slipped through the slats. Then, as it got hotter, they returned to normal size, leaving him embarrassingly stuck to the chair. He was freed after the beach maintenance guys found him and got someone to cut the chair in half.'

Kirsty's shoulders shuddered with laughter. 'My goodness, Robbie, what newspapers do *you* read? You gotta be pulling our legs with that one!'

Kulsoom clapped her hands. 'My turn, my turn! I read that a patient in Denmark was having a mole removed from his bottom with an electric scalpel when he broke wind, igniting a spark from the scalpel and accidentally setting fire to his pubic hair. The hospital staff put it out with a fire extinguisher.'

Lynette snorted with laughter. 'You must read the same newspapers as Robbie!' She rolled her eyes, a smile on her face. 'Count me out of this storytelling. I can't come up with anything that would beat those yarns.'

'Looks like you're lucky last, Kirsty.' Ron said.

Kirsty thought for a minute. 'Okay . . . Well, I can explain where the saying "dead ringer" comes from.'

'Great, do tell,' Ron replied, slipping another marshmallow on the end of his twig.

'In the old days in England, they began running out of places to bury people so they would dig up coffins, remove the bones and then take them to a bone house so they could reuse the grave and coffin again. Apparently, upon opening these coffins, some had deep scratch marks on the wood, and they realised people had been buried alive.' A gasp from the group made Kirsty smile, stoked she had their undivided attention. 'So to combat this, they would tie a string to the wrist of the corpse, lead the string up through a hole in the coffin then up through the soil, and tie it to a bell. Someone would have to sit out in the graveyard all night after the funeral to listen for the bell just in case the poor bugger was buried alive. Hence the expression "dead ringer".'

'Holy shit! I haven't heard that one before but I reckon it could be true. That's probably where the saying "graveyard shift" comes from too,' said Aden.

Kirsty laughed and held her thumb up in the air. 'I reckon it's a pretty good explanation, but whether it's true I'm not at liberty to discuss.'

Aden grinned back at her as he admired her smile, the feeling of Kirsty's body pressed up against his own only an hour before having roused dormant feelings inside him. He hadn't meant to grab her like that. It had been totally spontaneous, his intimate gesture surprising him just as much as he was sure it had surprised her. And at that very moment, when he'd had her in his arms, all he'd wanted to do was kiss her. He wondered if she had felt the same. It had taken everything he had to stop himself. Fuck! What had gotten into him lately? This was his best mate's little sister. He'd been warned by Robbie not to go near Kirsty when they were teenagers and he wondered if that still stood now they were all adults. Not that he was going to ask. Blokes just didn't do that. And not that he *needed* to ask. He shouldn't be making a move on her anyway. Aden knew he had to tread carefully. He didn't want to upset Robbie; he'd been so good to put him up in the cottage. But Lord help him, with her athletic body and feisty spirit, Kirsty Mitchell was so damn desirable – she always had been.

Mumbling in her sleep, Kirsty kicked off her doona and thrashed about her bed as she felt the Commodore tumbling once again, the cries of her friends so loud she thought her eardrums might split. She threw her hands over her ears, trying to drown out their blood-curdling screams, her own voice mute, no matter how hard she tried to call back to them. Then she was scrambling out of the car and trying to run away, but her legs weren't moving, as though her feet were made from lead. Blood dripped from her battered torso, and her arm hung loose from the open flesh of her shoulder. She ran her hand over her face, only to see it covered in blood as she pulled it away. Primal sounds came from the confines of the bushes beside the road, an eerie sound that made her skin prickle. Had someone been thrown in there from the impact? Shouldn't she go and help them? Once again she tried to lift her feet from the gravel of the road, her pulse hammering in her throat, finding herself completely frozen to the spot. In front of her, bodies began to emerge from the wreckage of the car, one after the other, skin dripping from their blackened flesh, bones protruding in places where the skin had been completely burnt away, their arms reaching out for her, begging her for help . . .

Screaming silently, eyes flashing open, her consciousness now back in the safety of her bedroom, Kirsty panted for breath and scrambled up to sitting, her body covered in sweat. Hastily reaching across, she switched on her bedside lamp, needing the flood of light for comfort. She swallowed hard, her eyes wide, her mouth dry. Taking a few deep breaths, she slowly released them, trying to calm herself down. The nightmares had plagued her ever since the accident. At times they would come night after night and then she would have a few months with none. Her psychiatrist had told her it was part of the healing process and that eventually the nightmares would stop, once she had fully dealt with the accident. She hadn't had a nightmare in over two months, since she'd returned home – what had brought this one on? Her brief encounter with Aden in the dark? Still shaking, she slid from her sheets and padded off towards the kitchen, in need of a glass of water or maybe something a little stronger.

An hour and one glass of red wine later, Kirsty wearily climbed back into bed, switched her lamp off and pulled the sheet over her, kicked it off, then pulled it up again with a groan. Who was she kidding? There was no way in hell she was going to sleep tonight after that nightmare; and on top of that, thoughts of Aden with his arms wrapped around her waist were playing havoc with her mind. What was Aden doing? Why, after all these years of knowing her, was he showing signs of liking her? Was he lonely, suffering from the breakdown of his marriage? He didn't appear to be, but who knew? It was only going to be worse on a camping trip with him. She was almost certain of it: Aden Maloney had feelings for her. And she couldn't have him. How cruel life could be. How much heartache could it throw at her before she finally broke into a million little pieces?

Chapter 8

THE country road narrowed as Robbie drove the Land Cruiser along the well-worn track to Lake Tinaroo, the twangy country voice of Keith Urban on the radio. The tropical heat of Hidden Valley was gradually left behind as the lush rainforest closed in on both sides, creating a thick canopy overhead. Amazing to think they were only two hours from Flame Tree Hill and yet the landscape was so distinctly different.

Sunlight refracted through the trees, sending speckled golden light across the substantial undergrowth. Bromeliads flourished in the damp conditions here, their blues, reds, oranges and purples striking against the dark green forest floor. Kirsty imagined the insects and green tree frogs making their homes in the overlapping leaves, the bromeliads' centres resembling miniature lakes for the water-loving creatures.

The earthy aroma of the moist soil and the lush green rainforest made Kirsty feel so alive. It helped that they were on the road to Tinaroo – it was her favourite place to camp out under the stars. Walter, her grandfather, had helped build the dam in the fifties and its holding capacity was large enough to create a lake the size of Sydney Harbour, very impressive indeed for the small community of the Atherton Tablelands. In 1959 when the dam was filled, the small township of Kulara, which had suffered greatly during the Depression, was submerged, forever to stay in its grave beneath the dam.

Her dreamy attentiveness to the glorious scenery was broken as a trio of scrub turkeys scampered across the track and Robbie swerved a little to miss them, the Land Cruiser slipping slightly in the soft terrain as he gently pulled the old girl back onto the trail, his beloved speedboat bouncing around behind them.

'Bloody crazy-arse things,' he mumbled under his breath while he glanced behind quickly to check everything was all right.

Kirsty smiled as she watched the scrub turkeys disappear into the rainforest and then turned her attention back to Robbie and Aden. Opening a packet of peanut M&M's, she popped one in her mouth, then shook the bag in offering. 'Do you guys remember in 2003, when we'd had a few years running of a dry spell, and the old town beneath Tinaroo resurfaced because the dam had started to dry up?'

Aden dug into the packet and pulled out a handful of M&M's. 'Hey yeah! We all came and watched the Pioneers cricket match that they played on the old Kulara cricket field. It's bizarre to think they were playing on a pitch that had been laid to rest for years under the dam and we were walking around on roads and bridges that used to be the main thoroughfares of the old town. It was a day in history, I reckon, and one I was proud to be a part of. We even had our photo taken all together and published in the local newspaper, remember?'

Kirsty nodded, smirking as she recalled the picture in the paper, her huge metal braces amid her broad teenage smile. 'Yeah, the three of us looked like right dorks and yet we all thought we were so cool getting into the paper. The entire school was talking about it, taking the piss out of us. I took heaps of photos, too, which I'm so glad that I did. According to the weather bureau it could be another sixty years or so before Kulara is visible again.'

'Bloody oath,' Robbie said between crunching on M&Ms. 'Especially considering the shed at home is built with the timber from some of the buildings they removed before they flooded it. Grandad Walter was always a stickler for reusing materials, never throwing anything away.'

The sheltered rainforest suddenly gave way to endless views of crystal-clear water, surrounded by gently sloping grasslands. It was a scene straight from a painting.

With swags unpacked, camp fire prepared with a stockpile of gathered timber, and the portable table and chairs erected, Kirsty, Robbie and Aden got busy preparing their ski gear, the speedboat lapping at the shore in readiness.

'So who's up first?' Robbie asked as he slapped on some sunscreen.

'Oh, me, me!' Kirsty said, hopping on one leg as she hastily pulled on her wetsuit. She couldn't wait to get in the water.

Aden grinned at her, clearly amused by her eagerness. 'I'll get your skis ready, K. One or two?' he asked.

Kirsty was struggling with the zip of her wetsuit, cursing under her breath as it refused to budge. 'I think I better stick to two skis for now. It's been a long time since I last did this. I'm not even sure I'll be able to get up on them.'

Aden walked up behind her and placed his hand over hers

on the zipper. 'You'll be fine. It's just like a riding a bike. You never forget how to do it. Here, let me.'

'Well said, by the master of barefoot skiing,' Kirsty said as she cautiously let her hand drop back down beside her, a shiver travelling over her entire body as Aden pushed her long hair over her shoulder and slowly zipped her suit up. He was dangerously close. All she had to do was turn around and she would be close enough to kiss him.

The zip finally locked into place and he whispered in her ear, 'There you go, all set.'

Kirsty gave in to temptation and turned, meeting Aden's eyes as he stood casually before her, his wetsuit hanging from his waist. They held each other's gaze, something passing between them for the briefest of moments, the intensity of it unfathomable. Kirsty fumbled with her hair, throwing it up into a quick ponytail, unable to look into Aden's chocolate-brown eyes any longer for fear of falling into them. The deep grumble of the speedboat broke the silence and Kirsty breathed a private sigh of relief. 'Um, thanks for zipping me up. We better get in the water before Robbie takes off without us.'

Moments later Kirsty was strapped to the skis, gripping the handle of the rope tightly as Robbie hit the throttle. She wobbled to her feet, swaying, the challenge of the feat filling her with sheer determination to accomplish it. She could do this! She'd done it a thousand times before. She gritted her teeth, her concentration totally focused on balancing, and then she gained her footing and was gliding over the water like it was ice, sprays of water arcing out behind her. She looked at Aden, who was watching her from the back of the boat, ready to tell Robbie she had fallen if the need arose. He gave her the thumbs up and she grinned back at him, chuffed she had proven her skiing abilities after all these years. The three of them had spent many school holidays out here on the lake with their families and she'd always found herself showing off in front of Aden. But they weren't schoolkids any more, and a flicker of sadness crossed her mind at the thought of how much had changed.

After a light lunch they all hit the water again, this time with the wave biscuit. Kirsty and Aden held on for dear life as the huge inflatable ring they were clutching bounced erratically over the water at top speed, the fine sprays of water hitting them in the face, making it impossible to see. Aden chuckled and Kirsty couldn't help but squeal delightedly; it was unadulterated fun at its best.

Robbie hooked the boat to the right and the rubber ring hit a wave of water, lifted into the air, then slammed back down seconds later as Kirsty fought hard to hold on and Aden tumbled on top of her, both of them grappling for leverage. He stretched his arms out wide, grabbing hold of the handles and pinning them both down to the ring, every inch of his well-built body now pressing into hers. She closed her eyes, enjoying the sensation, wishing they could stay in this position all afternoon.

At that moment, they hit another wave and the rubber ring lifted once again, this time twisting upside down in the air and dumping both Kirsty and Aden into the lake. They tumbled under the water, grabbing for each other as they resurfaced, laughing and struggling for breath. Aden wrapped his arms around her waist, holding her up, his deep throaty laughter making her dizzy with desire as she tried to blink her eyes back to some sort of normalcy; her eyelids had almost folded backwards after she was dunked so forcibly into the water. It felt wonderful, like they were teenagers again, without a care in the world.

Their laughter subsided and Kirsty bit her bottom lip as Aden brushed her sodden hair from her face. He moved in nearer, pulling her closer to him under the water until she could feel the heat of his body against her own. She held her breath, wondering if he was about to kiss her, her heart trying to hammer its way out of her chest as she imagined what his lips would feel like. Then Robbie was there again, the boat rocking from side to side in the water as he motioned for them to hop back onto the ring, completely oblivious to what was going on.

Aden's hands slid slowly from her highly responsive body, the sloshing water making it impossible for Robbie to know what was going on beneath the surface. Kirsty's mind raced. What was Aden doing to her? And what was she thinking, letting him? She sighed as she swam over to the ring, joining Aden back on it.

The scraping of tin camping plates signalled the end of the night's lip-smacking dinner of rump steak, eggs and jacket potatoes that had been wrapped in alfoil and baked in the camp fire. Kirsty relaxed back further into her chair, contently full, as she immersed herself in the peacefulness of the evening. She had missed this, spending time out in nature. She could hear the water lapping gently at the lake's edge and the boat softly rolling from side to side. An owl hooted nearby and she glanced up to the tops of the tall pine trees that circled their camp, trying to spot the bird's glowing yellow eyes with the beam from her torch. She switched it off, the only light now coming from the embers of the camp fire glowing red in the darkness and the kerosene lantern on the fold out table.

Aden pushed himself up and began gathering the dirty plates. 'I reckon it's time to boil the billy. The damper I stuck in the camp oven earlier should be almost ready. Who'd like a cuppa to go with it?'

Robbie grinned, the whiteness of his teeth glowing in the dimness. 'Sounds like a plan. I'll go grab the butter and golden syrup from the Esky. Heart attack on a plate! Yummo!'

Kirsty licked her lips. 'Aw, yes please. That sounds delicious. And leave the dishes, Aden. I'll wash them up while you two look after the dessert.'

Aden carefully dropped the pile he was carrying into the washing-up bowl, which was already filled with hot water and suds, leaving them to soak. 'That's a done deal, K.'

A lazy spiral of smoke swirled upwards as the trio said their goodnights and climbed into their swags. Kirsty was weary and she yawned loudly, stretching her arms high, spellbound by the blanket of sparkling stars above. 'Just beautiful.'

'Pardon?' Aden asked as he wriggled in his swag.

Kirsty chuckled softly. 'Oh nothing, I was just talking to myself. Admiring the stars. I just love sleeping under them.'

'Me too. There's no ceiling more beautiful than the night sky. I sleep so peacefully when I'm camping. It's just so quiet out here.'

With a few little snorts, Robbie began to snore stridently.

'Well, it *was* peaceful!' Kirsty said, unimpressed. 'How are we meant to sleep with that bloody racket?'

'I reckon I'm that tired I'd sleep through a cyclone at the moment,' Aden replied.

Kirsty snuggled further into her swag. 'Yeah, you're probably right. Every inch of me is aching. I'm not used to how much skiing takes it out of you.'

'Night, K. Sweet dreams.' Aden's husky voice sounded sleepy, his last word trailing off as his breathing deepened.

Sweet dreams indeed, Kirsty thought as she closed her heavy eyes. I'm sleeping beside the most gorgeous man in the world, with the most amazing views surrounding me. Now if I could just find a way to change the past, I'd be the happiest woman in the world.

Chapter 9

ADEN honked the horn briefly as Kirsty took one last look at herself in the mirror. She scowled at her reflection, annoyed at the pimples that had so inconveniently decided to erupt on her face today. She hadn't had pimples since she was a teenager. Could it be her new face cream? She picked up the offending bottle and tossed it in the bin beside the bathroom sink, sighing as she swiftly pulled her hair into a ponytail.

Robbie stuck his head in the doorway of the bathroom. 'You better hurry up, sis. Aden has heaps on today. Don't want to keep the man waiting.'

'Okay, okay. Hold your horses,' Kirsty replied gruffly as she heard Robbie's footsteps padding down the hall. She'd had a bad night's sleep, tossing and turning all night after another nightmare, and had felt like death warmed up when she got out of bed that morning.

She hung her towel on the rack, wincing as her arm brushed against her chest. Her breast still felt sore but her period had been and gone. She wasn't due again for another week so that couldn't be the reason behind the discomfort now. She idly thought about getting it checked out, just to make sure she didn't have some sort of weird infection under her nipple. She was due for her pap smear anyway so she'd make an appointment to see the local doctor before she ran out the door this morning. She couldn't leave it any longer.

Hanging up the phone, Kirsty was pleased to have scored an appointment the next day thanks to a cancellation. She hurried into the kitchen and grabbed the packed lunch she had prepared. She shoved it in her backpack along with a freshly made flask of tea and two pannikins.

Robbie poured hot water into his mug, the pungent scent of coffee instantly filling the kitchen. 'It's nice of you to help Aden today. The poor bugger is so snowed under. I don't know how he keeps going.'

Kirsty reached up on her tiptoes and gave Robbie a quick peck on the cheek. 'I don't mind being busy. It'll be fun learning about the horse acupuncture biz.' She took off down the hall. 'Catch you tonight. It's your turn to cook dinner, too.'

'Spaghetti it is then!' Robbie called after her as the door slammed shut.

In the driveway Aden's four-wheel drive was waiting. Kirsty opened the passenger-side door and Aden tipped the front of his hat and nodded. 'I thought you'd fallen down the plughole. I was just about to send in a search party.'

'Sorry, didn't mean to keep you waiting. I brought lunch for us both if that's any consolation.' Kirsty slid into the Land Cruiser, feeling slightly frazzled from rushing. A whiff of Aden's aftershave tantalised her senses, earthy woods mixed with a hint of musk and spice. It reminded her instantly of their trip to the lake a few weeks back, when he had held her close beneath the water. The very recollection of it made her nervous. They'd been acting like it hadn't happened.

'I dunno . . . It depends on what it is,' Aden responded with a smile as he started the four-wheel drive, the motor turning over noisily.

'Cheek! You won't get any if you keep that up. I've packed corned beef and pickle sandwiches and a generous slab of chocolate cake, which I made myself.' Kirsty raised her eyebrows. 'And not from a packet either.' She smiled smugly as she struggled with her seatbelt. 'Bloody thing!' The seatbelt locked and refused to budge. She yanked at it in frustration, only making matters worse, and then gave up the tug of war as she huffed and slumped back in the seat.

'Here, let me help.' Aden chuckled as he leant across and gently pulled the seatbelt over Kirsty's breasts and stomach, clicking it easily into the lock. He turned his head, his lips now only centimetres away from hers. 'Seatbelts can be a bit temperamental, like people. You just gotta have the magic touch.' He stayed where he was for a moment, holding Kirsty's blue eyes with his own before pushing himself back into the driver's seat and pulling his own seatbelt on with ease.

Kirsty didn't realise she'd been holding her breath until her burning lungs reminded her to breathe. Her temperature seemed to have risen considerably and she could feel a red tinge burning her cheeks. She hastily diverted her attention to Hank, who sat outside the open window of the Land Cruiser, giving her his best puppy dog eyes. 'Sorry, buddy. Not today. I promise I'll take you for a burn on the quad to check the cattle when I get home this afternoon.'

Hank whimpered. His head and tail hung low as he slowly headed back towards the cottage, stopping once to turn around and stare back at her, giving it one more try. Kirsty smiled at his efforts and shook her head while shaking her finger at him. 'Go on, back on the verandah, mister.'

'He's persistent, got to give him that,' Aden said as he turned the Land Cruiser around and headed down the long drive, a trail of dust flaring out behind them.

'Poor bugger. I haven't had much time for him with all the work around here. Between tending to the horses, feeding the cattle and mending broken fences and water lines, I haven't really had time to scratch my own butt.'

Aden switched on the stereo, the alluring voice of Waylon Jennings filling the cab. Kirsty hummed away to 'Rainy Day Woman'.

'You *do* work hard, Kirsty, harder than a lot of blokes I know. It's admirable. Thanks for offering to give me a hand today. It's probably the last thing you feel like doing on your first day off since we went camping.'

'Seriously, I don't mind. It'll be nice to have a day out doing something different. I'm looking forward to watching you work.'

'It'll be nice having the company. I like hanging out with you. You're easy to be around,' Aden replied casually, his eyes on the road.

Kirsty couldn't help but smile; she was enjoying Aden's company more and more each day and was happy to hear he felt the same. She'd been feeling increasingly upbeat of late, too, the past not eating her up so often. It was a welcome change. Being back in Australia had had the opposite effect to what she'd feared. She didn't feel like she was running away any more. Aden was here and they were getting on great, and life felt like it was going back to normal. She prayed it would continue that way.

'How's your Aunty Kulsoom enjoying her stay?'

'Oh, she's loving it. She reckons the country air is healing her from the inside out.'

Aden nodded. 'I can vouch for that. I think she's put on

a little weight over the last few weeks, thanks to your mum's awesome cooking. God knows she needed it.'

'Yeah, it's wonderful to see her looking healthier. She was so skinny when she got here. The cancer has really knocked her about.' A familiar lump of emotion caught in Kirsty's throat. 'It would be terrifying to think that you could die in a matter of months if the chemotherapy didn't work.'

'I understand a bit about what she's gone through after watching my granddad die from lung cancer. It's a bit different though . . . his cancer was caused by his smoking, but your aunt's – it was just totally random. When Grandad started smoking as a teenager the health risks of smoking weren't even known and he'd given up years before being diagnosed, but it still got him in the end. It's so bloody unfair.' Aden's voice trailed off as a frown creased his brow.

Kirsty stared out the window for a moment, trying to control the emotions raised at the thought of Kulsoom's cancer. 'Tell me a bit about horse acupuncture so I can at least look like I know what I'm doing today.'

'Well, the Chinese have used acupuncture and herbal medicine to treat horses for over five thousand years, with brilliant results. We westerners have a bad habit of shunning anything that veers away from textbook veterinary practice, but in my opinion we should be embracing traditional Chinese medicine. I've worked with horses that have been deemed untreatable, and acupuncture has cured them in a matter of months – everything from lameness and leg injuries to physical and mental stress, right through to horses afraid of being tied up or mares that are just plain bitchy.'

'It must be that magic touch you were just talking about,' Kirsty said, her interest in the subject growing. 'So, tell me, how does it all work?'

Aden shoved the sun visor to the right of him, partially blocking the powerful morning sunshine that was streaming through his window. 'The theory behind traditional Chinese medicine is that energy, or "chi", flows through every living body. The chi is disturbed by injury, stress or disease, and this disturbance can be altered by stimulating certain anatomical points with the insertion of the acupuncture needles . . . which in turn increases the circulation. Before treatment I often administer a shot of vitamin B12, too, as it seems to increase the potency of the acupuncture and helps the effects to last longer. The results really speak for themselves. You'll see.'

Kirsty nodded slowly as she tried to take in all the information. 'What do you do if a horse freaks out while you're trying to put the needles in? I mean, does it hurt them? I *hate* getting needles, so I couldn't imagine have ten or so of them hanging out of me.'

Aden glanced at Kirsty and smiled. 'Acupuncture needles are nothing like the needles you get when you're having a shot for tetanus or chickenpox. They're really thin, and in my opinion they don't hurt a bit going in. In severe cases I can sedate a horse if I have to, but to be honest, it's never been necessary. All horses tolerate the needles fairly well. Acupuncture actually causes the body to release endorphins, so I find the horses relax quite deeply during the thirty or so minutes I'm working with them. It's really cool to watch.'

'I'm impressed. You certainly know your stuff. I think I'll have to give acupuncture a go myself one of these days. I could use some harmonising effects on my body.'

Aden chuckled. 'I reckon everyone could benefit from acupuncture. From headaches, anxiety, backache to period pain, it'll fix you. Wish I'd know about it earlier – I would've recommended it to my sisters.' The smile faded from Aden's face at the mention of his sisters. No doubt he was reminded of Bec, as was Kirsty. A silence fell in the Cruiser. Aden broke it.

'I miss her so much.'

'I know, Aden. So do I. I miss them all. I'm so sorry about what happened to Bec.'

'Please don't be sorry, K – you've got nothing to be sorry for,' said Aden.

Kirsty pulled a tissue from her bag and wiped at her eyes. 'I just wish I could believe that.' She took a deep breath to compose herself. 'So, where are we heading today?'

'Over to Harry and Mary Mallard's place, Diamond Racing Stables. Harry needs me to work on a few of his thoroughbreds that are set to race next month in Sydney. He's a big fan of acupuncture because it's drug- and chemical-free. There's no need to worry about anything showing up in blood tests, and it doesn't affect the animals' health in any adverse ways. I've been working with his racehorses over the last few months and Harry's been amazed at the improvement of the horses' wellbeing and performance. He reckons he might even win the Melbourne Cup this year. Time will tell.'

'Wow! Grumpy old Harry Mallard. He must think you're the bee's knees. He doesn't let just anyone near his prized thoroughbreds. I remember him chasing me away with a broom at the racecourse in town one day because he thought I was trying to make friends with his beloved racehorses. But I was there to clean up all the crap his horses dropped for a little pocket money in the school holidays. I was that scared of him I refused to go back to work and then he had to clean it all up himself. At least Mary is cheerful and kind-hearted.'

Aden pulled up at the servo, laughing. 'Yep, Mary is lovely.

But Harry, well, he can be a cranky old coot when he wants to be. But I respect him because he respects his animals. Let's hope there's no repeat of the broom incident today. I'm just going to run in and grab a can of Red Bull. Do you want anything?'

Kirsty looked at her watch. 'God, you're drinking Red Bull this early in the morning, Aden? I'd love a vanilla malted milk, please, if you don't mind. Oh, and a Snickers for later.' She leant down to grab her wallet off the floor. 'Here, let me grab you some cash.'

'My shout, back in a tick!' Aden said, jumping from the Land Cruiser and shutting the door before she even had time to argue with him.

Kirsty watched him saunter away. Aden looked so good in his jeans, he always had. He walked tall and proud, a rough-around-the-edges persona emanating from his every pore. Without thinking, she found her eyes travelling down the length of his back and halting on the full curve of his butt – it was utterly divine in his jeans. Her captivation was only broken when the servo's door slid shut behind him.

'Well, well, if it isn't Kirsty Mitchell.' Harry's deep voice rumbled like thunder as he held out a weather-beaten hand to her. The strong smell of pipe tobacco wafted in the air and the hint of a smile pulled at the corners of his leathery lips. 'I haven't seen you for years, girl. Where've you been hiding?'

Away from you and your broom, Kirsty thought. She smiled broadly as she shook his hand, wincing slightly at his vice-like grip. 'I've been overseas for the past three years, doing a bit of travelling. I lived in the UK for some of the time.'

He gave a few short clucks with his tongue, a frown creasing his already wrinkled face. 'Too many of you youngsters go overseas to holiday when we have the best places to travel right here in Australia. That's what's wrong with our bloody economy. You're not keeping your cash where it should be – in Aussies' pockets.' He pulled his hat down further on his head and directed his steely gaze at Aden. 'Come now, you've got work to do. I've got the horses ready to go in the stables. I just have to duck home and make a few phone calls but you know the way, lad.'

Aden heaved his heavy veterinary case from the tray of the Land Cruiser. 'No worries. Kirsty's here to give me a hand today. I'll come over and let you know once we're finished, Harry.'

Harry turned to Kirsty, his eyes almost burning a hole right through her skull. She couldn't help but take a small step backwards. 'Just make sure she knows what she's doing.'

Aden briskly nodded his head. 'Don't you worry. She's trained by the best, Harry.'

Harry let a small snort escape as he nodded his head. 'That's what I like to hear.'

'Say hi to Mary for me,' Kirsty said as she watched Harry turn on his heel and hobble towards the homestead, the distinct limp in his right leg caused by an accident he'd had as a young jockey. Mary Mallard had been head of the tuckshop at the local high school for years, and had been like a granny to Kirsty and lots of her schoolmates.

He gave a quick wave of his hand as he continued walking, motioning for her to follow him. 'Why don't you come say hello yourself? Mary would enjoy that. Always had a soft spot for you, she has.'

'Uh, sure, I'd love to. If Aden can spare me for a few moments.' Kirsty turned to Aden, her voice a low whisper. 'Trained by the best, hey?'

Aden grinned playfully. 'Well, I had to say something.'

'I'll be back in ten. Is that okay? I just want to say a quick hello.'

'Sure, no probs. It'll take me about that long to set up.'

Kirsty half jogged after Harry, catching up to him just as he rounded the stables and the Federation-style homestead came into view.

Harry gestured for her to go up the stairs. 'I'm going around the back to the office. Just give a few raps on the door. Mary won't be far.'

'Thanks, Harry. Catch you later.'

After a few knocks, Kirsty could hear footsteps coming towards the door and she readied herself for one of Mary's wholesome hugs. The door swung open and Mary appeared, her mass of purple-grey curls styled to perfection as always, her heart-shaped face lighting up as she swept Kirsty into her arms. 'Oh, love! It's so good to see you after all this time. My word, you're all grown up, too.'

Kirsty squeezed her back, the frailness of Mary startling her, her dear old friend not as plump and rosy-cheeked as she used to be. Were her seventy-odd years starting to take their toll? 'And it's lovely to see you too, Mary. It feels like it's been forever.'

The women pulled apart, both smiling broadly, Mary's lack of height causing her to look upwards at Kirsty, her grey-green eyes prominent against her sun-freckled skin.

'Come in for a coffee, dear,' said Mary. 'It'd be wonderful to catch up. I'd love to hear about your years overseas. Your mum has been filling me in on your adventures whenever I run into her in town.'

'Sorry, Mary. I can't today. I'm here with Aden, the vet, helping him work on the horses. But I'll come back another day, promise.'

'That would be nice. I hope you enjoyed yourself, dear, travelling the globe. I would have loved to have done that myself . . . just never got the chance,' Mary said wistfully, dabbing at her brow with a handkerchief, her face pale.

'Oh, I had a wonderful time. I'll tell you all about it when we have time to sit down and chat.' Kirsty couldn't help but notice how exhausted Mary looked. She had aged tremendously in the past few years. It was part of life, growing old, but it was still sad to see. Mary had always been so full of energy. 'All right then, I'd better get back to it.' She gave Mary a kiss on the cheek. 'See you soon.'

'Yes, dear. Say hi to your mum and dad for me – oh, and Robbie too.'

'I will, Mary. Take care. See you again soon.'

Aden slowly ran his hands over the jet-black stallion, talking gently, placing pressure in certain points on the horse's neck and back to gauge its reaction, checking to see if there were any points where the horse was in pain from its strenuous training regime. The horse whinnied gently then bent to nibble at his shirt collar. Aden chuckled and gave the horse a scratch behind the ears. 'You're in pretty good shape this week, buddy – just a bit sore in the back, by the feel of it. I'll have you feeling like a million bucks in about half an hour.'

He looked over to where Kirsty was casually leaning against the timber railing. Her beauty took his breath away. The sun was sending golden shafts streaming through the stable doors, illuminating her blonde hair, her blue eyes sparkling as she watched him work. He quickly steered his train of thought back to the job at hand, his gaze lingering momentarily on her lips as a wave of regret washed over him. He should've kissed her when he'd had the chance. Too bloody late now. 'I'll get you to pass me the acupuncture needles, K, if you don't mind.'

Kirsty beamed. 'I'd love to.' She hurried over and squatted down beside Aden, who was rummaging through his case. 'What were you doing just then? It looked to me as though you were just giving the horse a bit of a rub-down.'

Aden pulled out a box of acupuncture needles and opened the top for Kirsty, passing the pack to her. 'I was applying pressure to different points and feeling for differences in the tissue quality. Things like firmness, yielding to my pressure, tightening up under pressure, warmth, cold . . . all those sorts of things. We basically follow the meridian lines but I also like to trust the reactions of the horse I'm working on. It's a very simple yet very precise technique that allows me to work out where those little babies need to go.' He pointed to the box in Kirsty's hand.

Kirsty raised her eyebrows. 'Intricate stuff, this acupuncture.'

Aden squirted some strong-smelling antiseptic into his hands and rubbed them together vigorously, smiling at Kirsty as he motioned at the bottle for her to do the same. 'Raised eyebrows – good, that's what I want to see. I only ever get two reactions when I explain acupuncture to people. The one you just had or the opposite, when they lower their eyebrows in disbelief, like they're scowling at me. I'm happy yours was the former.'

Twenty minutes later, the horse looked as if it had just been given a shot of Valium. It had dropped its head onto the timber railing and was resting the left side of its rump up against the stable wall, its bottom lip quivering gently.

'He looks drunk, Aden. What have you done to him?' Kirsty asked, giggling as she opened the thermos of tea she'd brought along, a puff of steam erupting from the opening as she carefully filled two pannikins.

Aden looked up from where he was crouched on the stable floor, inspecting the horse's legs. 'Told you. Great, isn't it?'

'Bloody oath it is! I don't think I've ever seen a thoroughbred so relaxed. They're normally twitching with anticipation. I really have to try this out for myself one day.' Kirsty unwrapped two pieces of chocolate cake from the lunchbox, licking the rich chocolate icing from her fingertips as she did so. She passed Aden his share and sat down on the floor of the stable, leaning her back against the railing. 'So what's next on the agenda, boss?'

Aden took a gulp of tea. 'Only another four horses to go for acupuncture and then we have to check out a pregnant mare. I think she's going to give birth any day now.'

'Fantastic. I'm really enjoying this. I might have to apply to be your assistant,' Kirsty said jokingly.

Aden shuffled closer to Kirsty and threw his arm over her shoulder, giving her a quick peck on the cheek. 'I'd have you as my assistant any day, Miss Mitchell. You're very helpful *and* good-looking, too!'

Kirsty went to reply but her breath caught in her throat.

Aden's friendly kiss had left a lusciously hot spot on her skin. His eyes met hers, his gaze lingering, their faces so close their warm breath mingled. Aden's cheeky smile faded, replaced by an intense look that sent Kirsty's pulse into overdrive. He reached out slowly and traced the outline of her face, his fingertips feathering over her lips. He smiled softly, the dimples in his cheeks creasing. Kirsty's control snapped and she gave in to her desire, running her hands up his chest and wrapping her arms around his broad shoulders. Aden responded and threw his arms around her. She fell into his kiss, savouring his scent. At first the kiss was soft and sensuous, as he caressed her tongue with his own, but it quickly turned passionate as the heat between them transformed into a raging inferno.

Aden reluctantly pulled away, his breath fast and heavy as he looked deeply into Kirsty's eyes. 'I've been waiting to do that for a very, *very* long time.'

Kirsty just stared at him, her head swimming with questions. None of them seemed to find a way out of her lips.

Aden studied her expression. 'I hope you're okay with me kissing you? I mean, it seemed to me like you were okay with it.' He grinned. 'I'm so sorry if I was out of line . . .'

Kirsty looked over at the stallion briefly, then down at the floor, then back at Aden in a bid to prevent her nerves from stealing her ability to speak. This was it. She had to decide. Was she going to push away the man she had wanted all her life? Or was she going to jump in feet first and see where she landed? She wanted his love, wanted to love him. If she rejected him now she would never get a second chance. She touched his arm tentatively. 'I'm just a little taken aback, that's all. I mean, I thought you saw me more like family, considering you and Robbie are like brothers.'

Aden held her eyes. 'I've never seen you as family, K. Far from it. I've had a thing for you for as long as I can remember.'

Kirsty gasped, covering her mouth in surprise. Reality seemed to vanish around her as the impact of his words left her breathless, all her promises to herself to steer clear of Aden evaporating in an instant. 'My God! Why have you waited until now to tell me?'

Aden grinned sheepishly. 'Robbie warned me years ago that he would rip my head off and shove it up my arse if I ever touched you. I knew he was serious; he's very protective of you, K. Then, well . . . Bec died and I felt the need to get away from here, like you did. Our lives went in different directions for a little while, but here we are. Things are a bit different now and I don't think Robbie would rip my head off these days. Kind of fluky, don't you think – for both of us to arrive back here at the same time? I reckon the universe is trying to tell us something.'

'I like the way you think, Aden.' Kirsty leant in and kissed him hard on the lips then, pulling back, she placed her hand on his cheek. 'I'm glad you kissed me. I've wanted you to do that since I was a teenager.'

Aden took her by the hand and tenderly kissed it, his voice husky. 'It makes me so happy to hear it. Now come on, my gorgeous assistant; as Harry said, we've got work to do.'

Chapter 10

KIRSTY re-read the faded Murphy's Law poster that was tacked to the ceiling, trying to distract herself as she lay on her back in the doctor's surgery. It was just a regular procedure, one that all women had to go through, but Kirsty wasn't a fan of going to the doctor's at the best of times. She closed her eyes and let her thoughts wander back to the night before. It had been strange returning home with Aden, their relationship at a whole new level after the heart-stopping, mind-blowing kiss in the stables. The past receded further from her mind – yet she couldn't shake that bedrock of guilt from her consciousness. But what good would dredging up the past do now? Even thinking about it made her feel nauseous.

Kirsty and Aden had agreed to keep their burgeoning romance quiet for now, just until they knew where they were heading – if they were heading anywhere. They didn't want everyone knowing their business until they had got their own heads around the fact they were together. It all felt surreal, for both of them. She admired the fact that Aden had kissed her goodnight and headed off to his own bed, a look of longing in his beautiful brown eyes. She certainly wasn't ready to tear her clothes off for him – yet. She told Aden she wanted to take it slowly, *really* slowly, and he'd agreed, respecting her decision, making her care for him all the more.

'There we are, all finished,' Dr Nichols said as she pulled off her surgical gloves and tossed them in the bin beside the table. 'Now, would you like me to do a breast examination also?'

Kirsty sighed inwardly. All she wanted to do was get out of there. But her right breast was still tender, and it wouldn't hurt to get a professional opinion. She mustered up her most carefree voice as she wriggled up on the table into a sitting position, making sure the sheet was over her bottom half. 'Yeah, why not?'

'Okay then. Just remove your bra and raise your hands up in the air.'

Kirsty tipped her head to the side. 'I've never had to put my hands up in the air before.'

'It's a new technique. We're finding it works very well. You can see if there are any inconsistencies in the breast tissue by any wrinkling or gathering of the skin once your arm is raised. Too many women find it hard to feel for lumps because we naturally have so many in our breasts, and we are finding this technique is much easier to do at home on your own, in front of a mirror.'

Kirsty removed her bra and threw her hands up in the air, feeling slightly stupid, like she was in a stick-up. She looked at the ceiling again and rolled her eyes at the bloody poster.

'Just drop your right arm for me, Kirsty, but leave your left one up in the air. Really stretching, that's it.'

Kirsty felt cold fingers touch the suppleness of her left breast, making her jump slightly. Dr Nichols' fingertips moved professionally around her breast, and after a few moments she asked Kirsty to swap arms. She soon began to probe Kirsty's right breast, and as her fingers moved expertly she let out little *hmms*. That wasn't exactly the sound Kirsty wanted to hear. She began to feel nervous.

'Is everything all right?' she said. A sudden blinding pain shot up her right arm and she gasped loudly as Dr Nichols stepped back, a frown creasing her face.

'Have you had any tenderness in your right breast lately, Kirsty? Even a feeling of fullness or something similar?'

Kirsty felt the blood drain from her face. She didn't like the direction this appointment was taking. She nodded slowly. 'Actually, yes, I have. I felt pain there just over three weeks ago, when I was out mustering, and I gathered that maybe my period was on the way. Then it arrived a few days afterwards and I put the discomfort down to that. My period's due again in about a week's time but my breasts haven't really stopped aching and I've been noticing the occasional stinging sensation in the right nipple. So I'm gathering the cause can't be my menstrual cycle.'

'And how have you been feeling generally?' asked Dr Nichols. 'Full of energy? A bit lethargic? Normal?'

Kirsty paused before answering. 'I've been feeling a little run-down lately, to be honest. I often feel tired. I'd just put it down to working long hours on the farm.' She didn't want to tell the doctor about her sleepless nights because of the nightmares. There was nothing anyone could do about them anyway.

The doctor clasped her hands together and inhaled deeply. 'Well, there's a small lump in the right breast. Before you panic, take a deep breath. I don't want you getting concerned over it just yet. Let me write you a referral to the Cairns Breast Clinic for an ultrasound and, if need be, a biopsy, and we'll take it from there, okay? It may just be a cyst, Kirsty, so please don't worry. I'm going to ring the clinic myself now, and try to get you in as soon as possible.'

Kirsty smiled meekly. 'Okay.'

What else was she meant to say?

Kirsty slid into the driver's seat of her Holden ute, her hands shaking uncontrollably as she tried to slip the key into the ignition. She gave up and let her hands fall into her lap, resting her head against the steering wheel to ward off another flash of dizziness.

'Oh my God, I have a lump. It could be cancer. Please, I'm too young to die,' she whispered as tears poured down her cheeks. She shook her head gently, causing the horn to honk and scaring an old couple passing by. She quickly wiped her eyes and sat up straight. 'Shit, get a hold of yourself, girl! It might just be a cyst – nothing to worry about. It's all going to be okay. You'll get the test done and it will all be fine. You'll see.' She took a deep breath and let it out with a forced sigh as she pushed the key into the ignition and revved the Holden to life. 'It's all going to be okay,' she repeated over and over as she drove towards Flame Tree Hill, the tears rolling down her face once again.

Aden greeted Kirsty at the front door, holding a can of beer out for her. His smile faded when he noticed she'd been crying. He wrapped his arms around her and pulled her towards him. 'K, what's wrong? Are you regretting yesterday? You can tell me if you are. I'm not going to pressure you into anything.'

Kirsty stood silently for a few moments, enjoying the comfort she felt in Aden's arms. She stepped back and rubbed her face with both hands. 'No, it's nothing like that.' She sighed heavily, her lips quivering. 'I'll cut to the chase. The doctor found a lump in my breast. I have to go to the breast clinic in Cairns on Thursday. It might just be a cyst, though. Please, don't tell my parents – or even Robbie, for that matter. Not with Aunty Kulsoom in remission. They'll all be worried sick. No need to stress them out until I have the ultrasound, and even then I'm sure it will be all right anyway.'

Aden's face creased with worry as he reached out and held her hands. 'So it might be something more than a cyst? Shit. I don't know what to say. I promise my lips are sealed. I'm sorry you have to wait until Thursday, though. Can't they get you in any sooner?'

'My doctor tried but they were pushing it getting me in *this* week.'

Aden cupped her face gently and met her eyes. 'I'll be taking the day off and driving you there. You can't be expected to go by yourself.'

'But —'

Aden put his hand up to stop Kirsty's protests. 'No. I'm taking you and that's that.'

Chapter 11

SUNLIGHT filtered softly through the window as Kirsty sat in the waiting room among all the other women dressed in blue hospital gowns. She was exhausted after not sleeping much the last few nights. When she did manage to sleep, her dreams were terrifying ones that would leave her waking up in a cold sweat, unable to shake the feeling of dread from the pit of her stomach. She was in hell when she was awake and then the nightmares toyed with her when she tried to sleep. She couldn't win.

A middle-aged woman looked up briefly from her magazine and caught Kirsty's worried gaze. She smiled kindly, as if she knew what Kirsty was feeling right now. Kirsty wriggled in her seat, nerves making her feel as though she was going to throw up.

She longed to feel Aden's arms around her; in his embrace was the only time she felt truly safe, as though this wasn't really happening to her. Aden had argued with her in the car park for five minutes about wanting to come in to wait with her but she had bluntly refused, saying it wasn't a place for men and she didn't want to make all the other women in there feel uncomfortable. She was going to ring him on his mobile once she was finished. Looking around the waiting room, she was relieved she'd insisted.

Kirsty watched uneasily as one of the doctors walked into the waiting room with a clipboard in her hand. *Oh God, what if it's my turn next? How am I going to get through this?* Her fight-or-flight instincts kicked in and yet again, all she wanted to do was run. Typical – that was how she seemed to handle all her problems in life. She sat stone still, her heart racing and her limbs tingling from the surge of adrenaline.

'Miss Kirsty Mitchell.'

The doctor's soft yet confident voice soothed Kirsty. She stood, smiling faintly, as she gathered her handbag from the seat beside her with shaking hands.

The doctor motioned the way down a long corridor. 'Hi, Kirsty. I'm Dr Maria Little. Follow me, please.'

The doctor's shoes tapped lightly on the linoleum floor, and her long black ponytail swung from side to side with each step as she disappeared into a doorway. Kirsty followed her through, her clammy hands clasped tightly in front of her, feeling as though she was about to pass out.

'I'll be doing the ultrasound for you this morning. When you're ready, can you take your top off, slide up onto the bed for me and put your right arm above your head. I'll just pull the curtain closed until you're settled.'

A few moments later Dr Little came back and opened the curtain. Calmly, she applied gel to Kirsty's right breast then ran the transducer backwards and forwards, capturing images on a computer screen as she went. Kirsty closed her eyes and prayed harder than she'd ever prayed before, begging that there would be nothing to worry about, begging that she would walk out of there and not be fighting for her life, that this was all just a big mistake. Promising God that if it was a mistake she would reveal the truth about what she'd done to Aden – to everyone.

After years of fretting about her past, all she hoped for now was that she had a future.

'Kirsty, I'm seeing a small lump there, so we are going to do a needle biopsy to determine whether the lump is benign.'

Kirsty gasped, a flood of panic filling her as she struggled to breathe. 'Is it going to hurt?' Her voice was almost a whisper.

Dr Little shook her head gently. 'No, I'll give you a local anaesthetic so you won't feel a thing. Then I'll make a very small incision in the skin on the right breast so I'm able to insert the biopsy needle and remove some of the breast tissue for a sample. It will be a little sore afterwards, so I'll write you a script for some painkillers.' She placed her hand on Kirsty's arm. 'You just stay there and I'll be back in a few minutes with a nurse. It won't be much longer. Promise.'

'Okay.' Kirsty watched meekly as the doctor left the room, half of her wanting to scream and then the other half wanting the doctor to wrap her arms around her, to tell her everything was going to be all right. She felt as though she was drowning in a mixture of heartbroken emotion, devastation and absolute terror. What were they going to find?

Aden absentmindedly flicked a piece of the beer coaster across the table, watching as it landed among the other pieces he had already torn off. He'd been wandering aimlessly around Cairns for the past two hours, his tension growing as he waited for a phone call from Kirsty, fighting the urge to sprint into the clinic to see how she was going. What was taking her so long? What was he going to say to her if it was bad news? How would *he* take it if it were bad news? He couldn't lose another woman he cared so much for. Life couldn't be that ruthless. Could it?

The not knowing was killing him. He'd finally decided to try to eat some lunch but after taking two bites of his steak burger he'd pushed it away. He looked out over the Cairns Esplanade at all the holiday-makers enjoying the sun, swimming in the lagoon or barbecuing. It was such a happy scene and such a contrast to the turmoil that was crashing around inside him. Kirsty meant so much to him . . . she always had. To lose her now that he had just found her again was almost more than he could bear thinking about. But he was getting ahead of himself.

He took a sip of his Coke and checked his mobile for the hundredth time, just in case he'd missed a call. Fuck, this waiting was killing him. Maybe he could go and buy Kirsty something nice? His low mood lifted a little. Now that was an idea. Some flowers perhaps, to make her feel special, with a little card to let her know he was here for her and always would be. He'd noticed a shop a few streets back with bunches of native Australian flowers. Kirsty would love them. He stood and gathered his mobile and wallet off the table, heading in the direction of the florist, relieved he'd found a mission.

Halfway through paying for the flowers his mobile rang. It was Kirsty. He passed the money over and told the shop assistant to keep the change as he hurriedly flipped open his phone. 'Hi, beautiful. How's it going?'

'Hi, Aden. I'm all finished now. I'll meet you out the front of the clinic. See you soon?'

The urgency in Kirsty's voice was unmistakable and his heart sank. The street began to close in around him and he leant against a parking meter for support. What wasn't she telling him? He had a fair idea. 'I'll be there in a few minutes.'

Kirsty sat in the shade of a frangipani tree as she waited for Aden, a soft breeze wrapping itself around her. She picked up a white and yellow flower that had fallen on the grass and rolled the stem between her shaking fingers, the scent from the bloom suddenly overpowering her. She tossed it to the ground as waves of emotion washed over her and she fought hard to control the images that were rushing through her mind. She didn't want to go there; she didn't want to think about dying. She couldn't. It would mean she had accepted the devastating news the doctor had just delivered. Her life had suddenly become so very precious. She had a strange feeling of separation, like she was standing outside her body – a body that was diseased and that she couldn't run away from.

Maybe she should have died the night of the accident. She had cheated death, while everyone else has lost their lives, and now it was *her* time to go. How was she going to tell her family and friends? And how was she going to tell Aden, the man she had wanted for so long, and whom she was falling hard for, that her life might be cut short? Could she stay with him and put him through all of this? Damn it, she felt like everything was working against her.

Kirsty closed her eyes and dropped her head into her hands, wanting to block out the world. There were too many things to think of and way too much uncertainty. There was only *one* thing she was sure of right now: she had invasive ductal carcinoma breast cancer. It was too aggressive to operate on, and she would be starting a course of chemotherapy the following week. Twenty-one weeks of chemotherapy, to be exact. And that wasn't the worst of it. Doctor Little had also explained to her that there was a possibility of the cancer having metastasised into her bones. She had to undergo more tests in two days to determine that. The battle had only just begun.

Aden gripped the steering wheel, his knuckles white, as he weaved his way through the traffic and around the roundabout, his tyres screeching as he came to an abrupt stop in front of Kirsty. She was slumped against a frangipani tree, her face as pale as a ghost as she stared off into space. She hadn't even noticed he'd pulled up. He jumped out of the driver's seat and ran towards her. Kneeling down he took her into his arms, his heart breaking into a million tiny pieces.

Kirsty, suddenly realising he was there, wrapped her arms around him and began to weep, loud, heart-wrenching sobs escaping her as she tried to speak. 'I, I have aggressive breast cancer, Aden. Oh God. I don't want to die. Please, don't let me die. I'm so frightened about what's going to happen to me.' She began to shake uncontrollably in his arms, her tears soaking his shirt.

Aden squeezed her tighter. Tears burned his own eyes but he blinked them away, wanting to stay strong for her, every inch of him wishing he could take her pain away. Why, after almost losing her once, was he faced with losing her again? How fucking cruel could life be? He kissed her face, his lips wet with her tears, his eyes coming to rest on her own. 'I'm here for you, beautiful. And I will be with you every step of the way. No matter what.'

Kirsty nodded and rested her head against his chest.

Chapter 12

HIDDEN Valley was only halfway through autumn but winter was already whispering its arrival, with the early mornings becoming fresher. North Queensland was not blessed with four distinct seasons; there was only really summer and winter, with slight variations in autumn and spring. Kirsty loved the cooler months at Hidden Valley. The mornings were cold enough for her to wear her fluffy slippers and robe, and with the way she was feeling that was a godsend. Over the past week she'd experienced a mixture of emotions – fear, denial, anger, sadness, helplessness and despair, her mood changing at any given moment. At times she felt strong, like she would be able to face the cancer and beat it hands down, while at other times she would roll herself into a ball on the couch and cry until she had no tears left.

Kirsty straightened up the flowers that Aden had given her the week before, touched he had chosen natives – her favourites – and then stirred two teaspoons of sugar into her pannikin of tea, enjoying the fact that the house was all hers for the day. She wandered out to the verandah, welcomed by endless blue skies and golden rays of sunlight dancing across the worn timber floorboards. Hank came to greet her, his tail wagging furiously as Kirsty gave him a rub behind the ears. She slumped down on the couch, her spirits lifting slightly as she spotted Kulsoom heading over from the main house with a cuppa in her hands.

'Morning, Aunty, how are you?' she called when Kulsoom was in earshot.

Kulsoom held onto the banisters and slowly made her way up the stairs. 'I'm good, love. But more importantly, how are you?'

Kirsty wriggled over so Kulsoom could sit beside her. 'I'm okay, I suppose. I'm trying to remain positive but I think I'm still in shock. I'm just finding it hard to believe I have cancer – you always think something like this will never happen to you. And I'm terrified about tomorrow.'

Kulsoom took Kirsty's hand and squeezed it tightly; the compassion in her face made Kirsty want to burst out crying for the third time that morning. 'Cancer can be a tough battle, my love, but you've just got to be tougher. Try not to think about it. I'll be with you tomorrow, darling, along with your mum. Strength in numbers, as they say.'

'I know, and I really appreciate you coming along. I know it'll be hard for you, going back to an oncology ward.'

Kulsoom smiled softly. 'Don't you concern yourself with me. I'm an old hand at this, and a lot tougher than people realise. You focus all your energies on getting better.'

'How are Mum and Dad coping? They act strong around me but I know Mum has been crying endlessly – unless there's another reason her eyes have been red and puffy for days.'

'They're doing as well as can be expected, Kirsty. They're trying to be strong for your sake. Your dad has gone terribly quiet and your mum, well, she's pretty upset. But she's a strong lady and she will deal with things as they crop up.'

Kirsty blinked back tears. 'I hope they understand my wishes to keep this to ourselves. The only person outside of here who knows is Jo, and she's all the way over in the UK. I don't want to be a hot topic among the Hidden Valley locals – I don't want people feeling sorry for me.'

Kulsoom squeezed Kirsty's hand. 'We all understand that, and we will respect it. I was the same when I found out. You'll eventually find that you open up to people, whether it's in a week, a month, or longer, but I think at first, until you get your head around it all, you're a bit like me and like to keep things close to your chest.'

Kirsty nodded and glanced out over the paddocks, taking a few sips of tea while she watched Cash nibble on some grass. 'Tell me, what does chemotherapy feel like? I'm expecting to feel really sick, since that's what the doctors have said. But is it all the time?'

Kulsoom sighed. 'I'm not going to lie and say that chemo is a walk in the park. Yes, it can make you very sick, and there will be days where you don't even feel like getting out of bed. But what's making you sick is killing the cancer in the most effective way we know of. You're strong-willed, Kirsty, always have been, and I *know* you will get through this. You come from a strong line of country women, remember. And you have all of us here to support you, to love you, to carry you through this. Please promise me you will accept our love and support along the way.'

Kirsty looked back at Kulsoom, a little taken aback. 'Of course I will. Why wouldn't I?'

'The journey ahead of you is one that will make you question so much about life, about the people you know, about what you've done in the past, about all the things you want to achieve and about what's really important to you in the long run. These thoughts can sometimes make you so angry that you take it out on the people who love you the most. In those times, remind yourself that we love you very much. Can you do that for me?'

Kirsty leant in and hugged Kulsoom. Little did her aunt know just how much she already questioned her past. It was such a heavy burden to carry and with the new stress of breast cancer on top of it, the weight was almost crushing her. 'Okay, I promise.'

'Good. I'll hold you to that,' Kulsoom replied gently as she patted Kirsty on the knee. 'Now, tell me, how's it all going with Aden? How is *he* managing with all this?'

Kirsty couldn't help smiling as she thought of Aden. It had been a week now since they'd come clean about their feelings, and despite the cancer diagnosis, Kirsty felt a tingle inside her every time she thought of him. They still hadn't got past the stage of kissing and cuddling, but she liked it that way for now. Aden wasn't pushing her for anything more, which she appreciated. Even though she'd dreamt of being with him for so long, she just couldn't focus on anything other than her cancer right now. She adored him all the more for understanding that.

'Oh, he's smothering me with love and affection . . . but I think I can handle it. The timing is incredibly bad, and I think we're both sad we didn't open up about our feelings earlier.' Kirsty sighed. 'But, Aden being Aden, he's keeping all that to himself. I'm sure it's because he doesn't want to add to my worries. I think he's a bit upset that I won't let him take me to my chemotherapy session, but as I explained to him, he has to work – he's put everything into his business and I don't want him jeopardising that because he has to take days off to look after me. I would feel guilty if he did.' Kirsty felt the all too familiar lump in her throat as tears filled her eyes. Aden was being so wonderful to her. Deep inside, the guilt rose and she tried to push it down. She'd missed her opportunity to come clean with him.

She fumbled with the handle on her cup, not wanting to meet Kulsoom's gentle eyes. There was another matter sitting heavily on her heart too – but at least she could talk to Kulsoom about that one. 'Do you think I'm selfish asking him to stay with me when I've just found out I have cancer, Aunty? It isn't going to be easy for us to make it work, even if the chemo goes well. I could die.'

Kulsoom gasped. 'Don't you ever think like that, my darling girl. You're *not* sentenced to death. And in no way are you being selfish staying with him – by golly, you only just got together after all these years. He's a wonderful man and he doesn't care a whit about your cancer. You hang on to him, you hear?'

Kirsty pulled a tissue from her pocket and wiped her eyes. Hang on to him? She was trying to do just that. Even though Kulsoom's words comforted her, she couldn't shake a feeling of selfishness from her mind. It was so much to ask Aden to commit to her when her future was so uncertain. 'Thank you, Aunty. Thank you for all your advice. It helps. I'm so happy you've cancelled your flight back, otherwise you'd be leaving this weekend. I can't believe almost five weeks have gone already. It only feels like yesterday that you got here. Uncle Harry has been wonderful, encouraging you to stay for me. Bless him.'

Kulsoom leant over and gave Kirsty a kiss on the cheek. 'I'm not going anywhere until you're out of the woods.' She sat back on the couch and motioned for Hank to jump up. He obliged eagerly, his tail slapping Kulsoom and Kirsty as he got comfortable between them. Kirsty could only laugh; he was a delightful distraction from her turbulent mind.

'How did Robbie take the news that you and Aden are an item now?' Kulsoom asked. 'Aden mentioned something to me about Robbie warning him not to go near you when you were teenagers.' She smiled. 'Poor Aden – although I thought it was adorable that Robbie was so protective of you.'

'He still is!' said Kirsty. 'But it all went very well, better than expected. I think my cancer news outweighed any concerns Robbie may have harboured about me and Aden being together.' She shook her head and pulled at a thread on her robe, her smile fading as she blinked back more tears. 'I'm worried about Robbie, though – I haven't seen him smile in a week.'

'We all love you dearly, Kirsty, and it's scary to find out a loved one has cancer. Give him time and trust me, he'll smile again soon. It was great news that the test results came back clear. I was so relieved when you told me the cancer hadn't spread to your bones. I finally felt like I could breathe again.'

'Tell me about it! I felt like I had been given some sort of lifeline. Those three days of waiting for results were agonising. I couldn't believe I needed so many darn tests in the first place. I know the doctors needed to find out exactly what stage my cancer was at so they could treat it appropriately, and also if it had spread anywhere else, but between a nuclear, a CT, various blood tests and an MRI scan, I felt like I had been prodded and poked all day long.'

'It's not nice, going through all of them. I had to do all of that too. But you got the best result possible – that the cancer is contained to the breast area.'

Kirsty drank the last of the tea in her pannikin and stood resolutely, holding her hand out to Kulsoom to help her up from the couch. 'Right, enough talking about my cancer. How would you like to help me clean out my darkroom and dust off all those photographs I have in there? Aden has offered to knock up a few frames for me out of some old timber that's been stored in the shed for years. He reckons going through my photos will be therapeutic for me, and help inspire me to follow my dream of owning a gallery in town one of these days.'

Kulsoom eased her way out of the couch. 'I reckon he's onto something there. I'd love to help. I'll just go and get changed out of my pyjamas first.'

'Thanks.' Kirsty smiled gratefully. 'I might pop over to the homestead after I have a quick shower, to see if Mum wants to help too. We could make an afternoon of it, us three girls. Mum's been nagging me to clean the darkroom out for years, and to hang up my work, especially the photos I won awards for, so she'll be chuffed I've finally decided to.'

'Right you are, darling. I'm all yours for the day,' Kulsoom said.

Kirsty kicked her thongs off at the front door and made her way into the homestead. Everything was silent, other than the ticking of the massive grandfather clock in the corner of the lounge room. The rhythmic noise was echoing around the house eerily. It was so quiet. She looked at her watch and shook her head. The place was usually a hive of activity at smoko time. She wandered down the hall and into the kitchen, half expecting to find her mum in there baking like she normally would be, but it was empty. Where was everyone? Kirsty leant against the kitchen bench and had a peek out the bay window. Her heart clenched in sorrow. Outside, Lynette stood at the clothes line in Ron's arms, her body trembling as she sobbed on his shoulder. He was stroking her hair and kissing her on the forehead. Kirsty knew it was because of her. Should she go out there? She jumped as Kulsoom walked up behind her.

'Go on, love, go out there. Your mum has to learn that it's okay for you to see her cry.'

'Okay,' Kirsty replied quietly, opening the screen door and heading into the yard.

Lynette pulled free from Ron's embrace when she spotted Kirsty, hastily wiping her eyes with a handkerchief and straightening her apron. Ron stood back, sniffing loudly, not able to look in Kirsty's direction.

'Morning, dear, how are you feeling today?' Lynette said, all too cheerily, as she shook out a pillowcase and hung it on the line. Reaching into the clothes basket she began to pull out another, but Kirsty stopped her by placing her hand gently on top of her mother's.

'Mum, you don't have to pretend that you're all right. It's okay for me to see you upset.' She turned to Ron. 'And that goes for you too, old fella.'

Lynette's reserve broke and she began to cry as she pulled Kirsty into a tight cuddle. 'I love you so much. And it hurts like you wouldn't believe to see your child go through something like this. It's not like I can put a bandaid on it and make it all better for you, like when you fell out of that tree or stacked your bike. This is so different, and I feel so helpless.' Lynette's lips quivered, her eyes meeting Kirsty's as she pulled back and placed her hands tenderly on Kirsty's cheeks. 'It's bringing back all the fear I experienced the night of the accident, when I thought we'd lost you. You mean everything to me, my darling. I don't want to see you go through physical and emotional pain like that again. It's not fair; you've had enough trauma in you life. If I could change places with you I would – in a heartbeat.'

Kirsty's heart ached for her mum and she reached out to brush away Lynette's tears, her own falling freely, a wave of guilt washing over her for what her parents had gone through on that earth-shattering night six years ago. They'd had to see her hooked up to tubes in the hospital, battered and bruised, unable to breathe on her own, while trying to comfort the parents of her mates who had died in the accident. 'It's okay, Mum. It's not your fault. I love you too.'

Ron wrapped his arms around his wife and daughter and the three of them cried together. At that moment, Kirsty felt more loved than ever, and her will to live, to survive, filled her with a yearning she had never experienced before. A yearning to get married, to have children, to fulfil her dream of owning a gallery, to live to a ripe old age with Aden by her side. And before all that, she yearned for the courage to open up about her past. It wasn't too much to ask. Was it?

Kirsty placed the last of the photographs she wanted to frame on the spare bed, admiring the beauty of the shots, quietly impressed. She hadn't looked at these photos in years. Her favourite one was of teenaged Robbie and Aden and two other stockmen riding into camp after a long day out mustering on Flame Tree Hill, their faces dusty and shaded by their hats, the sun setting magnificently in the background. Maybe it was worth giving photography a go again? Not that it mattered now. It might be too late to do anything about it. She might not even live until the end of the year.

She turned as she felt someone's presence in the room and was met by Aden's handsome face. He was leaning against the wardrobe, smiling at her, his hands behind his back. 'Hey, gorgeous, I missed you today. I'm happy to see you've sorted through your photographs. It's time they were on the walls for everyone to admire.'

Kirsty tried to peek behind him, to see what he was hiding. 'I missed you too. What have you got there?'

Aden walked towards her, his dark eyes almost entrancing her. 'I'd like a kiss first, and then you'll get your present.' His lips met hers, his kiss soft and tender as he gently caressed her tongue with his. Kirsty felt her body respond, a pleasurable tingle travelling through her, leaving her breathless. Aden pulled back, grinning playfully, placing a wrapped gift in her hands. 'I hope you like it.'

Kirsty gently tore open the gold wrapping paper to reveal a beautifully embellished diary. She ran her fingertips over the cover, which was handcrafted. 'I love it, Aden. It's absolutely stunning.'

Aden smiled, a look of relief flitting across his face. 'I'm glad. It took me over an hour to pick it out. I thought it might be nice for you to write down how you're feeling . . . You know, express yourself privately. I thought it might help.'

Kirsty felt her heart swell at his kindness. The brochures the cancer clinic had given her had mentioned keeping a diary. Aden must have taken the time to read through them. She wrapped her arms around him. 'Thank you, thank you so much. It's such a thoughtful gift.'

Aden kissed her tenderly again. 'Well, if you reckon *that's* thoughtful, come into the kitchen. I have another surprise for you. Close your eyes.'

Kirsty grinned. 'What next?' But she closed her eyes obediently as Aden led her by the hand into the kitchen. The familiar scent of Gucci perfume gave the surprise away before she had even opened her eyes.

'Oh my God! Jo!' Kirsty screamed as she ran into her best friend's arms, emotions overwhelming her. 'What are you doing here? You should be in the UK, enjoying your promotion!'

Jo hugged her back fiercely, her eyes brimming with tears. 'I've packed up and moved back home, mate. I couldn't leave you to go through all of this without me here to keep you on your toes, now could I?'

Kirsty was overwhelmed, and for a moment she couldn't speak. 'Thank you for coming home. It means the world to me that you did,' she finally managed between sniffles. 'Not that I would have expected you to.'

Jo grabbed hold of Kirsty's hands, her wet eyes full of determination. 'You're going to get through this. And I'm not taking no for an answer.'

Kirsty nodded and squeezed Jo's hands tightly. 'Yes, sir! You're the most wonderful friend, Jo. I'm so happy you're here.' She tried to look strong, positive – determined, even – and for a moment she convinced herself. But uncertainties possessed her, haunted her, like they did every day. She wasn't sure she was going to make it through this. Even the doctors weren't sure. But she had to believe in something right now. She just *had* to believe she was going to live, for it was all she had to hold on to.

Chapter 13

KIRSTY was out of the comfort of her bed and into the saddle before anyone else that morning. But the azure skies were now giving way to threatening black clouds, the air thick with tension. The sunlight began to fade quickly as dark shadows stretched across the paddock. Kirsty glanced skywards as a lightning bolt shot its iridescent veins through the clouds, igniting the skies with an electric-blue flash as it sent its many tentacles down towards the darkening landscape. A rumble of explosive thunder followed in its wake, so powerful Kirsty could feel it shudder through the ground beneath her and Cash. What a perfect photograph it would have made – but Kirsty didn't have time to stop and admire it. It was dangerous to be out in lightning like this, especially when she and Cash were so exposed. And it looked like this storm was going to be a whopper.

Kirsty gave Cash a firm nudge with her legs and leant forward in the saddle, gripping the reins, urging him to pick up the pace and head back to the stables. Small droplets of rain began to fall as Cash broke into a gallop. Riding made Kirsty feel free and intensely alive, even if it was just for a few hours. The only noise she could hear over her own breathing was the thumping of Cash's hoofs on the earth, and that was a soothing sound in itself.

Another loud crack of thunder boomed overhead, reverberating off the distant mountains, and seconds later the skies opened up, the heavy downpour soaking Kirsty through to the skin. Cash whinnied and Kirsty called out to him, calming him with her words. He was none too keen on storms, and she would never have taken him out for a gallop if she had known the weather was going to take a turn for the worse.

It had seemed like a great idea at dawn when she had woken, feeling pent-up and nervous about the day ahead, despite the night spent in Aden's arms. Today was the day: her first chemo treatment. She had made sure to leave a little note beside the bed for Aden, telling him where she had gone, then she had snuck out of the bedroom, willing the floorboards not to creak too loudly beneath her feet.

It had been a rough night. From the minute they had crawled into bed together Aden had held her close, never complaining about her tossing and turning, quietly soothing her when she had woken in the early hours drenched in sweat after endless nightmares. In one dream, she was about to be buried alive in a coffin, the faceless mourners standing above the grave chanting the word 'revenge'. It was one of the many dreams that had haunted her after the accident, only now it seemed more menacing, like it had gathered power from her malignant cells. Aden had kissed her tenderly, his fingers gently stroking her hair, his husky whispers in her ear making her body ache with desire. She had almost given in to the moment but Aden had stilled her gently, telling her she needed her rest. She was silently relieved. Her mind was in turmoil and her body ached, and she wanted the first time with Aden to be as special as she'd always imagined.

She had watched him as he drifted back to sleep, his handsome, rugged features so beautiful in the soft moonlight filtering through the curtains. Part of her wanted to wake him up and tell him everything. But she couldn't bring herself to fracture the perfection of what they had.

She hadn't slept a wink after the nightmares, instead lying in Aden's arms, listening to his heartbeat while he slept as though it was the most magical sound in the entire world. And to her it was magical, for it was life itself, beating within his chest, reminding her just how much she had taken everything for granted. But as always, the guilty thoughts kept returning to her mind. Just how much would Aden hate her if he knew the truth?

After driving down the Kuranda Range at a snail's pace due to the monsoonal storm that had descended so suddenly that morning, Lynette pulled up outside the Cairns Base Hospital with Kirsty in the passenger seat and Kulsoom in the back. Kirsty silently prayed for courage to get through her first bout of chemotherapy – and courage to even walk through the front entrance of the hospital in the first place. When she'd got back from her ride, Aden had already left for work, but he'd left a note for her on her pillow: *My beautiful Kirsty, I missed waking up beside you, but I hope you enjoyed your ride. I'm thinking of you every minute today, wishing I could be right there with you. Please know you mean the world to me. You always have and forever will. Love Aden xxxx*

She held the note tightly in her hand and pushed it against her thumping chest, willing it to give her the strength she needed. She had cried as she read it that morning. Did she deserve this beautiful man? Deserve his unconditional love? She took a deep breath, opened the car door and stepped out. It was time for her to face her fears, to begin the battle. And she was going to fight with everything she had. The cancer was *not* going to win. It was *not* going to take her life away from her! She had way too much to live for.

Even with Lynette and Kulsoom beside her, the journey in the lift to the oncology ward seemed to take forever. Kirsty kept her gaze fixed on the floor, not wanting to meet anyone's eye, trying to muster her inner strength. The first thing that struck Kirsty as she stepped through the lift doors and onto the ward was the smell. It was similar to that of moth balls, or some sickly aftershave. The rest of the hospital didn't smell like that – it was unique to the oncology ward.

An elderly nurse with a kind face greeted them from behind the reception desk. 'Good morning, how can I help you?'

'I'm, um, here for my, um, chemotherapy,' Kirsty stammered as Lynette gently rubbed her back. The room was beginning to spin around her and she was suddenly worried she might fall over. She grabbed hold of Kulsoom's hand. Her aunt knew exactly what she was about to go through.

'And what was your name, dear?' the nurse asked gently as she glanced over the list she was holding.

Kirsty tried to answer but nothing came out of her mouth.

'Kirsty, Miss Kirsty Mitchell,' Kulsoom replied, smiling tight-lipped and holding Kirsty's hand firmly.

The nurse tapped the board with her pen. 'Oh yes, here you are.' She looked up and smiled. 'Is it okay if I call you Kirsty?'

'Oh, yes, I'd prefer it,' whispered Kirsty, her heart hammering a million miles a minute. All she could hear was the blood pumping in her ears as she struggled to breathe normally.

'All right then, Kirsty, follow me.' The nurse turned her gaze to Lynette and Kulsoom. 'You two ladies can wait in the reception area if you like. There's tea and coffee in there, and a telly and magazines to pass the time. We should only be about an hour or so.'

Lynette pushed Kirsty's fringe back and kissed her on the forehead while blinking back tears. 'We'll be waiting for you when you've finished. Love you.'

Kirsty nodded, unable to speak, and cautiously followed the nurse into a huge room with a long line of chairs. The nurse led Kirsty to a chair next to a young girl, who looked like she was no older than fifteen. The girl smiled and Kirsty smiled weakly back. Noticing the girl's bald head she blinked back tears. What courage this young girl must have to be going through cancer treatment.

As Kirsty settled herself, the nurse went to get an IV drip and came back to her side. 'Now I've got two different kinds of drugs here, and they'll just go quietly in over the next little while – you don't need to do anything but relax. I'm also going to give you an injection, but that will be over very quickly.'

Kirsty froze. She was petrified of needles. She'd been so wound up thinking about the cancer that she hadn't even stopped to consider she would be getting needles. How in the hell was she going to get through this every three weeks for twenty-one weeks? She nodded apprehensively as she bit her quivering bottom lip, closing her eyes, wanting the sounds, smells and sights of the room to vanish. The entirety of it was terrifying.

'You'll just feel a little sting,' said the nurse, and immediately afterwards Kirsty felt an injection into her vein. She wasn't sure if she was imagining it but a feeling of nausea immediately washed over her. And she hadn't even got the drip in yet. She gritted her teeth, knowing this was just the beginning – if she couldn't get through this part she was never going to make it. And she *had* to make it through this.

19 April 2012
Dear Diary,

Today was my first experience with chemotherapy, and it was hideous. I feel like I've been electrocuted and my head wants to blow itself off my shoulders. My ears are buzzing, I feel very dizzy and very unsteady on my feet. My jaw is trembling constantly and I vomited twice on the way home. Poor Mum, she was pulling the car over every ten minutes just in case. Everything is making me feel nauseous: smells, sounds, moving objects, movement generally . . . I feel as though I have a furnace burning inside of me, but on the other hand I can't stop shivering. Aden and Robbie have just carried me from the toilet and put me to bed so I can get some rest. I didn't even have the strength to walk. Aden is just having a quick shower and then he's going to come and lie with me. I need to feel him beside me; he makes me feel so safe, so loved.

Robbie keeps sticking his head in every two seconds. Bless him! He's trying to act so strong around me but I know it's tearing him apart. Mum didn't want to leave me here at the cottage, but I told her she had to go home – Dad needs her too – and I'm not moving into the homestead, like she asked me to, because this is my home. Aunty Kulsoom offered to stay with me for the night but I kindly told her that I would rather have Aden sleep with me. She just laughed and said she would prefer a hot young man sleeping beside her over an old woman any day too. Thank goodness for her humour. Lord knows I need it. I'm so afraid of what is going to happen to me. I think that is all I can write at the moment. I feel so weak, so exhausted. I'm hoping that tomorrow I might feel a bit better.

K x

Chapter 14

ADEN and Kirsty stood together under the night sky, the new moon just a hint among the millions of stars. It was two weeks since her first chemo session, and Kirsty still felt like she had an extremely bad case of the flu, every part of her body aching. Everything was quiet apart from the whinnying of a few horses and the soft scrape of the bougainvillea vine against the metal rainwater tank. Aden pulled Kirsty in to him, his hands lightly caressing her back as he placed a lingering kiss on her mouth.

Kirsty's pulse quickened as he ran his lips down the side of her face, butterflying soft kisses along the way. Her breath caught as he moved along her neck, releasing a long warm exhalation that sent pleasurable shivers all over her. Kissing Aden was one of the only things that took her mind off the pain. He brought his gaze back to meet her own, a mischievous twinkle in his chocolate-brown eyes. 'It's freezing out here. We'd better head back inside before you catch a cold.'

'Yes, Dr Maloney.' Kirsty rolled her eyes but she let him take hold of her hand and lead her towards the door, every inch of her wanting to keep going, willing him to keep going, although she knew damn well that with how she was feeling it wouldn't be physically possible.

The doctors had been adamant that Kirsty avoid any illnesses, as her immune system was weakened by the chemo, and Aden was meticulously trying to do everything by the book. She knew he was only trying to do the very best for her, but sometimes his insistence on things annoyed her, as though every day she was losing a little bit more of her independence. She was trying hard not to snap at him for it, knowing it would be nasty of her to do so, but sometimes she found herself biting her tongue hard.

The first day of June was officially the first day of winter in Australia, but it was only the fourth of May and the frosty, haze-shrouded mornings were already starting to emerge, the westerly winds sweeping across Flame Tree Hill's paddocks chilly enough to warrant Kirsty stoking up the open fire in the cottage. She padded inside while Aden headed down the hall and towards the shower, leaving behind him an earthy, horsy scent from his day at work. Kirsty relished it. She missed coming home at nights covered in dirt and dust after working outside with the cattle and horses. How she prayed she would be able to do it again.

After making herself a hot chocolate, Kirsty headed for the lounge, where Robbie was installed in his favourite chair. 'Hey, Robbie, thanks again for dinner.' She put her hot chocolate down on the coffee table. 'I'm still full.'

Robbie smiled at her as he grabbed the remote and switched off the telly. 'You're welcome, sis. I'm just glad you've been able to eat this past week.' He swiftly avoided her gaze and picked up the newspaper from the floor, sniffing loudly. 'You've lost too much weight already and it's only been a couple of weeks since you started chemo.'

Kirsty moved closer to him, leaning over his chair and wrapping her arms around his shoulders, willing the lump to diminish from her throat. 'Don't you worry, Robbie – I'll be back to myself in no time. You'll see.'

She picked up the matches and knelt down on the sheepskin rug in front of the fireplace, not quite avoiding Hank's affectionate lick of her face. With a giggle she wiped the slobber from her nose and gave him a quick cuddle before pointing to his blanket in the corner of the room. Hank obeyed and strutted off, his head high in the air and his tail proud. He was allowed to sleep inside due to the wintry weather and he clearly felt like the king of the castle. His antics were a welcome relief from the emotional roller-coaster Kirsty had been on for weeks.

She turned her attention back to the fireplace, crumpling up some old newspaper and tucking it beneath the ironbark before striking a match and tossing it in, the scent of sulphur lingering for a few brief moments. She leant back against the couch and took a sip of her hot chocolate, mesmerised as the rising flames fed off the oxygen in the atmosphere and engulfed the kindling with their red hot tongues. The flames grew higher as she watched, dancing and flickering spectacularly. It reminded Kirsty of the way Aden's fingers left trails of heat on her skin that seemed to tingle forever. If only she had the energy to respond.

The past two weeks had been a living hell and the worst of it was she still had another nineteen weeks of it. How was she ever going to make it through? Every inch of her body felt as though it was conspiring against her. The cancer was fighting to live, yet she was fighting to live too – it was a vicious battle that only one would win. She was constantly dehydrated, but on the other hand she found it hard to keep anything down, even water. There were fleeting moments where she almost wished she would die, the pain and the nausea taking their toll. And to make matters even worse, her immune system had deteriorated, leading to a whole host of other problems: her mouth and tongue were now covered with painful ulcers, and her sinuses had blocked up. But worst of all was the smell, that horrible pungent smell that she'd first had a whiff of in the hospital. It clung to her, and she knew now it was the smell of the chemo toxins seeping out of her pores. It was on her sheets and on her clothes, and no matter how much she bathed it was still there, persistently reminding her that she had breast cancer, that she was full of poisons, and that if these poisons didn't do their job, she would die. In one week's time she would have her second session of chemo, and she bloody well hoped it was working.

Both her family and Aden had offered their support to her by trying to get her to eat and drink, embracing her when she was overcome with tears, holding her hand while she was being sick or had trouble falling asleep, and carrying her around the cottage when she was too weak to walk. Kirsty appreciated it, and at times she desperately needed their help *and* encouragement, but she was also fiercely determined to do things on her own. For her own self-worth she needed to hold tight to what she had left of her independence, much to everyone's apprehension, but they knew better than to argue with her about it, knowing that when she had her mind set on something there was no way in hell they would be able to talk her around. She wasn't about to become a pity case where everyone had to stop his or her life to take care of her. She needed to see the normalcy of life going on around her; it gave her comfort, like her life was normal too.

Sometimes she would feel a small pang of jealousy when the guys headed off to work, wishing she could join them, but she knew bed rest was imperative for her right now and she just had to accept it.

During the first week after her chemo Kirsty's family had driven her nuts ignoring her request to be left alone. Yes, she required help but she also needed some space and time to be with her own thoughts. Everyone except Kulsoom found this very hard to understand. Thank goodness Kirsty had her aunty there to explain. At the odd moments when no one was with her and she needed to go to the toilet, she refused to use the phone beside her bed to call the homestead for help. Instead she would stubbornly crawl, wanting to prove to herself that she could do it, having to stop along the way to lean against the wall as she squeezed her eyes shut and panted. Then the exhaustion would wash over her, the task seeming almost impossible, as tears poured down her face. It was moments like these that Kirsty really doubted herself, doubted her ability to survive. She knew from what Aunty Kulsoom had told her that it was going to be a scary and soul-searching journey, but nothing and no one could have prepared her for just *how* terrifying it was going to be. And it was only just beginning. In her desolate moments she'd made a pact with God that if she lived then she would be totally honest – with everyone, in minuscule, agonising detail, no matter what the consequences.

Aden came into the lounge after his shower and sat on the couch behind Kirsty, who was still on the floor, clutching her empty mug and staring into the flames. Without a word, he wrapped his arms around her shoulders and kissed her cheek, his warm, freshly showered scent enveloping her. Then, placing his hands on her shoulders, he began to massage firmly. Instead of relaxing Kirsty it hurt and she yanked herself away from him, instantly annoyed. Didn't he know how sensitive and sore her body was from the chemo? God, she'd told him enough times. She scowled at him while clutching at her now throbbing shoulder, not wanting to make a scene in front of Robbie.

Aden stared at her, wide-eyed, clearly taken aback, worry clouding his features. He looked down at his hands, then back at her, suddenly understanding. 'Sorry, K, I forgot. Well, not forgot, but you know, didn't think,' he whispered.

She instantly felt guilty. He was only trying to do something nice. Geez, she had been snappy lately. And Aden didn't deserve for her to be so short-tempered with him.

'Well, I'm off to bed, you two,' Robbie said, completely oblivious to the tension that had been and gone, yawning and tossing the newspaper onto the coffee table. He pushed the footrest from the recliner back into the chair and it settled with a loud clunk.

Kirsty blew him a kiss. 'Night, sleep tight, don't let the bed bugs bite.'

Robbie chuckled. 'I'll try not to. Night.'

'Night, mate,' Aden said.

Once Robbie had left, Aden slipped off the couch and carefully snuggled in closer to Kirsty, pulling a silky cashmere blanket up and over the both of them. 'I'm really sorry I hurt you. I didn't mean it.'

Kirsty turned and met his concerned gaze. 'Don't apologise. I'm the one who should be saying sorry. I shouldn't be so grumpy. I know you're only trying to help me feel better.'

'Yeah, I am, but I can be a bloody doofus sometimes.'

'Yeah, but you're my doofus,' Kirsty teased as she rested her head on his shoulder.

They sat in comfortable silence for a few minutes, the light from the fire flickering softly over their faces. Kirsty entwined her fingers with Aden's and squeezed his hand, craving some normal conversation, away from the subject of her cancer; it seemed to be the only thing she got to talk about lately. 'How was your day at work?'

'It was good. I got to do some acupuncture on a ten-year-old Shetland pony called Rodger. He has terrible arthritis, the poor bugger. The little girl who owns him was so concerned. It was adorable. She gave me a big kiss and a cuddle before I left for coming to help him.'

Kirsty had a little chuckle at the horse's name. 'And how did *Rodger* find his acupuncture? Did it help him?'

'It sure did. I mean, it's not going to cure him, but it will relieve the pain. A regular monthly session of acupuncture will do the trick, along with a drink of strong homemade ginger ale every day.'

Kirsty giggled. 'Ginger ale?'

'Yep. Ginger ale. I have a recipe I give out that is made from plenty of fresh ginger, and the horses love it. Ginger is a great natural anti-inflammatory, so it's perfect for arthritis.'

'Wow, you really are a clever man!'

Aden gave her a gentle squeeze. 'Gee, thanks, gorgeous.'

Kirsty snuggled in closer and Aden began to run his fingers delicately through her hair. Usually this would have been pleasant but now it made her recoil like a threatened snake. Poor Aden, he couldn't win at the moment. He was only trying to be affectionate but she was petrified he would pull his hand free of her head and take half her hair with it. Not that any had fallen out yet, but it was going to happen at some stage. Aden didn't seem to notice her flinch, or if he did, he didn't make a big deal of it, giving her hair one last stroke before stopping. 'Are you sure you don't want me to come with you tomorrow? I mean, I don't mind having the day off. I feel awful going about my normal day when you're at the hospital. I really want to be there with you, for you.'

Kirsty placed her hand over his and gently squeezed it, feeling the strength in his hands. 'Thanks, but no. Like I've told you, I don't want you missing work. And to be honest I really don't want you to see the oncology ward. It's not a nice place to be. Mum has to work at the old people's home tomorrow; it's her turn to cook meals. She said she would tell them she couldn't do it but I insisted she go in. She's been volunteering there for years. Aunty Kulsoom and Jo are taking me.'

Aden cleared his throat, his body stiffening slightly as he pulled his hand away from hers and quickly wiped his eyes. 'Oh. Righto.'

Kirsty's heart broke. Was he crying? She manoeuvred herself so she could look at him, his handsomeness accentuated by the soft glow from the fire. She tenderly cupped his face with her trembling hands, the silence between them suddenly deafening, the intensity of the moment tearing her heart to shreds. His eyes were wet with unshed tears. She ran her fingers over his chiselled features, pausing to trace the scar above his lip, a short gasp escaping her parted lips as she scrambled to find words, her heart pitter-pattering within her chest. Why couldn't she let him in, let him take care of her? She could see she had hurt him and it cut her deeply. Taking his hand, she placed it on her heart, still unable to talk, wishing he could reach inside her and feel exactly what she felt for him. Aden went to speak but she placed her finger over his lips.

'Aden, I love you, I love everything about you. You mean everything to me. Please don't think otherwise. It's just, it's just . . .'

Now it was Kirsty's turn to cry, the wall she had put up crumbling as her body was racked with sobs. Aden scooped her into his arms and she fell into his warm embrace, her tears flowing freely. He pushed the hair from her face so he could whisper in her ear as she nestled in closer to him, the heartfelt passion in his voice unmistakable.

'I love you too. I love you so much it hurts. I'm not going to let you go through this on your own, K. I can't. You have to let me help you. Please. What are you so afraid of?'

Because I've done something you'll never forgive me for, Kirsty thought as she edged out of his protective embrace and reached over to the coffee table to pull a few tissues from the box. She blew her nose and wiped her eyes, although the tears were still falling. Aden reached out for her hand. She took a deep breath, knowing that she owed him some sort of explanation. She looked down at the floor, weighing up how much she should tell him. 'I'm so afraid I might die, Aden, and I don't want you to be with me if that happens. It's not fair to you. You don't deserve to be with a woman who has a death sentence hanging over her. And there's so much you don't know about me, Aden . . . I've done things I'm so ashamed of. Trust me – with my past, I'm not worthy of your love.'

Aden's face twisted in sadness as he shook his head, staring at her. 'How could you say such things? I don't care about what you've done in your past. All I care about is right here, right now. Nothing could stop me loving you, *ever*. And I think it's for me to decide if I can handle the heartache of your cancer, not you. Please don't push me away – I want to stand by you through all of this, and celebrate with you when you beat it. And I know you will – I believe that with all my heart.' Aden gently raised her hand to his lips, kissing it softly, leaving warmth searing through her skin.

Kirsty didn't know what to say. This was the closest she'd

come to being honest with him, and her conscience was screaming for her to tell the whole truth. But she had to get through her cancer first.

'Okay, you can come with me to chemo the next time. I promise,' she whispered as she reached out and pulled him close to her.

Chapter 15

10 May 2012
Dear Diary,

Today is my second bout of chemo. I wish I didn't
have to go any more, that my life didn't have to revolve
around this stupid cancer. I want to go outside and
ride Cash all day long, and help Dad and Robbie with
the horses and cattle, but I can't, I'm just too exhausted – and Dad won't let me, anyway. I tried to tell him I
could handle it but he wouldn't hear of it, telling me to
go and lie down. Does he have any idea what it is like
to lie down all frigging day? It's making me feel really
pissed off and I think I may be taking it out on others.
I don't mean to but I can't help it.

I bit Aden's head off this morning when he tried
to make me eat breakfast. He looked so upset when I
pushed the plate back at him, and now I feel horrible
about it. He just doesn't understand that I'm going to
throw it all up again on the way back from the hospital. But then again, how can he? He's not the one who
has cancer. And Robbie couldn't even look at me this

*morning, like he had to hide his emotions from me
in case I got upset. Well, ignoring me upsets me even
more! I feel like everyone is tiptoeing around me, and
I can't stand it. I'm stuck in this diseased body and
there is nothing that I can do about it. No one under-
stands – well, other than Aunty Kulsoom. It is so nice
that she acts normal around me. I just wish I could run
away from it all. It's weird. I have never felt so alone in
my life even though I have everyone around me.*

*I know I need to be more understanding towards
Aden. I keep hearing Kulsoom's words when she asked
me to promise I would accept everyone's love and
support. At the time I didn't know what she was talking about. Last night Aden cried in my arms, and it
just about broke my heart. I've been so wrapped up in
myself that I hadn't even noticed Aden was suffering.
I feel terrible. I love him with all my heart, but still the
same old doubts keep going through my head. I wish I
knew all the answers.*

K xx

The hospital loomed menacingly as Kirsty, Kulsoom and Jo
piled out of Jo's ute, which Kirsty had parked in the shade
of a huge weeping bottlebrush tree. Kulsoom and Jo hadn't
wanted her to drive but she had insisted. Driving made her feel
free, it always had, and she at least felt well enough to drive
to the hospital. It was her small way of holding on to some
kind of independence. It would be a different story on the way

home, when she could barely sit up for the nausea. A flock of noisy seagulls descended upon the tree's swaying branches, the strong sea breezes causing the birds to hover slightly before coming to rest. A month ago Kirsty would never have noticed such a thing, but she was learning to slow down, to take an interest in the life that was going on about her. It was as though she was looking at life through a child's eyes again, noticing the amazing facets of the world that surrounded her. Why did it take such a dreadful disease for her to realise how wonderful living could be?

The Cairns Esplanade was across the road from the hospital, and on such a gloriously clear and sun-soaked day Kirsty could see all the way out to Green Island. The ancient, lush green coral cay located in the Great Barrier Reef shimmered in the distance like a beautiful mirage. Kirsty and Jo had spent many a day on the island among the hoards of tourists, sunbathing and snorkelling, the marine life so colourful and unique to North Queensland waters. Kirsty took pleasure in the short distraction, imagining what it would be like to enjoy a tropical holiday right now, before turning back to the entrance of the hospital. Immediately, her pulse quickened and her senses readied themselves, her body deciding whether to fight or flee.

With immense effort she slowed her rushing thoughts and took a deep, calming breath, silently telling herself that she could do this, and that she had done it once before. Although this time it was different: it wasn't really *getting* the chemotherapy that she was afraid of, it was the agonising sickness afterwards. She'd felt better in the last three days than she had since before the first treatment, and it was a cruel irony that she was about to submit herself to the whole thing again just when she felt on the mend. She knew all too well what she was in for.

Kulsoom moaned as she stretched her legs and rubbed the base of her back. 'I'm not sure that front seat is built for three people. I reckon my butt is going to be numb for a month.'

Jo giggled. 'It was all right for you, Kulsoom, you had the window seat. I had my legs twisted all over the place trying to squeeze into the middle.' She lifted her foot off the ground and tried to wriggle her toes. 'I think I've lost all circulation to my feet.'

Kirsty raised her eyebrows. 'Why do you two ladies think I offered to drive?' She tapped her head. 'Not just a pretty face, hmm?'

Jo and Kulsoom looked at each other, realising they had been outsmarted, and laughter erupted between the two of them. Kirsty joined in, wishing she could relax a bit and enjoy Kulsoom and Jo's company, but it was hard to quell the anxiety in her stomach.

Kirsty glanced at her watch, realising it was almost midday; she only had a few minutes to go before her appointment. 'How about you two go and get yourselves some lunch down on the esplanade while I'm doing this? I think it would be much better than sitting in the waiting room.'

Jo and Kulsoom began to disagree but Kirsty shook her head. Jo bit her bottom lip and Kulsoom pretended to zip hers.

Kirsty continued, 'I really don't want you both to wait for me up there. I'll feel much better knowing that you're out and about, enjoying such a glorious day. Please. I'll just give you a call when I'm finished.'

Kulsoom put her arm around Kirsty's shoulders, giving her a quick loving squeeze. 'Okay, boss, if you insist.'

'And only if you're one hundred per cent sure?' Jo added as she rifled through her bag and pulled out her mobile, checking it was switched on, and then shoved it in her pocket. 'But I'll have you know that I don't feel comfortable leaving you to go into the hospital on your own, Miss Bossy Boots.'

Kirsty was touched, but her friend's willingness to do as she'd asked meant even more. 'I'll be fine, Jo, really.' She turned to Kulsoom for moral support, crossing her arms over her chest and tapping her right foot gently to feign a strength she was not feeling inside. 'Won't I, Aunty?'

Kulsoom reached out and cupped her face. 'Yes, you will.'

Kirsty entered the hospital and cursed when she saw that the elevator doors were just about to close. She made a short dash towards them, barely jumping inside as they clamped shut. She didn't want to wait for another – she wanted this over and done with. She excused herself a few times as she tried to squeeze in among the group of people, avoiding any eye contact in the cramped space, following elevator etiquette. She impatiently tapped her hand against her thigh as the lift stopped at every floor, leaving only a few people still in there with her by the time it reached the oncology ward. The doors slid open and the horrible sickly smell hit her once again like a slap in the face. She instantly felt like vomiting and covered her mouth as she stepped out of the lift. A strong hand squeezed her shoulder firmly and she jumped.

'Kirsty.' The deep, gruff voice sounded familiar. Turning around, she was surprised to see Harry Mallard standing before her, his hands resting on a wheelchair. Mary Mallard shifted uncomfortably in the seat to look up at Kirsty, her usual head of thick purple-grey curls missing, her head entirely bald. Swallowing her shock, Kirsty gripped her hammering chest, fighting hard to smile without her lips trembling. Mary had had a full head of hair when she'd seen her a month ago. It must have been a wig.

'Hi, Harry, you scared the living daylights out of me.' Reaching out, she placed her hand on Mary's frail arm, feeling the bones under the skin. She'd had a hunch that something had been up with Mary the last time she'd seen her but she'd put it down to Mary's age. Now Kirsty found herself reeling with the implications of what she was seeing. Why hadn't she called in for a cuppa as she'd intended? To be honest, with all the stress of the cancer, she'd forgotten all about it until now. 'Hi Mary. I, um, didn't know that, well . . .'

A faint smile crinkled Mary's already wrinkled face. 'Of course you didn't, dear. Harry and I have kept my cancer quiet. I've just been telling everyone my diabetes is playing up. I don't want the whole town checking up on me all the time. I need my rest these days.'

Kirsty nodded. She had a sudden flashback to how Mary used to be at the school tuckshop – always laughing, always up for a joke. An uncomfortable silence fell between the three of them as they stood in the hospital corridor, and Kirsty wished she could evaporate into thin air. She chewed on her bottom lip, her emotions welling like a dam about to burst its banks. Mary looked like she was knocking on death's door.

Harry broke the silence, sounding a little too cheerful for an oncology ward. 'So, Miss Mitchell, I think you've got off on the wrong floor. Who are you visiting today? Did one of your friends have a baby? The maternity ward is one floor down.'

Kirsty took a sudden interest in the scuff marks on the lino-leum floor, softly running her shoe over the top of them. 'Oh, I'm not in here visiting anyone. I'm here to have my chemo. I, um, have breast cancer.' She blurted the words out like they were poisonous. When she finally looked up, Harry locked his grey-blue eyes on hers. They were filled with compassion and understanding. She took a shaky breath, feeling a chill creep up her spine, as though a ghost had just run its icy fingers over her flesh. Harry opened his mouth to speak, but nothing came out. She watched him as he inhaled deeply, shook his head and then rubbed his hands over his face.

Mary reached out and took her by the hand. 'Oh, my dear, we're so sorry to hear that. You're so young. How many chemo sessions have you had?'

'This will be my second. How about you, Mary?'

'This is the last one, thank goodness. I don't think my old body could handle any more. I've been here so many times that I've lost count. You see, this is my second bout of breast cancer.'

'Oh Mary, that's terrible. I'm so sorry to hear that. It's not an easy battle and to have it twice —' Kirsty glanced up at the wall, panicking as she spotted the clock and realised she was now ten minutes late. She lightly squeezed Mary's hand. 'I'm running late, but I'd love to come over and visit you one day, have that cuppa I promised. Would that be all right with you?'

Mary smiled. 'I'd love that, dear. And Kirsty, please keep my cancer to yourself for now. Like I said, I don't want people fussing over me.'

Kirsty forced a wobbly smile, nodding. She knew exactly what Mary meant; she felt the same herself. 'I promise I will, Mary. And could you do the same for me?'

Mary patted Kirsty's hand before letting it go. 'Of course.'

Gritting her teeth, Kirsty slid the bedsheet off her shoulder and ever so slowly pulled herself up to sitting, using the tension of the sheet for leverage. She had to stop along the way, taking small shuddering breaths before continuing. The pain coursing through her body was nothing short of excruciating. Sights, sounds and smells were intensified beyond belief; virtually everything sent her into the next fit of vomiting. The bucket sat beside her, at the ready. She had given up trying to walk to the toilet to throw up; when she stood up, the bones in her feet felt as though they were breaking through her soles. The deep bone pain was so intense it was twisting her muscles agonisingly in response. When she had the strength, she would cry out in agony. At other times, lacking the energy to cry out, she would suffer in silent agony.

She closed her eyes. She wasn't sure if she could do this any more. As she ran her fingers through her hair, a handful of it came free. She hung her arm limply over the side of the bed and let the clump of hair drop to the floor, along with the rest that had fallen out that day. Another sharp pain shot through her and she couldn't help but scream; the pain was almost too much for her to bear. How much more could her body take before it packed it in?

Lynette and Kulsoom appeared at her bedside. Lynette tenderly placed her hand on Kirsty's cheek. 'What is it, sweetheart? What can I do to help you?'

Kirsty writhed in pain beneath the sheets. 'Oh Mum, it hurts so much!'

Kulsoom sat on the edge of the bed. 'You haven't been to the toilet for four days now, love. It's another bloody side effect of the chemo. How about your mum and I take you there and you sit for a while and give it a try?'

Lynette nodded, clearly shaken as she glanced nervously towards Kulsoom. 'Yes, that's a good idea.'

Kirsty's only response was to screw her face up in pain.

Kulsoom and Lynette slowly helped Kirsty up from the bed. Then, gently placing her arms over their shoulders, the two women carried her down the hall to the toilet. Kirsty sat slumped there, her mum and Kulsoom on either side of her to hold her up. She felt utterly humiliated. Imagine if Aden was home – how would she feel about him seeing her like this?

Kulsoom tucked the last of the sheet back in underneath Kirsty as Lynette brought in a small cup filled with homemade chicken broth. She carried it on a tray along with a glass of water and some antinausea medication.

'Thank you both for taking care of me,' Kirsty said, wiping tears from her cheeks.

Kulsoom waved her hand in the air, insinuating that it wasn't a big deal. 'Pffft! Chemo does dreadful things to your body, and there's nothing you can do about it. Just one of the many things we have to deal with.' Kulsoom dropped her voice to a whisper. 'I like to call it a TT.'

Kirsty scrunched her eyebrows up. 'A TT?'

Kulsoom nodded. 'Yep. A toxic . . . well, you know the last word.'

For the first time in hours Kirsty smiled. 'Ahhh. Yep, I get it. Oh my God. What a fitting title, Aunty!'

The three women looked at one another and Lynette's sad expression gave way to a huge smile. They exploded into glorious laughter, the seriousness of Kirsty's condition temporarily forgotten.

After only a few mouthfuls of soup, Kirsty couldn't eat any more. She closed her eyes and snuggled into a pillow, wishing the exhaustion she was experiencing would finally give way to deep, peaceful sleep. It was the only reprieve she got from her nausea and the growing doubts about her relationship with Aden. Gruesome images of her dying in his arms circled in her mind like vultures waiting to consume their prey.

Chapter 16

GENTLE movement at the side of the bed stirred Kirsty from her sleep. She slowly opened her eyes to see Aden's handsome face softly illuminated by the morning sunlight that was creeping beneath the closed curtains. He sat down beside her on the bed and rested his hand on her thigh, giving her time to wake up.

She smiled sleepily at him and sat up, straightening her pyjamas, admiring him in his black boxer shorts, his chest bare. 'Hey there, my sexy man. What time is it?'

'It's eight o'clock, my gorgeous lady, and I thought I would bring you breakfast in bed today.' He pointed to the bedside table, where a steaming pannikin of tea and a plate with two pieces of Vegemite toast were sitting.

She smiled, her heart swelling with his thoughtfulness, and leant in to give him a kiss on the cheek. 'Aw, thanks, you're the best.' She tipped her head to the side. 'But seeing it's a Thursday, shouldn't you already be at work?'

'Hmmm.' Aden rubbed his chin, pretending to be in deep thought while a wisp of a smile tugged at his lips. 'It's a beautiful day outside so I thought I'd take today off. But don't dob me in to the boss. I don't want the sack.'

Kirsty crumpled her brows. 'Oh, Aden, I don't want you

feeling like you have to take time off to —'

Aden held up his hand, waving her worry off. 'I didn't have anything urgent on so I've moved all my jobs to tomorrow. I think it's about time you and I had ourselves some fun, away from the confines of the cottage. What do you say?'

Kirsty's face lit up, her belly somersaulting with the knowledge that she would be spending an entire day out with Aden. She knew she should really be in bed resting up – doctor's orders – but to hell with her treatment for just one day. She needed some fun, to act like she didn't have cancer.

'Really? Oh Aden, that sounds fantastic. Not that I can do anything *too* energetic, I still feel a little sick from last week's chemo. But I'll certainly give it a go. What are you thinking of doing?'

Aden grinned, wriggling his eyebrows. 'I want to surprise you, so that's for me to know and you to find out. All you have to worry about is eating a bit of breakfast while I go and run you a nice warm bath. We have about three hours before we have to be anywhere, so no rush. And then tonight, I am taking you out on a dinner date. If that's okay with you.'

Kirsty's broad smile faltered. 'Oh, I don't really want to go to town for dinner. I'm kind of avoiding it at the moment. Don't want people seeing me so sick if I can help it.'

'Don't worry; I know you're worried and I've taken that into account. I'm sure you're going to love what I've got planned.'

Kirsty traced her finger over the tattoo of the bucking horse on Aden's chest as she bit her bottom lip; she yearned to make love to him but knew it was impossible with the fragility of her body right now. 'Just what *are* you up to, Mr Aden Maloney?'

Aden visibly shivered from her touch, his deep brown eyes locked with hers as he tugged on her pyjama top and slowly pulled her to him. 'Let's just say it's nice and private. That's all the clues I'm going to give you,' he whispered, his voice husky.

Aden's voice oozed over her like melted chocolate, his unkempt bed hair suiting his rugged charisma. A moan escaped her as they kissed, and she explored his lips with hers, the tingles in her body intensifying as he cupped her face and deepened his kiss.

Sitting in the passenger seat of Aden's Land Cruiser, Kirsty gazed dreamily out the window – everything looked so gloriously alive. As Aden had said, it was a magnificent winter's day, the sky cloudless and the temperature a comfortable twenty-one degrees. One of her favourite country music artists, Jasmine Rae, was playing on the radio and she hummed along, feeling the best she had in weeks, and all thanks to Aden. Her bath had been wonderful, filled with strawberry-scented bubbles, and when Aden had joined her it was even more enjoyable. He had tenderly washed her back, butterflying kisses along her neck as he did so, and then they had sat and talked about everything and anything – other than her cancer – until the water grew cold. It was a brilliant start to the day and from the sound of all the surprises he had planned, the day was only going to get better.

Kirsty snuggled into the pillows and blanket Aden had thoughtfully packed into the Land Cruiser just in case she needed to rest on the journey, but she was too busy enjoying the excitement of being out among life to close her eyes. She glanced over at Aden, taking all of him in: his hard-working build, his strong bull rider's forearm resting on the windowsill, his well-worn, wide-brimmed hat tugged down. He reminded her a little of Patrick Swayze, one of the sexiest men to have walked the earth, only Aden had a little more country ruggedness to him. How lucky she was to have him in her life. If only the situation could have been different, where she wasn't at risk of dying from cancer, but it wasn't and she had to accept that and make the most of their time together, in case it was cut short.

Opening her eyes, Kirsty realised she must have dozed off. She stretched her kinked neck, smiling as Aden gave her a nod.

'Good morning once again, my sleeping beauty. We're nearly there.'

'Where are we?' Kirsty whispered sleepily as she glanced out the window just in time to spot a sign announcing they were coming into the small township of Ravenshoe, which meant she had probably been sleeping for a good hour. In less than a minute they drove past the famous Top Pub, aptly named because Ravenshoe was the highest town above sea level on the Tablelands by a whopping 930 metres, then on past the numerous timber craft shops and quirky cafes. Kirsty hadn't been to Ravenshoe for years and had forgotten just how pretty the little town was, the Misty Mountain Wilderness trails surrounding the area famous for their natural beauty. She recalled that the last time she'd visited there had been talk about the town of sightings of the Malaan Rainforest Monster, a yowie-like creature that had apparently been spotted by a few locals over the years. Kirsty didn't know whether to believe it or not, but the myths were fascinating all the same.

Just past the town centre, Aden took a left turn and pulled up in front of an old weatherboard house surrounded by well-tended gardens. A small sign out the front announced it was the home of Colin Chang, Master of Acupuncture. Kirsty suddenly felt nervous and excited all at once. Should she be getting acupuncture when she had cancer? Was it going to hurt getting the needles in?

Aden switched off the ignition and undid his seatbelt, then, as if sensing her apprehension, took her hand in his. 'I'm gathering you've figured it out now, K. And you look really scared so I hope I've done the right thing. You only have to do this if you want to. No pressure. I just thought it might be nice for you to try it out, seeing you mentioned ages ago that you'd like to.'

Kirsty smiled nervously, his tender touch and soothing voice snapping her out of her thoughts. 'Oh, no, I mean, yes, yes, you've done the right thing. I just don't know what to expect, that's all. You know, if it's going to hurt or not.'

'It's exactly the same as what you've watched me do to the horses. It shouldn't hurt at all and you'll find it really relaxing *and* it will help to ease some of the pain and nausea you're feeling, as well as give you a boost of energy. I know Colin well and he is very good at what he does – he's been practising acupuncture for forty years. He'll take very good care of you.'

Kirsty squeezed Aden's hand, finally smiling, wriggling eagerly out of the blanket. 'Well, in that case, what are we waiting for? Let's get in there!'

After a ten-minute consultation with Colin, which included him checking her pulse and inspecting her tongue, Kirsty climbed up on the massage table as Colin gathered a few things from a tray, his back turned for her privacy. Feeling a little anxious and clad only in her bra and pants with a towel over her,

Kirsty settled down on her back and looked around the softly lit room, impressed by the many framed diplomas on the wall and intrigued by the number of foreign-labelled bottles of liquids and strange-looking therapeutic gadgets. Soft relaxation music was playing and the aroma of sage, lavender and mugwort wafted from the smudge stick Colin Chang had lit and was now waving closely around her body. He explained softly that it was to cleanse her physiologically and spiritually before he began her acupuncture treatment. Kirsty nodded. Colin wasn't a man of many words, only speaking when the need arose, but Kirsty found herself instantly comfortable with his calm and kind demeanour, likening his appearance to Mr Miyagi out of the movie *Karate Kid*.

Placing the smudge stick down on the tray, Colin then asked her to roll over while holding the towel up in front of his eyes for discretion. Once Kirsty was settled he placed the towel back down over her legs and began to run his fingers down her back, pushing on certain spots. She then felt a slight prick as Colin guided a thin needle into her skin, tapping the top of the needle very gently and asking her if it was comfortable. He worked rhythmically, his hands steady. A count of twelve needles later, including some in her scalp and legs, Kirsty's tension eased. Aden had been right, it hadn't hurt a bit. And in a strange way, it was quite relaxing.

Colin placed his hand gently on her arm, his accent strong even after being in Australia for twenty years. 'I be back in thirty minutes, Kirsty. You just relax. Okay.'

'Uh huh,' Kirsty replied sleepily, her body already beginning to feel light. She vaguely registered the soft thump of the door as Colin closed it behind him before her heavy eyelids drooped closed and she had a pleasurable feeling of weightlessness.

She began to drift along with the soothing music, as though floating on a cloud, the sensations in her body delightfully calming as she wafted into a daydream state of mind. All her pain was forgotten, her body feeling somewhat sedated. After a month of physical, mental and emotional suffering, this was absolute heaven.

Kirsty sat on the front steps of the cottage, the sweeping views of Flame Tree Hill hypnotising her. Her body felt at peace from the acupuncture and so did her mind. It was a welcome change. She'd made sure to make another appointment for a few weeks' time, the benefits of acupuncture nothing short of amazing. She rested her head on her hands, jiggling her legs as she waited for Aden to pick her up. He'd vanished from the cottage about an hour ago, asking her to dress warmly as he'd kissed her goodbye and requested for her to be on the steps at six o'clock. Wherever was he taking her? A clip-clop sound pulled her attention from the landscape, her eyes widening as she spotted Aden riding Cash bareback towards her, looking as handsome as ever in his going-to-town hat. Ahh, so they were having dinner somewhere close by. But where? There were no restaurants within a cooee around here. She stood and padded down the steps to meet him, her heart fluttering.

Gesturing for Cash to stop, Aden smiled charmingly as he sat back and gently tugged the reins. 'Howdy. You're looking mighty fine tonight, Miss Mitchell. Would you like to climb aboard and ride off into the sunset with me?'

Kirsty found herself blushing under Aden's penetrating gaze

as she pulled her woollen coat in tighter then put her hands in her jeans pockets. 'Thanks heaps, so do you, Aden. And yes, I'd love to. I just have to figure out a way to get up there first.'

'Follow me.' Aden directed Cash towards a small stepladder off to the side of them and Kirsty grinned. God, he'd thought of everything. He held out his hand as Kirsty climbed up, helping her as she threw her leg over the top of a very subdued Cash.

Aden turned around to face her, the reins hanging softly in his hands. 'You right to go?'

Snuggling her body in behind his, Kirsty wrapped her arms around Aden's waist and placed her cheek on his back. 'I sure am. I'm one lucky girl having my date pick me up on a horse for dinner. It's certainly a first.'

Aden gave Cash a squeeze and off they trotted at an easy pace, Kirsty noticing they were heading in the direction of the bottom paddock. Her curiosity was getting the better of her now but she chose not to ask any questions, instead enjoying the beauty of the bush as it began to hush, the expanse of it glowing in the jaw-dropping sunset. She breathed in Aden's familiar scent, feeling so safe and secure in his presence, her body responding as she pressed up against his.

Near the top of the ridge the countryside sprawled out before them, giving an awesome view of this part of Flame Tree Hill, which made the hilly terrain they'd left behind look as though it had been ironed flat. Ahead of them, Kirsty saw a candlelit table set for two, enclosed in a circle of more lit candles. Kirsty felt happy tears fill her eyes and she allowed them to fall down her cheeks freely, the effort Aden had made overwhelming her. She covered her mouth, gently shaking her head from side to side.

Aden turned to face her, wiping her tears with his thumb. 'I hope they're happy tears, K.'

Kirsty met his tender gaze. 'Oh my God, Aden. This is absolutely beautiful. I can't believe you've gone to all this trouble for me. First breakfast and a bubble bath, then the acupuncture . . .' She swept her arm over the romantic scene. 'And now this.'

'And you deserve every second of it,' Aden said, pulling his eyes from hers as he turned and enticed Cash into a canter.

Reaching their very own private spot, Aden slid smoothly from Cash and then gently helped Kirsty down. Then leaving Cash to chew on some grass he took hold of her hand and led her to the table.

Aden took a swig from his wine glass – filled with grape juice because Kirsty couldn't drink alcohol – smiling at her over the rim. 'So are you still feeling relaxed from the acupuncture today? You certainly look it.'

'Yep. I can't believe how much acupuncture works, it's powerful stuff. And it was nice to have a natural therapist instead of a doctor giving me treatment for a change. In a weird way, I felt I had more control over what was being done to me, like I was taking an active role in my treatment and working more positively towards a recovery. Not at all like when I go for my chemo and I'm told what I have to do, knowing the entire time I'm going to be sick as a dog afterwards because of all the toxins going into my body. It was wonderful to know that I was going to actually feel *better* when Colin was finished with me.' She chuckled. 'I might get kind of addicted to it now.'

'That's great, K. I knew you'd love it and it makes me a very happy man to know I've done something to help you feel a bit better.' Aden's smile wavered. 'I feel so helpless sometimes. Like I should be trying to do more for you.'

Kirsty reached across the table and placed her hand over his. 'Today has been incredible, one of the best days of my life. So thank you, Aden, for loving me the way you do. I know you're always trying to help me feel better and I appreciate it from the bottom of my heart. Even though sometimes, when I snap at you, it may not appear that way.' She paused, her emotions welling. 'I love you so much.'

'I love you too. I always have, and always will,' replied Aden, his eyes filled with raw emotion.

Kirsty smiled softly. 'That means more to me than I could ever put into words.'

They sat for a few moments, gazing into one another's eyes, words not needed, and then, leaning back in her fold-out chair, Kirsty sighed, the meal of honey chicken and fried rice Aden had bought from her favourite takeaway in town hitting the spot nicely. She hadn't been able to eat as much as before she'd got sick, but she'd still given it a good go, managing more than she had in weeks. Aden pulled his chair in beside her, placing his arm over her so she could rest her head on his shoulder. They remained quiet, enjoying the peace of the country, the conversation that had flowed freely over dinner fulfilling their need for chatter. Around them were the soft noises of night animals as they scurried about, the occasional *thump thump* as kangaroos bounced nearby, and above was a blanket of flickering stars and a full moon so bright it illuminated the countryside as if it were daylight. For Kirsty, this was like a scene right out of a romantic movie, but the most beautiful thing was, this was her real life.

Chapter 17

IT had been one of those days when Kirsty had felt tired from the minute she'd woken up, the acupuncture's benefits having worn off over the week. She'd decided to retire to bed after a light lunch and was taking an afternoon nap when a thunderous racket stirred her. She edged herself up to a sitting position, clutching the sheet to her thumping chest, her ears straining to discern where the commotion was coming from. Someone was in the house – and it sounded like they were ransacking it! The very thought sent panic rushing through her. In her state she was too weak to fight off a burglar, and there was no one around on the farm to protect her. The men were all at work and her mother and Aunty Kulsoom had headed off to bingo for the afternoon. What was she going to do? Scare the burglar away with her bald head? Kirsty paused for a moment when she realised Hank wasn't barking. He would never allow a stranger near her front door.

She quickly calmed herself down – there would be a perfectly reasonable explanation. She slipped out of bed cautiously and tiptoed over to the door, opening it a crack. Shit! She couldn't see a darn thing!

A loud clip-clop reverberated around the cottage, and then a stampede of footsteps followed. What in the hell was going on out there? It sounded like one of the horses was in the house. She knew from previous experience that the scenario wasn't completely impossible. Cash had been caught out a couple of times helping himself to the contents of her pantry. The clever bugger would wrap his teeth around the doorknob and then just yank it open. She'd once found him covered in cheesy orange powder, several empty Twisties packets strewn at his feet, his lips slopping delightedly as he devoured the contents. Kirsty had tried to reprimand him but had been laughing too hard – even his long eyelashes had orange flecks all over them. Cash had bobbed his head at her while giving a mischievous, cheesy smile.

Kirsty pulled on her pyjama bottoms, straightened her singlet and crept slowly down the hallway to investigate. The racket was getting louder, a mixture of hoofs and heavy footsteps on the timber floorboards, with a few swear words thrown in. She knew then, from the huskiness of the voice, that Aden was home early. She smiled, her belly flip-flopping with the thought of seeing him, touching him, kissing him.

Just as she entered the lounge room Aden went hurtling past her, barely holding himself upright as he stumbled over the rug, his arms outstretched as he chased a tiny black and white lamb. He dodged the coffee table, giving her a quick sideways grin, his eyebrows raised to the ceiling in a 'help me!' gesture as he vanished down the hallway in pursuit of the runaway animal.

Kirsty's jaw dropped. What in God's name was a lamb doing in the cottage? And where had Aden found it? Flame Tree Hill didn't have any sheep and neither did any of the neighbours. Since the unrelenting heat lasted for at least six months of the year, Tropical North Queensland was cattle country, through and through. Fluffy sheep would find it very difficult to survive the harsh weather conditions, and their wool would be the perfect hiding place for the paralysis ticks endemic to the area. And if the sheep somehow survived all that, their meat and wool would be very poor quality anyway. It wouldn't be financially viable to breed them and it would be cruel to even try.

A splendid bubble of laughter rose from her belly, a sensation she had only enjoyed fleetingly over the past month and a half. She fell to the floor as tears of glee ran down her face. She knew she should go and help Aden but her legs were so weak from her mirth that she couldn't bring herself to stand up. She slumped against the back of the couch, laughing. She hadn't realised until this moment how glum she'd been, the only reprieve she'd had from her grumpiness at the world being the romantic day she had shared with Aden the week before.

Aden's voice travelled from the bedroom, carrying a hint of amusement. 'Shit! Come here, you little blighter! I'm not going to hurt you! I saved you, for Christ's sake! Come on, that's it, come on, come to me. Good girl.'

With a deep sigh, Kirsty gathered herself together enough to stand upright again. She really should go and help Aden. Then, out of the blue, everything went silent, the chaos of the past few minutes over.

Aden's handsome face peeked around the corner of the lounge room door, his eyes twinkling naughtily. 'I've put Hank outside in the kennel for now. I wanted you with me when we introduced him to his new playmate.'

Kirsty put her hands on her hips and tipped her head to the side. 'And who or what might his new playmate be? What are you up to, Mr Maloney?' She took a step forward. 'May I see what you're hiding there, behind the safety of the wall? It looked to me like a lamb, but I must have been hallucinating, surely?'

Aden stepped forward and casually leant on the door-frame, the tiny black and white lamb now cradled in his arms, its big shiny eyes darting about the lounge room. It let out a strident bleat and then another. Aden cuddled it tighter as he smiled at Kirsty.

She tapped her foot lightly, feigning impatience as she raised her eyebrows. He glanced down at the lamb with a shrug, giving it a light scratch behind the ears. 'This is my new little buddy.' He glanced back up at Kirsty, uncertainty crinkling his rugged features. 'Well, yours, to be exact . . . If you want her?'

Kirsty crossed her arms, her brows creased. 'But where is its mother? It looks barely a week old.'

'A week and six days old, to be exact. Bit of a sad story there, though. Its mother died today, bitten by a snake. I went on an emergency call-out to a farm in Mutchilba but I couldn't save the mother. I'd say it was a king brown that got her.' He gently ruffled the lamb's head. 'But I saved this little one from being knocked on the head by the farmer. The miserly old bastard didn't want to spend the time feeding it. Said he had enough to bloody do. I couldn't let him kill her.'

The lamb bleated again and the noise melted her heart. Kirsty couldn't resist the urge to touch it. She walked over and stroked it soothingly. 'You're so sweet saving her, Aden.' She pushed up on her tiptoes and placed a lingering kiss on his lips, smiling as she pulled away. 'Of course I'll take care of her. I'd love to. But how's she going to survive the heat up here, especially in summer? They're not really ideal conditions for a sheep.' She shook her head. 'What was the bloody idiot thinking, having sheep out here in the first place?'

Aden chuckled, touched by her sincerity. 'Oh, this isn't your average lamb, K. She's a Dorper poddy, bred for the tough drought conditions. There are not a lot of them around Hidden Valley but the ones that are here are usually kept as pets. That's probably why you've never seen them before. You're not likely to see a mob of them out in someone's paddock.' The lamb wriggled in Aden's arms and he cautiously placed it back on the floor. He and Kirsty stood silently for a moment, watching as it clip-clopped across the floor on wobbly legs and then clumsily collapsed on the rug. It rested its head on its front legs, eyeing them drowsily.

Kirsty went over and sat beside it, hugging her knees into her chest as she watched it drift off to sleep. 'Before I get too deep into this, how do I take care of her? I wouldn't know where to start when it comes to shearing and stuff like that. I'm a cattle girl, not a sheep farmer. And what happens when I'm really ill for those few weeks after chemo? I can barely look after myself. I'm not going to be finished it until the first or second week of September, which is still sixteen weeks away. And then who knows what's going to happen to me . . .'

Aden sat beside her, gently placing his arm around her shoulder. 'Stop right there, K. Don't worry, we'll all pull our weight to help. I'm sure Kulsoom would love to give you a hand. The little thing will be a cinch to take care of, anyway. Dorpers don't need shearing, crutching or docking and they don't suffer from flystrike. They're incredibly hardy, and they graze like goats, too, feeding on bush shrubs, grass and even weeds. A brilliant little lawnmower, I reckon. We just have to watch she doesn't eat the entire garden.'

Kirsty raised an eyebrow. 'Sounds too easy. I've never heard of this breed before.'

Aden leant in, cupping his hand around Kirsty's ear and dropping his voice to a whisper. 'I've been told they're really good eating too.'

Kirsty gasped, pretending to cover the lamb's ears while Aden chuckled. 'Don't talk like that in front of her. She's not going to be on anyone's dinner plate!'

Aden grinned. 'I know. Just kidding. Look at you, the protective mother already!'

Kirsty's stern expression gave way to a relieved smile as she wrapped her arms around him, resting her head on his shoulder. 'I'm going to call her Joy. Because I know that's what she's going to give me, and loads of it too, with how sweet she is.'

'That's just perfect.' Aden smiled as he closed his eyes and snuggled in to Kirsty.

As Aden held the woman he loved, he could feel happiness emanating from her. It was wonderful, and such a contrast to the past month or so. The day he had taken off to spend with her the week before had been amazing, exactly what they had needed, but the tranquillity between them hadn't lasted long – Kirsty woke up two days later back in her despondent mood. If he could, he would make each day as romantic and magical for her as that one but the reality of everyday life made it impossible. With each week that passed she was becoming more and more withdrawn from him, and from life. He couldn't deny the cancer was putting a strain on their relationship; it cut him deeply that she didn't allow him to look after her more and sometimes he felt like he couldn't do anything right, and her short-temperedness was always directed at him. The lamb had been a spontaneous decision, with the aim of taking her mind off the cancer. Maybe it would ease some of the tension that had been growing between them lately.

'Is anyone home?' Robbie called from the kitchen.

'Yeah, we're in the lounge room, Robbie!' Kirsty called back sleepily.

Robbie walked into the room, pulling his tattered hat off. 'Why aren't the lights on? And Aden, you lazy bugger, it was your turn to cook so where's our dinner? I'm starving.'

Kirsty hurriedly looked at her watch and was shocked to see it was a little past seven. Shit! She and Aden had fallen asleep. She patted the rug beside her, panicked when she noticed the lamb was nowhere to be seen.

She shook Aden and he sat bolt upright, blinking his eyes frantically. 'What, what is it?'

Kirsty pulled herself up from the floor, using Aden's shoulder to do so. 'It's Joy – she's not in here. Where the heck has she wandered off to?'

Aden leapt up beside her. 'Bugger! Great parents we are.'

They both hurried out of the lounge room, calling Joy's name, a bemused Robbie behind them.

'Have you two gone stark-raving mad?' Robbie asked.

'No time to explain right now, bro,' Kirsty called as she vanished into Aden's bedroom, searching everywhere: behind the cupboards, behind the door, under the bed. 'All you need to know is that there's a lamb gone MIA on us.' She reappeared, huffing as she waved her hands around. 'Come on, Robbie, help us find her. Please!'

The search party split up, turning over everything in sight as they searched the house. Kirsty was just about to lose hope when Aden emerged from the laundry with Joy wriggling in his arms and Hank at his heels, tail wagging vigorously. 'I've got her!'

Kirsty clutched her chest. 'Oh, thank goodness! Where was she?'

Aden grinned as Hank sat down at his feet, whining as he looked up towards Joy. 'She and Hank were snuggled up together underneath a pile of towels, happily sleeping until I rudely woke them.' Joy glanced down at Hank and bleated at full volume. Aden chuckled. 'It looks like they're best mates already.'

Kirsty giggled. 'Yeah, seems that way. But how in the heck did Hank get inside?'

'You might want to have a look at the laundry door – it's kind of missing the flyscreen. I think Hank must have pushed it in so he could get to Joy.'

Kirsty scowled at Hank before a warm smile returned to her lips. 'Hank! You little terror!' She gently took Joy from Aden's arms. 'And you're a little terror too! You and Hank make a good couple.'

Robbie broke in, his eyes glued to Joy. 'Does someone want to tell me what's going on here?'

Kirsty smiled at him, delight twinkling in her eyes. 'Sure, but how about we order some pizzas first? I can't believe I'm about to say this, but I'm hungry. Even if I can only get one piece down, it's nice to feel like eating for a change.'

'That's great news, sis! I haven't heard you say that in ages!' Robbie looked impressed as he directed his gaze towards Aden. Aden winked back at him.

Chapter 18

THE dawn sunlight crept over the scrubby mountain tops that surrounded Flame Tree Hill, creating a blanket of diffused golden light across the vast fields. The sky acted as a massive filter, sending a shifting series of cool blues, pearly pastels and warm hues across the countryside, creating perfect inspiration for Kirsty's photography.

She'd finally got some of her old photos framed thanks to Aden's handiwork and the images now hung in pride of place on the walls of the cottage. After weeks of looking at them, and feeling increasingly proud with every compliment from her family, Kirsty had decided it was time to dust off her camera and get back into what she loved. It was the perfect distraction from her treatment.

Perching her freshly made pannikin of tea on the verandah banister, she carefully placed her camera on the tripod and bent down to peer through the viewfinder, exhilaration filling her at the view. Slowly she applied pressure with her fingertip and the shutter clicked repeatedly, capturing a wedge-tailed eagle as it lifted off from a rocky outcrop, a lifeless snake in its deadly grasp. It met its partner in the sky and they circled each other with ease, hovering on the gentle morning breeze.

Kirsty swiftly lifted the camera from its stand and followed the magnificent birds' path, wanting to capture more, to tell the whole story of the two eagles that were partners for life. Kirsty found it so touching that when one passed away, the other would never mate up again. It was the way of most birds. What a perfect love story. Not that she expected Aden to live out his days alone if she died. Humans needed to love, to be loved. She understood that fully. The birds eventually vanished from sight, but the magic of the moment reminded Kirsty just how much she loved photographing the landscape and nature.

She sighed contentedly as she lowered her camera. She hadn't realised how much she'd missed taking photos. It made her feel so alive and in touch with the land she called home. And of course it helped to take her mind off the pain of her cancer, emotionally, mentally and physically. Although Joy was also doing a very good job of that. The little lamb needed to be bottle-fed three times a day and was constantly getting into mischief. Joy had helped herself to a number of Kirsty's favourite plants in the cottage garden and only yesterday, Kirsty had discovered her eating a pair of Aden's socks.

A short playful bark followed by a string of animated bleats broke Kirsty's concentration and she turned her attention to the garden, where Joy and Hank were frolicking together. Aden and Robbie sat on the lawn beside them, eating their bowls of cereal, delighted grins lighting up their faces. Kirsty stole a few shots, catching the two men unawares.

Aden looked over and, noticing the camera, posed and smiled sexily. Robbie pulled a stupid face, making Aden laugh hysterically. Kirsty couldn't help but laugh too, and it felt damn good.

After a few hours' work that morning Aden had the rest of the weekend off, a rarity for him. Once he got back home they were going to the shops to buy her a wig, and afterwards they were off to have lunch with Harry and Mary Mallard so she could finally have that cuppa she'd promised to have with Mary almost six weeks ago at the hospital. She felt bad for not catching up with Mary earlier but between her chemo and feeling ill she just hadn't had the strength to socialise. They'd spoken a few times on the phone, which was nice, but it was never the same as catching up in person and Kirsty was really looking forward to it.

Thinking about wearing a wig saddened Kirsty and she hoped she could find one that she didn't look ridiculous in. Needing one in the first place also made her feel a little irritated because it made her feel like her cancer was winning, even though it was only a side effect of the chemo. It had been very traumatic watching her long blonde mane fall out day by day, but she had to accept what was happening to her. She was tired of wearing scarfs whenever she went out, which wasn't often. The only time she normally left Flame Tree Hill was when she went down to Cairns for her chemo and she managed to do whatever errands needed doing down there. She was still trying to hide the fact she had cancer, not because she was ashamed of it but because she refused to accept anyone's pity. She just hoped she wouldn't run into anyone she knew this morning. She wasn't in the mood to explain her lack of hair.

At least she was feeling well enough to be out of bed – but not for long. Monday would be her fourth chemo session and the extreme sickness would start all over again. It was a cruel cycle, and the constant battle was beginning to wear her down. Every time she looked at her reflection in the mirror, at her bare scalp and her pale skin, her faith in her own survival slipped away from her a little bit more, no matter how hard she tried to remain positive. The only reprieve she seemed to get from it all was the few days after her acupuncture. And she could only get over to Ravenshoe every two weeks for that.

Kirsty was beginning to wonder what Aden had ever seen in her. She looked dreadful *and* smelt dreadful, thanks to the chemo. Her self-doubt and anxiety lay just below the surface. At times she even found herself almost resenting Aden. She loved him, but on the other hand she envied his healthy life. And a deep, hidden part of her wondered how long it would take him to move on to another woman if she did die. Would it be a week, a month, a year?

Some days she felt as though she were hanging off a towering cliff with lethal waves crashing treacherously beneath her, her fingers slipping from the edge little by little as she fought to hold on. Wouldn't it just be easier for everyone, including herself, if she let go? She wished she had the courage that her Aunty Kulsoom seemed to have. Not that she was going to admit any of her darker feelings out loud. Those were her own demons to deal with. Opening up to her loved ones would only upset them and she felt like she had already upset their lives enough. She didn't want to be any more of a hindrance to anyone. As long as she seemed happy and strong on the outside, that was all that mattered. Wasn't it?

As Aden steered the Toyota along the long dirt driveway, Kirsty glanced down at the illuminated screen of her camera and flicked through the hundreds of shots she had taken that morning, smiling. Joy was such a cutie! Hank seemed to adore her company. It was lovely to observe them together, and even better to photograph them. The one of Robbie and Aden laughing that morning was a beauty, too. It had so many elements in it, from the flecks of dust shimmering in the sunlight and the guys' joyful emotions, to Joy and Hank prancing about beside them and the magnificent bushland backdrop. Kirsty felt she could fall right into the photograph and relive the happy moment with them all over again.

She loved the way a camera operated like a human eye. The aperture was the pupil, which allowed light in, while the shutter was the eyelid, determining the speed at which the light entered – and for how long. It never ceased to amaze her, the way she could capture a single moment and suspend it in a photograph forever.

'Here we are,' Aden said chirpily as they pulled into the car park of the local shopping centre.

Kirsty sighed loudly, glancing about to see if she was familiar with any of the cars or four-wheel drives already parked there. In a small community like Hidden Valley, it was common to know what most of the locals drove, although there were quite a few new residents who had moved here while she'd been away because of the mining boom. She was relieved to discover that none rang any bells. 'Right then, let's go find me some hair.'

Aden slipped off his hat, reached over and planted a kiss on her cheek. 'You look beautiful as you are, you know. If you don't want to do this today we don't have to.'

Kirsty undid her seatbelt and began gruffly tying her scarf around her head. 'You don't have to say things like that just to make me feel better, Aden. I *do* know what I look like. I see myself in the mirror every day and the mirror tells the truth. I look terrible without hair. Stop being so damn nice all the time.'

The second the words were out of her mouth, she regretted them.

Aden placed his hand on Kirsty's leg, circling his thumb around her knee. 'I'm not lying to you, K, I mean it. You still look as gorgeous as ever to me.'

Even though she knew she shouldn't, Kirsty ignored him as she slid out of the seat. There was no way he could be telling the truth, and she wished he wouldn't say those things. It felt patronising.

She caught the look of hurt in Aden's eyes, but at this moment she just didn't care. In a way she preferred Kulsoom's no-nonsense approach to her cancer, rather than Aden's attempts to make her feel better all the time. She closed the door to the Land Cruiser a little too firmly behind her and waited for Aden to lock the car, looking into the distance so she didn't have to see his sad eyes staring at her.

In the shopping centre, Kirsty tried on stacks of wigs: red ones, blonde ones, black ones, curly ones, long ones and short ones. To her delight, she found a couple that really suited her. The sombre mood lightened between her and Aden, and soon they were laughing and having fun as Aden tried on every wig that she did. They *really* lost it when he tried on an afro, forcing the small wig onto his head then proceeding to model it in the shop, sending customers into fits of giggles. Aden took it all in his stride, his mischievous behaviour even winning over a pair of elderly ladies who looked like they wished they were forty years younger. Kirsty admired his confidence as she wrestled the afro off his head, panicking momentarily when it looked like it was stuck there then gasping as it suddenly came free, flew across the shop and landed on a display of shower products.

'Aden – Aden Maloney, is that you?' A woman's voice broke their moment of mirth and Kirsty's heart sank before she'd even turned around. She'd know that voice anywhere. Why, when she was feeling so hideously unattractive, did they have to run into Aden's drop-dead gorgeous ex from high school, Linda Lovell? Kirsty hurriedly pulled on the wig she had chosen, a long blonde one similar to what her hair used to look like, not wanting Linda to know she had cancer. She was *not* going to be the object of Linda's pity, or her notorious town gossip.

Aden's broad smile faltered as he looked over Kirsty's shoulder towards Linda, and he quickly ruffled his hair back into place, cursing under his breath.

He and Linda had had a pretty acrimonious break-up and he hadn't seen her in years. This was going to be a little awkward. 'Linda, hi. Um, how are you?'

Kirsty forced herself to smile briefly at Linda, praying silently that her wig was sitting straight. She couldn't help but notice how stunning Linda was, perfectly groomed from head to toe with make-up on and the most up-to-date clothes. Kirsty hardly ever bothered with anything more than a dab of lip gloss, and lately she hadn't even been bothering with that. As for fashion, it was jeans all the way. She tried not to feel self-conscious. 'Hi, Linda.'

'Oh, wow, Kirsty Mitchell! I haven't seen you in years. I heard you'd skipped town and were travelling the globe,' Linda said, eyeing Kirsty up and down. 'And you've lost a lot of weight, good for you! You look much better for it.' Linda smiled fleetingly then returned her attention to Aden. 'It's *so* good to see you, Aden, it's been too long. Are you home on holidays? Where are you staying?'

Aden shuffled uncomfortably. 'Nah, I'm home now, for good. I'm living with Robbie and Kirsty, over at Flame Tree Hill.'

'Great, we'll have to catch up sometime! I still have the same mobile number, so give me a call.' Linda touched Aden's arm, her lips curling into a flirtatious smile. Kirsty was filled with a sudden urge to reach out and slap her. Aden stood there, mute. Kirsty had no idea how to interpret his behaviour – was he acting weirdly because he couldn't wait for Linda to leave, or because he wished Kirsty wasn't standing beside him so he could have a private conversation with Linda?

Linda glanced at her watch. 'Oh, damn, can't stand and chat. I have a nail appointment.' She reached out and touched Aden's arm once more. 'Make sure you call me.' And with that she was gone, leaving the scent of her perfume wafting ominously in the air, fuelling Kirsty's uncontrollable feelings of jealousy. She glared at Aden.

'What was all that about? You looked like a stunned mullet.'

Aden shrugged as he gently took Kirsty's hand. 'Nothing. I haven't seen her for ages and I wish it'd stayed that way. I feel uncomfortable around her. That's all.'

Kirsty gruffly pulled her hand away and folded her arms firmly across her chest. 'Why? Do you still like her?' She kicked herself mentally for asking such a dumb question, but she couldn't help it.

Aden sternly shook his head. 'Are you kidding? I can't believe you even have to ask. I only have eyes for you, my beautiful cowgirl.'

Kirsty stood for a few moments, searching Aden's face for the reassurance she craved. He smiled humbly at her. She let out a flustered sigh as she pulled the wig off and scratched her itchy head. 'I'd better go and pay for this before they think I'm going to steal it.'

Aden pulled his wallet free from his weathered jeans and grabbed a handful of notes. He pushed them in Kirsty's direction. 'Please, my shout.'

Kirsty defiantly shook her head, staring at Aden until he reluctantly placed the money back into his wallet. She didn't need his money. The thought flashed through her head that Aden hadn't made any attempt to let Linda know he was with her now. Why? Was it because he wanted to keep his options open in case she died from the cancer? Or was she just over-reacting? But with everything going on in her life at the moment, she was still allowed to be a little jealous. Wasn't she? 'Thank you for the offer, but I don't feel right taking your hard-earned money. I'll pay for my wig.'

Aden watched Kirsty walk over to the counter, cursing himself for acting like a bloody fool in front of Linda. He'd been shocked running into her, a bit lost for words. She was a piece of his past, one that he hadn't thought of in a long time – with good reason. What a darn goof he could be sometimes. But Kirsty's jealousy was disconcerting. Her mood swings were really starting to wear him down, although he was reluctant to admit that even to him-self. He knew he had to push past her low moods and not take them to heart. Kirsty had every right to be bitter towards the world at the moment. He just wished it wasn't directed towards him like it had been lately. Their bickering had increased in in-tensity over the past week. Kirsty was becoming increasingly agitated with him, and he didn't know why. He tried to support her but also give her space; to suggest things to take her mind off the cancer, but also let her do her own thing. He adored her and wanted to be there for her but she was making that a huge task in itself. He knew he had to try to understand her behaviour in the context of her illness, but it was really starting to break his heart. Taking a deep breath, he exhaled slowly, trying to rein his emotions back in before joining Kirsty at the counter.

Aden knocked firmly on the hardwood door once again, listening intently. Only silence answered him. Strange. 'Anyone home?' he called again as he tried to peer through the curtains of the front windows.

Kirsty and Aden had barely spoken during the drive to Harry and Mary Mallard's house. Now Kirsty stood resolutely beside him, the small Esky that contained her famous potato salad grasped firmly in her hands, her gloomy mood unchanged. She hoped seeing Mary and Harry might take her mind off Linda.

Finally, heavy footsteps came to an abrupt stop as the front door swung open with a creak. Harry stood before them, unshaven, bleary-eyed and dishevelled, his usual tough demeanour missing. He glanced down at the Esky then back at their faces, surprised to see them. 'Oh dear . . . I'm so sorry. With everything that's happened in the past week it had slipped my mind that you were both coming for lunch today. I'd forget my head at the moment if it wasn't screwed on.' He motioned for them to come in as he limped off down the hallway, not uttering a word as they settled themselves in the lounge room. Kirsty sat beside Harry, uneasiness creeping into her stomach as Aden sat opposite, his eyes full of foreboding.

Harry cleared his throat, looking down at the floor as he clasped and unclasped his hands. 'My darling Mary has taken a turn for the worse. I'm afraid she doesn't have the will to fight any more. She's not eating much at all and can barely speak. She's so weak. Her doctor told me that she hasn't got long, maybe a few weeks at the most. She's come home from hospital to be here for the end.' Harry dropped his head into his hands as his body began to shake with unshed tears. 'I don't want to lose her. She's *everything* to me. I know I have to let her go, but how am I meant to do that after fifty-two years of marriage?'

Aden stood up and placed his hand on Harry's shoulder. 'Oh mate, I'm so very sorry. If there is anything that we can do, anything at all, please let us know.'

Kirsty choked back the tears that were threatening to fall. The big comfortable house suddenly felt dark and lifeless. She wrapped her arms around Harry, shocked to see him so distraught. Harry Mallard had always been so strong, so composed, but underneath his armour he was just as human as the rest of them. The notion made her heart ache for him even more.

'But I only spoke with Mary on the phone a few days ago and she sounded really good. She must be having a bad few days, that's all – we all do. I'm sure she'll pull out of it. She has to. She can't die. She's one of the strongest women I've ever met.'

Harry lifted his gaze from the floor, holding Kirsty's anxious stare with his bloodshot eyes as he cupped her cheeks. 'Oh dear girl, cancer is something that you cannot predict the outcome of. Mary has given the bloody awful disease everything she has but it's still won, and has destroyed her spirit in the process. We've decided that it's time to let the community know of her cancer, so they can come and say their goodbyes.' He shook his head sadly. 'I have to find a way to accept that she's ready to meet her maker. She needs relief from the pain and suffering. It would be selfish of me to expect her to stay in this world for my sake. She's fought long enough.'

Kirsty stood, feeling dizzy, and then sat down on the arm of the lounge chair, her face draining of colour, a million things running through her mind. How unfair could life be, to take someone who was so cherished and so loved by her husband and those who knew her well? To do this to a woman who gave so much of herself to everyone she met over the years?

Kirsty, Aden and Harry sat motionless. There was nothing left to say, just unfathomable emotions rippling through all of them, emotions that tore at Kirsty's very core, ate away at her belief in there being a happily ever after. Kirsty couldn't help but wonder if she would be next. If it would be Aden going through the devastation that Harry was experiencing. What type of woman would she be to put Aden through all this when they'd only been together for a matter of months?

'Can I see her, Harry?' said Kirsty, her voice cracking.

Harry rubbed his face and exhaled slowly. 'Of course you can. She may not seem coherent but she'll know you're with her. Lack of food and water makes you a bit disorientated, as you can imagine.' Harry smiled weakly. 'Thanks for coming today, Kirsty. She's always adored you – she'll be touched to know you've come to visit.'

He stood, groaning as he tried to straighten his crook leg. 'Follow me. She's in the guest bedroom. I put her in there because it has a beautiful view of the garden. My Mary has always loved gardening.'

Kirsty followed Harry down the dimly lit hallway, her hand gripping Aden's, feeling as though the walls were going to close in on her. How was she going to react when she saw Mary? Would she be able to keep her emotions in check? She didn't know. Thoughts whirled about in her mind like a ferocious cyclone, taunting her, mocking her, hurting her. Mary Mallard, beautiful, vivacious Mary Mallard, was going to die and there was nothing anyone could do about it.

Chapter 19

THE strident ringing of Aden's mobile phone broke Kirsty's concentration, sending her off-balance and toppling sideways into a potted bamboo palm. She tried to regain her footing but stumbled over a snoozing Joy and Hank, eventually saving herself when she grabbed hold of the verandah railing. Joy and Hank gazed sleepy-eyed at her, Hank cocking his head to one side while Joy let out a tiny bleat as if laughing at her.

Joy wasn't the only one. Jo, Kulsoom and Lynette tried to stifle their amusement.

'Are you all right, love?' asked Lynette while peering at Kirsty through her legs from the downward dog position.

'Nothing hurt other than my bruised ego,' Kirsty replied, righting herself. They'd decided to try doing some yoga together, and today was their first attempt. It showed. Kirsty and Lynette had done yoga classes together back when Kirsty was in high school but neither of them could remember many of the poses. Still, some exercise was better than none and Kirsty's doctor had recommended a little gentle exercise each day. Apparently it would help with her mood, which seemed to be getting worse as the months went on. She had been feeling particularity low since Harry had told her and Aden that Mary was not going to make it. Kirsty had visited her regularly over the past two weeks and each time Mary seemed to be slipping away that little bit more. It was devastating to watch her dear friend fading away in such a cruel way. Kirsty also found it impossible not to imagine herself lying in the bed instead of Mary. It felt a little selfish to be thinking like that but how could she not when she had the same disease eating away at her body as Mary did?

Of course, Kirsty had good days and bad days, but she could barely remember a time when she felt consistently robust and cheerful for days on end. She knew she'd never take good health for granted again, but it was small consolation now.

Aden's phone was still ringing from the kitchen, and Kirsty sighed as she headed to pick it up. Aden had forgotten to take his mobile phone to work with him and the darn thing had been ringing off the hook all morning. He had called her as soon as he'd realised he'd forgotten it, letting her know he wouldn't be back to pick it up as he was attending to animals out of town all day, and asking her if she could please answer it in case there was an emergency. He had a young bloke with him on work experience and had given Kirsty the guy's number so she could contact him if the need arose.

Grabbing the phone from the kitchen bench, Kirsty flipped it open, slightly out of breath. 'Hello, Aden Maloney's phone, Kirsty speaking.'

There was a long pause before a voice spoke. 'Oh, um, hi, Kirsty. It's Tammy. Tammy Maloney, Aden's wife – well, ex-wife, really. I've heard so much about you so it's nice to finally talk, even if it's over the phone. Would Aden be there?'

Kirsty felt her spine stiffen as she gripped the phone like a vice. She knew she shouldn't feel uncomfortable but it was hard not to. This was the woman Aden had once loved, had been married to, and she couldn't help but feel a little threatened by her. She quickly found her voice, a feeling of unease sitting in the pit of her stomach. 'Tammy, hi. Yes, it's nice to finally talk. No, he's not here, sorry. He's at work. He left his phone behind this morning so I'm his answering machine for the day. Would you like me to take a message for you?'

'Oh . . . no, I kind of need to talk directly with him about a few things. If you could just let him know I've called that would be great. He knows the number to call me back on.'

'Okay, no worries. I'll be sure to let him know.'

'Thanks, Kirsty. But before you go, can I just ask, how's he going? I mean, does he seem happy?'

Kirsty swallowed hard. Shit! What was she meant to say to that? *Oh yeah, he's doing really great. He and I are madly in love, and everything's great, except for the fact I have cancer.* She decided to opt for the safest reply; it wasn't her place to be telling Aden's ex-wife about Aden's life – or her own. 'He seems to be content, and really happy with how his business is going. Probably best if you ask him, though, when you speak with him.'

'Yeah, you're right. I'll know as soon as I hear his voice how he's doing. Guys can hide their emotions really well from their mates, but not from their wives. Now that we've had a bit of a break from each other I'm noticing how much I miss having him around. I wonder if he misses me too?' Tammy laughed nervously. 'Sorry, I shouldn't be telling you all of this. I'm just really emotional at the moment. I'll let you go, and I'll talk to Aden later. Bye, Kirsty.'

'Okay, bye, Tammy.' Kirsty stood for a few moments after Tammy had hung up, the phone still pressed hard against her cheek, her pulse beating noisily in her ears. She flipped the mobile shut and tossed it back onto the kitchen bench, the room spinning beneath her feet. Why was Tammy ringing? By the sounds of it, Tammy was having second thoughts and wanted Aden back. But would Aden ever consider going back to Tammy? Fuck, how much more pressure could life place on her? Between the crushing weight of her past, breast cancer, Mary dying and now Tammy – she couldn't take much more. When it didn't rain, it bloody poured.

7 July 2012
Dear Diary,

Oh, what a horrible day! Aden's ex-wife Tammy called, and it all just seemed to go downhill from there. And the nightmares, the ones of the accident, they just keep coming and once I wake up from one I find it so hard to go back to sleep. I'm so tired. I just wish I could sleep for two days straight.

This morning after yoga, I visited Mary with Mum and Aunty Kulsoom. I really don't think she's going to survive the night, but if she does it won't be much longer that she's with us. She's barely able to hold her eyes open and she looks so frail. Poor Harry, he's trying his best to be strong in front of her but as soon as he walks out the bedroom door he breaks down. Today I found him sitting on the floor in his office, tears rolling down his cheeks, photos of his and Mary's wedding day scattered about the floor in front of him. Mum, Kulsoom and I made him go and lie down because he hasn't slept in goodness knows how long. The stubborn old bugger tried to argue that he didn't need sleep, but he eventually gave in. Not surprisingly, he was asleep in minutes. I spent the rest of the day sitting by Mary and reading to her while Mum and Kulsoom cleaned the house for Harry and made him a week's worth of meals. Mary has always loved books, and even though she hasn't got the strength to say much I can tell by the little smile on her face that she enjoys me reading to her.

The doctors have increased her morphine so at least she's not in any pain now. She can no longer swallow and hasn't eaten or drunk for four days. She begged me for water today so I tried to soothe her thirst by rubbing a piece of ice along her dry lips. She kept nodding her head gently to let me know that she appreciated it. It's terrifying seeing her the way she is. I'm trying not to think of my own situation when I'm with her, but I can't help it. The fear of dying is almost too much to bear. It might be easier if I didn't feel like shit the whole time – there's still two sessions of chemo to go, my next one in four days' time. And on top of all of this I'm so confused about my relationship with Aden.

He returned Tammy's call after dinner tonight and apparently she was begging him to take her back. He told her that their chance had passed. He swears he wants to be with me, but I'm finding myself doubting everything these days. Why would he want to be with me, dying of cancer, when he could be with a woman who has her entire life ahead of her? I mean, he must still have some feelings for Tammy. He was married to her, for goodness sake. I've known Aden for most of my life and deep down I know I can trust him . . . but I can't help feeling shaken up by Tammy's phone call.

*I've asked him to give me a little breathing space
for a few days and to sleep in his own room. I think
it would be good for us to have time apart, to get our
lives into perspective. He was really upset, but with
everything weighing down on me I just need some time
to myself. I'm utterly exhausted and feel like I haven't
even got the strength to have a shower, let alone a
boyfriend! But I'd be lying if I said I didn't love him.
I'll just see how I feel in a couple of days – that's all I
can do.*

*I wish there was some way of knowing what to
do – some magical answer. But I just have to stand on
my own two feet and follow my head, not my heart.*

Kirsty xx

Aden heard a soft thump as Kirsty closed her bedroom door.
He'd hoped she might change her mind about sleeping on her
own, but it seemed unlikely as he listened to her climb into
bed. He lay in silence, the chilly winter winds outside sending a
scattering of leaves fluttering against his bedroom window. He
closed his eyes, willing her to come to her senses, holding his
breath in anticipation. Why did Kirsty doubt his love for her?
She kept pushing him away, over and over. It made it hard for
him to be near her, but his love for her hadn't wavered. Was
it just the cancer and the chemo? It was clear that Kirsty was
under an enormous amount of stress, but was there more to it?
He couldn't quite put his finger on it. He wished he knew so he

could take action – anything other than lose her. He could feel her slipping away from him, slowly withdrawing into herself and he had no idea what to do. Kirsty was only on the other side of the bedroom wall . . . so close, yet so far away.

And now she said she needed space. He didn't like the sound of that. It had been exactly what he and Tammy had said to each other a month before splitting up for good. He just couldn't understand why Kirsty didn't believe him when he said he wanted to stick by her through her cancer. And was she using Tammy's phone call as an excuse to distance herself from him? He banged his head against the pillow a few times in frustration before brusquely kicking off the blankets and sitting up on the side of the bed, staring out at the horse paddocks through his bedroom window. Sleep felt unattainable, his mind whirring and his heart breaking. He stood and pulled on his jeans, sighing as he dragged a T-shirt over his head. It was going to be cold outside.

Aden made sure his wrists were taped tightly before slamming his clenched fists into the punching bag in the shed repeatedly, billows of dust pluming out with every powerful thud. All the tension, all the stress – from his relationship with Kirsty, how busy he was with work, his sorrow at what he couldn't fix – came out through the force of his punches. With each movement, the burden was somehow lightened.

The bag jerked and Aden ducked and weaved as though the bag were a real opponent who was nimble on his feet. The chill in his bones rapidly left him as sweat began to drip from his face and trickle down the back of his neck. It felt good, so good, to purge his tumbling emotions and his anger at the world, his helplessness in the situation and his unrelenting grief at losing his sister.

He took a quick step backwards, whirled around on his heel and then slammed his foot into the bag with a loud smack, the force sending the bag swinging violently from side to side. Aden shot out a few more punches in quick succession, giving it everything he had, then wrapped his arms around the punching bag and slumped into it, his hot breath escaping in clouds of mist.

Groaning, he wearily eased himself down to the ground and hung his head in his hands, a heavy sadness creeping over him, making him feel as though he were plummeting into a dark abyss. Finally, he let his tears fall, the tears he had been holding inside for months. The ones he had been so afraid to cry. Men weren't meant to cry. Men were meant to be strong, to be able to carry the world on their shoulders. But he could hold his emotions in no longer.

Curlews cried out and a horse whinnied in the distance, the sounds of the country at night somehow making him feel as though he wasn't alone. It was a comforting feeling. Thank God he'd left the city and come back to Hidden Valley. He wiped his eyes and let out a long slow breath, then lay back on the dirt and tucked his hands underneath his head, allowing himself to calmly run everything over in his mind once again. Was Kirsty scared she was going to die and leave him a broken man? Or was he right in thinking there was something else going on? Maybe, deep down, it had nothing to do with Tammy asking him back. He was *never* going to give up on Kirsty, especially if she was going to give up on herself. He loved her too much, too deeply, to turn his back on her at a time when she needed him the most. He had to fight on, fight for her, show her just how much she meant to him. And if, in the end . . . if, God forbid, he lost her to the cancer, he would never regret that he had shown her just how much he loved her. But that wasn't going to happen. Kirsty was *not* going to die. Life couldn't be that cruel.

Chapter 20

THE aroma of lemongrass wafted delightfully around the bathroom as Kirsty lit the four candles Jo had given her a few days ago when she'd come around for yoga. Jo had bought the candles at the local markets and they were so pretty Kirsty was hesitant to burn them, but Jo had insisted that she use them daily; lemongrass apparently had strong healing properties. Kirsty wasn't convinced it was going to help her but she felt blessed to have a mate like Jo. Burning the candles was the least she could do after the countless hours Jo had spent taking care of her.

Kirsty sat down on the edge of the claw-foot bathtub and assessed the temperature, dipping her hand underneath the substantial layer of lavender-scented suds, mesmerised by Enigma's relaxing melodies floating from the stereo in the lounge room. The water was perfectly warm, and would help ease her intensely aching bones. Other than her fortnightly acupuncture sessions with Colin, a bath was one of the very few ways she found some relief from the pain of the chemo. Another two days and she would be getting her fifth lot of chemo and then she'd only have one to go. The fact that it was almost over gave her a small amount of comfort, but she was still filled with dread every time she thought about walking through the hospital doors. It never got any easier.

Turning off the taps, Kirsty stood and slipped off her robe, her attention caught by her own reflection in the vanity mirror. She hesitantly turned so she stood before it, feeling tremendously exposed. It was as though she were looking at a stranger. The young, spirited, healthy woman she had once been had disappeared.

The flicker of the candles softly lit her features, accentuating bones that protruded in places she had never seen them before. Pasty white skin stretched over her body. She poked at her hipbones, half expecting them to shatter beneath her fingertips, then cast her gaze upwards as she ran her hands over her bald head. She imagined her long blonde hair slipping between her fingers and cascading down her bare back. She ran her eyes back down to her chest, staring at the offending breast. She wished she could just cut the darn thing off and throw it away, but she knew that it wouldn't solve her problem. What if the cancer had already spread?

Her mind began to spin with unanswered questions, questions she had asked herself a million times already. What was to become of her? And what did Aden see in her? How could he be attracted to her when she looked like this and was so damn moody all the time? Fuck it all! Why her? A furious pent-up rage filled her; she felt powerless to rid herself of the disease that was eating away at her and ruining her life *and* her relationship with Aden. She lashed out at her reflection, smacking the mirror with her palms, over and over until her skin stung with every whack. She collapsed despairingly against the hand-basin, clutching the edges of the porcelain to stop herself from falling, panting loudly from the unexpected outburst. Turning her back to her reflection as if turning her back on an opponent, Kirsty shuffled over to the tub and eased her shuddering body into its warmth. Her emotions getting the better of her, she wept freely once again.

'Yes, Joy, I know it's time for your bottle!' said Kirsty, smiling as Joy clip-clopped around the kitchen, bleating loudly and gently nudging her leg. Wherever Kirsty was, Joy was never far behind. After her meltdown in the bathroom that morning, Kirsty was more thankful than ever for Joy's unconditional love.

Kirsty wandered into the lounge room with Joy hot on her heels and slumped down into the beanbag, finding it hard to believe it was only seven weeks ago that Aden had brought Joy home. Joy scrambled onto her lap, making loud suckling noises as she grabbed the teat of the bottle and began slurping away. Kirsty smiled. This would be the last time she bottle-fed her – Joy was almost two months old now and ready for weaning. And, at thirteen kilos, she was getting way too heavy for Kirsty's lap.

While watching Joy drain the last of the milk from the bottle, Kirsty thought about her treatment. Thank goodness she only had two more chemo sessions to go – and then she would have another series of tests to find out the long-awaited results. She would know whether the cancer was gone or not. And then maybe she would be able to have the operation to remove the part of the breast where the cancer had been, and she could get on with living her life. The thought of finding out the results of the chemo filled her with dread. She knew she had to stay positive, but watching Mary fade away had made it even harder.

'Kirsty, are you awake, love?' Ron's voice called from the front door of the cottage.

'Yeah, Dad, come in! I'm in the lounge room,' Kirsty called back as she wriggled a sleepy Joy off her lap. It was rare for Ron to pop in during the day as he was normally out in the saddle or tending to the horses. She tried not to think about how much she missed working with him and Robbie, spending the days out mustering cattle, fixing fences or exercising the horses. They were treasured chances to bond with her father and brother – but, Kirsty told herself, she'd have those chances again.

On the odd occasion her dad had called in to see how she was doing, he always seemed uncomfortable, like he didn't know what to say. He would fumble with his hat or stare at the floor while he was talking to her – anything but look her in the eye. She tried not to take it personally and she knew he loved her deeply, but sometimes his distance really hurt. Ron was a country bloke through and through, thick-skinned and bred tough, and taught from a young age that it wasn't *manly* to show emotions.

'Hi, love.' Ron smiled gently as he walked into the room and perched on the edge of the lounge chair. He took off his hat and began twirling it around on his fingers while clearing his throat. He looked utterly exhausted.

Kirsty could tell from his grim expression that this wasn't a social visit; something was wrong. She placed her hand firmly on his jiggling knee to stop it moving. Her heartbeat gained momentum by the second. 'What is it, Dad?'

Ron exhaled slowly as he stopped jiggling his hat and his leg. Then, placing his Akubra on the arm of the lounge chair, he patted it a few times and for the first time in months looked

Kirsty directly in the eyes. 'Love, I have some bad news, and I'm sorry to have to be the one to tell you this. I just got off the phone to Harry Mallard. Mary passed away this morning.'

Hot tears stung Kirsty's eyes and rolled heavily down her cheeks. She'd known Mary was going to pass away. She had looked so gaunt the last time Kirsty had visited her with Lynette and Kulsoom, but the actual reality of it was overwhelming and heartbreaking. Mary Mallard had taken her last breath; she was gone now, forever, and Harry had lost the love of his life. Kirsty felt as though she had a tonne of bricks sitting on her chest.

'Poor Mary . . . she didn't deserve to die, to go through so much suffering. Frigging bloody cancer! It's a pointless battle!' said Kirsty, her temper suddenly flaring. 'Why even bother fighting it when you're going to die in the end anyway?' Her eyes filled with tears.

'I'm just not sure I can do this any more, Dad, I just can't. I'm so sorry. I want to give up, tell the cancer it's won. I'm too tired to keep going. Please, Dad – please don't make me fight it any more. I just can't.'

Ron took her into his arms, his face livid with misery. 'Now, now, love, I don't want to hear you talking like that. It *is* terrible what's happened to Mary, I don't deny that, but you're a different person, and you will have a different experience. There are thousands of women out there who have beaten breast cancer and are living normal, happy lives. Look at Kulsoom, she's a perfect example. Don't lose faith, Kirsty – please, love, don't give up. You have to keep fighting. I love you so much . . . We all do.'

Kirsty sniffled as she squeezed her father tighter, moved at his rare show of emotion. 'I love you too, with all my heart.'

As Kirsty relaxed into her father's embrace a bizarre feeling of detachment washed over her. Her mind cleared and the months of hazy confusion evaporated, leaving only solid answers in its place. She no longer doubted what she had to do. It was as though the shock of Mary dying had finally allowed her to give in to her fears, to crumble, to fall from the cliff she had been fighting so hard to hang on to for so damn long. It was a strangely blissful feeling.

It was time for her to face up to a few things, to *really* accept the fact that there was a huge possibility she wasn't going to make it. And with that realisation came the undeniable awareness that there was something else she knew she had to deal with: she wasn't going to take Aden down that dark path with her. It was time to let him go. And after she'd told him the truth about her past, he was going to find it easy to walk away from her – and never look back.

Chapter 21

KIRSTY fanned her face with the piece of paper she had been clutching since leaving the church. Blackened clouds lumbered overhead and the scent of approaching rain hung heavily in the air, adding to the already sombre mood of the day. The humidity was thickening by the minute, the sunlight almost obliterated by the stormy afternoon sky.

Kirsty could feel her anxiety building, and her throat was tight with emotion. She closed her eyes for a few brief moments, trying to calm down. The last time she'd been to the cemetery was for Bec's funeral. The distressing memories of that day, watching Aden and his family in absolute anguish, stabbed at her heart once again. How was she ever going to let go of the haunting images of that fateful night? She would carry the guilt of being the only survivor until her dying day. Being here, at the cemetery, brought it all crashing back. She knew Aden came here once a week, sometimes twice, to place flowers on his sister's grave. But Kirsty couldn't face seeing Bec's name on the headstone and had avoided coming with him. Sometime soon she had to find the courage to visit Bec's final resting place – and those of James and Peta – but for today she had to get through Mary's funeral.

Reaching into the back seat of Ron's four-wheel drive, she pulled two umbrellas out, stumbling as she stepped onto the grass, her high heels sinking into the moist ground. She swore under her breath as Aden hesitantly placed his hand on the small of her back to steady her. Her bottom lip quivered as she fought with all of her might to control the urge to throw up again. It had only been three days since her second-last treatment of chemo and she was severely dehydrated, but as usual, no matter how much she tried, she couldn't keep anything down.

Harry had told her he would understand if she couldn't make it to the funeral, but she would never forgive herself if she didn't go. Not that Aden had understood her determination to be there. Or if he had, he hadn't damn well shown it. She'd found herself fighting tooth and nail with him this morning about attending. She'd been told by her doctors to rest, and he was hell-bent on making her stay home in bed. The tension between them had remained all morning, the strain of the hurtful words they had spoken showing in their cautious body language. She felt guilty for her outburst, but she was still undeniably mad at him. She was tired of him acting like he had to be her knight in shining armour all the time, like he knew better. She was a grown woman, for goodness sake, and could make her own bloody decisions. Yes, she had cancer, but that didn't render her completely incapable, she'd heatedly reminded him. And he'd walked away from her without a word, the hurt evident in his deep brown eyes.

Since her revelation in her father's arms five days ago, Kirsty knew she owed Aden more than an explanation, but there hadn't been time. It wasn't going to be easy to explain that she couldn't be with him any more. To explain that it was too selfish to expect him to waste his love on her when she was most probably going to die anyway. That he would be better off going back to Tammy, a woman who had her whole life ahead of her. Maybe he and Tammy could rekindle the flame, make a go of things again. She knew Tammy was keen; the woman was *still* calling him regularly.

But it was going to be even harder to talk to him about the accident.

'Righto, love, us lot better make a move before the skies open and leave us all looking like drowned rats. I just had my hair done, too,' said Ron a little too cheerfully as he patted his hair. 'That's the place to be.' He pointed to a large group of mourners huddled beneath a portable marquee.

Nodding, Kirsty passed the smaller of the umbrellas to Jo just as big droplets of rain began to fall. She quickly opened her oversized umbrella and Lynette and Kulsoom squeezed in beside her while Robbie, Ron and Aden made a dash for the marquee without umbrellas. Jo smiled across at Kirsty as they made their way through the rain, and her compassionate glance spoke a thousand words. Kirsty felt arms go around her waist as Lynette snuggled closer, and not for the first time Kirsty realised how lucky she was to have such support from her mum, Kulsoom and Jo.

The hearse arrived and came to a stop only metres from where the crowd was standing. Harry pulled his car in closely behind, his face full of anguish as he stepped from the driver's seat and joined a solemn group of men waiting to carry the coffin. Kirsty watched with a heavy heart as the men lifted the coffin, the rain steadily falling. They began the short walk to the marquee. At the centre of the marquee was Mary's intended final resting place. The darkness of the earth was shocking against the green of the surrounding grass, and

Kirsty couldn't help but recoil from the sight of it. The men placed the coffin carefully on the pulley stand above the grave, and then a couple of them helped Harry to a seat before the priest began the service.

Fifteen minutes later the coffin was being lowered into the earth to the tune of 'Amazing Grace', the mounds of brightly coloured flowers on top slowly vanishing from sight, Mary's body finally laid to rest as Harry sobbed uncontrollably from his seat. The past surged in Kirsty's mind and before she knew it she was by Bec's grave, watching Aden and his family weeping . . .

The bloodcurdling screams from the night of the accident came back to her yet again, and she had a sudden sensation that it was *her* body in the coffin instead of Mary's. She reached for Jo's hand, squeezing it tightly, just as her knees buckled beneath her and everything went black.

Kirsty woke in an unfamiliar bed, feeling woozy and disorientated. The stiff sheets over her and the pungent smell of disinfectant immediately told her she was in hospital. She had spent so much time in hospitals lately that she could smell them a mile away. She glanced down under the sheets, a little shaken to see a blue hospital gown in place of the long black dress she had worn to the funeral. How long had she been here? She registered the drip in her arm as she glanced around the room. Her body ached more than it ever had before and she struggled to take a decent breath, feeling her lungs wheezing. Low whispers caught her attention and she saw Lynette, Ron and Robbie talking with a doctor in the corner of the room.

'Mum, Dad.' Her voice was hoarse and her mouth felt drier than a desert.

Lynette pulled her gaze away from the doctor and hurried over to the side of the bed. She began to gently stroke Kirsty's forehead. 'Hi, love. How do you feel?'

'Not the best, Mum. I need a drink of water, please. What happened to me?'

Lynette reached over to the bedside table and picked up a cup with a straw, which she placed carefully to Kirsty's lips. 'Well, the doctor says that you have the beginnings of the flu and your immune system is dangerously low. Because of that he needs to keep you in hospital to keep an eye on you. We can't risk you getting pneumonia. He's also worried with how dehydrated you are, so he's giving you fluids intravenously.'

'So I've caught the flu, hey? I wondered why I was feeling worse than normal. I don't want to be stuck in a bloody hospital though, Mum. Can't we go home so I can rest there?'

Lynette shook her head. 'Now, Kirsty, you don't rest up enough at home and you can't afford to be getting sick like this. You have to stay in here for at least a week, maybe longer if need be, to rest up properly. Doctor's orders.'

Kirsty found the energy to roll her eyes, but she knew better than to insist. 'Fine. But I demand a constant supply of horse magazines, butternut biscuits and Chicos.'

Lynette chuckled. 'It's a deal.'

Ron came over and sat at the end of the bed. 'So, love, what do you reckon about your hotel room? They bring you all your meals in bed, you can watch as much telly as you like, *and*, best of all, you don't have to put up with Robbie.'

'Oi! Fair go, Dad.' Robbie gave Ron a shove while winking at Kirsty. 'You okay, sis? You had us all worried sick. Poor

Aden, he's still as white as a ghost. I just sent him down to the canteen to grab himself a cuppa and some fresh air. He looked close to passing out himself.'

Kirsty smiled fondly at her big brother. 'Thanks for taking care of him, Robbie. And I'm all right – I've survived worse than the flu – but I'd be better if I didn't have to stay in here. It's like a jail sentence being told I have to stay in here for at least a week.'

Robbie raised his arm and swept it in the direction of the windows, his eyes wide. 'Look at these views! You can see the Cairns Esplanade from here, and the ocean. Shit, I reckon I'd like to move in here. You got room in that bed for your brother or what? Shove over.'

Kirsty chuckled weakly at Robbie's antics. She knew that he was trying to make her feel better about the situation, and she appreciated it. It felt good to laugh, even though it was at her own expense. 'Rack off, Robbie, you spinner. You'd go mad being cooped up in bed all day long.'

Robbie laughed and poked Kirsty lightly in the ribs. 'I'm already mad. You know that better than anyone. You live with me.'

Jo and Kulsoom poked their heads around the door, both of them smiling when they spotted Kirsty. 'Knock, knock,' called Kulsoom.

'Come in if you're good-looking,' Robbie replied.

Despite her pain, Kirsty couldn't help but notice that Robbie's eyes followed Jo just that moment too long. Something passed between them, something unspoken, but it was so fleeting that Kirsty wondered whether she was seeing things. She'd have to find a way to get Jo by herself and quiz her. Knowing her best mate as she did, there was no way she'd get a straight answer if she asked Jo in front of anyone else.

Almost on cue, Lynette, Ron and Robbie announced they were going downstairs to check on Aden.

As Kirsty's family left the room, Kulsoom took Kirsty's hand and gave it a gentle squeeze. 'Hello there, little Miss Headstrong. How are you feeling? A bit better now that you're lying down and getting fluids, I'll bet. Hmm?'

'Yes, Aunty, I'm feeling slightly better than I did at the funeral.'

Kulsoom shook her finger towards Kirsty in a playful but motherly manner. 'Aden told me he tried to stop you going. You should have listened to him instead of pushing yourself to the limit. I hear you basically told him where he could shove his advice. We all only care about you, sweetheart. You have to understand that, and stop pushing him away.'

Kirsty jerked her hand away from Kulsoom's, annoyed at her sternness. If Kulsoom knew the whole story she would be on Kirsty's side, not Aden's. 'I'm sick and tired of him always telling me what to do. I'm my own person and I'll do what I want. He needs to learn that he's not the boss of me.'

Kulsoom gently reached out and took hold of Kirsty's hand once again, her eyes filled with understanding. Kirsty felt ashamed of snapping at her beloved aunty. Kulsoom was only trying to help, and she knew better than anyone what Kirsty was going through. She remained silent, patiently waiting for Kulsoom to continue.

'Remember, I spoke to you about this right at the beginning of your treatment, Kirsty. I told you that the cancer can sometimes make you so bloody angry that you take it out on the people who love you the most. I know all too well. I've done it myself. At these moments, when the cancer tests every bit of resolve you have, when it pushes you to the point of no return, remind yourself that we love you very much, and that you are a very strong young woman with her whole life ahead of her.'

Kirsty looked away from Kulsoom's intense gaze, wishing her tears would dry up, but instead they rolled freely down her cheeks. 'I know you all love me. That's what makes this so very hard. What if I die, and you all have to cope with that? It makes me feel terrible.'

Jo took hold of Kirsty's other hand. 'You're not going to die, mate. Please, you have to stop thinking that.'

Kirsty shook her head slowly, wishing she could tell Kulsoom and Jo everything. But she couldn't – she owed it to Aden to speak with him first. 'I wish I could believe you both, believe that I'm going to survive this and go on to live. But I can't. Not when I stare in the mirror and see how sick I look. The cancer is killing me. It's winning. Can't you see that? That's why I need to break up with Aden. I can't go on pretending that we're going to grow old together, because we're not. He deserves better than this, than me.'

Jo gasped. 'Don't you talk like that! He's lucky to have you. And you're completely deserving of his love. You should have seen him when you passed out at the funeral, Kirsty. He was distraught.'

Kirsty turned to look at Jo, her heart cracking open even further when she saw the tears in Jo's eyes. But she knew what she wanted to say. 'My point exactly – he was distraught. He shouldn't have to go through that. I'm going to end it today. I have to.'

Jo went to reply but Kulsoom put up a hand. She held Kirsty's gaze. 'You do what you have to do to get through this, and if that means breaking up with Aden, then that's what you have to do. He'll still be here for you as a friend, I just know he will. Aden is too much of a good man to act any differently. You *must* focus on yourself, on getting better, because right now that's all that matters. Okay?'

Kirsty cried tears of utter relief. Just knowing that someone understood her need to leave Aden was overpowering. 'Thank you, Aunty. Thank you for accepting how I feel and supporting me with the decision.'

Kulsoom smiled as she kissed Kirsty on the cheek. 'You're more than welcome, love. Now, I'm off downstairs to have a strong black coffee. I feel like I need it. I'll be back soon.' Kulsoom gathered her bag and waved as she disappeared through the door.

Kirsty sniffed, wiping her eyes with the corner of the sheet, and then turned her attention to Jo, who was blowing her nose loudly into a tissue. 'I'm sorry you're so upset, mate. I hope you can understand why I need to do this, too. I would hate for you to be mad. I know you thought Aden was the one for me. And maybe he is – if I survive. But I just can't put him through this now – and I can't put myself through it either. I spend every day wondering why he's with me, and what will happen if I die. I just don't have the headspace for it.'

Jo nodded fervently. 'Of course I understand. Kulsoom is right. You need to focus on getting better. I've always supported your decisions, Kirsty, you know that. How could I be mad at you for doing what you think is right, especially with what you're going through? There'll be plenty of time for love and romance in the future, you'll see.'

Kirsty clutched Jo's hand in gratitude, and the friends shared a moment of silence, broken only by their mutual sniffling.

Kirsty raised her eyes to Jo's face. 'Speaking of love and

romance... what's going on with you and my handsome brother?'

Jo's face flushed red. 'Oh my God! Me and Robbie? Nothing's going on with us. How ridiculous of you to even think such a thing, Kirsty!'

Kirsty grinned weakly, her eyes still wet with tears. 'I caught you two staring at each other like a pair of lovesick teenagers before. The cat's out of the bag, my friend. So spill the beans.'

Jo motioned towards the drip. 'What drugs have they put in that thing? They must be bloody good. You seem to be hallucinating!'

Kirsty laughed. 'Oh come on, Jo. If you go any redder you'll pass for a bloody beetroot. Liven up my day. Tell me you and Robbie are an item. Please, come on, tell me!'

Jo threw her hands up in the air in defeat, grinning like she'd been caught snogging behind the school tuckshop. 'I can't get *anything* past you, Miss Mitchell. I admit it: Robbie and I *are* dating, have been for the last month. We just didn't want to give you one more thing to contend with when you're going through such a hard time. Of course we were going to tell you once you were better.'

Kirsty clapped her hands in delight. 'Oh, you silly buggers! I'm over the moon you're together. How wonderful it is that my bro and my best buddy are lovers! You should have told me sooner! My health is not the only thing that matters, you know. Everyone has their lives to get on with . . . and get on with them you will. Juicy details, please – actually, on second thoughts, not *too* juicy. Robbie is my brother, after all.'

Jo took Kirsty into her arms, resting her head on the pillow beside Kirsty's. 'I think we'll leave the juicy details for another day. You're meant to be resting, remember? But God, I love you so much, mate. Trust you to put your own problems aside to be happy for me and Robbie. Mind you, he's going to kill me for telling you. I promised him I wouldn't.'

Kirsty tapped the tip of Jo's nose with her finger. 'Don't you worry. I'll deal with Robbie. But first and foremost, I'd better deal with Aden.'

Jo nodded slowly. 'I think that's a good idea. I'll go downstairs and get him for you, hey?'

'Thanks, mate, I'd appreciate it.' Kirsty gave Jo another heartfelt hug. 'And wish me luck. I'm so nervous. You *do* know I love him, right? I love him with all my heart. That's why I have to do this.'

Jo smiled. 'I know you love him. You've always loved him, since the day you first laid eyes on him.'

Kirsty couldn't hide her surprise as she covered her gaping mouth with her hands. 'You knew? I didn't think *anyone* knew. Was it that obvious?'

Jo rolled her eyes playfully. 'I'm your best buddy! Of course I knew. Blind Freddy could tell that you fancied him. You went gaga every time he was around, and you still do, for that matter. I just didn't want to make a big deal of it when we were growing up.'

'So I can't get anything past you either,' Kirsty said, giggling.

'Nope!' Jo replied as she got up from the bed and headed for the doorway. 'That's one of the many things that make us best buddies.'

'So true.' Kirsty's gaze turned serious. 'Jo, please tell me . . . am I doing the right thing?'

Jo turned and leant on the doorframe. 'I can't answer that. Only *you* know in your heart, so trust your instincts. But what I can tell you is that Aden loves you, and you love him. So, as the saying goes, if you love something, set it free – if it returns, it was always meant to be yours.'

And with that, Jo was gone, and Kirsty was left to her own thoughts. She was about to break her long silence and Aden's heart – and her own. This was the moment she'd been avoiding for years, and the damage it was going to cause was terrifying. But there was no turning back.

Chapter 22

KIRSTY'S bottom lip quivered. The silence of the room was deafening, and the miserable look in Aden's big brown eyes almost too much to bear. She looked away and stared out the window, wishing things could have turned out differently. This was horrible, heartbreaking, and she hadn't even told him the worst of it. She was building up her nerve, her mind scrambling for words.

'I'm so sorry, Aden. Please believe me when I say that I don't want to do this, but I have to, and I hope you can understand. I feel like a different person right now. This cancer is devouring me, every part of me – my body and my soul. All of my energy has to go towards fighting it, and there's just none left over for anything else, or any*one* else for that matter.' She sighed and gave a shaky grin. 'This would all be easier if we hated each other.'

Aden exhaled sharply, as if someone had just punched him hard in the chest. 'I could never hate you, Kirsty. I love you too much to hate you,' he said, his voice rasping with emotion. 'I will always be here for you, as a mate if that's what you want right now.' He fought the urge to reach out and stroke the side of her face, to wipe away her tears, the desire to feel the softness of her skin beneath his fingertips one more time crushing him, breaking his heart, filling him with a deep sorrow. How was he going to refrain from acting like her boyfriend when every time he was around her all he wanted to do was hold her close to him, to save her from this horrible disease, and to tell her over and over just how much he loved her?

They stared at each other for a few moments, the intensity between them building, connecting them in a way that went beyond words. Aden was the first to turn away, clearing his throat a little too loudly. He grabbed his hat from the armrest of the chair, flipped it onto his head and then shoved his hands deep into his pockets. 'Well, I should go, let you get some rest. Can I call in tomorrow to see how you're going?'

Kirsty turned to face him, the room closing in on her, her body trembling. She couldn't believe she was about to do this. She inhaled deeply, attempting to calm herself down.

'Aden, I think it would be best if we didn't see each other for a little while. Give us both some time to get used to not being together. If you want to stay in the cottage, I might just have to move into the homestead for a while once I'm back home.' She took another deep breath. 'And I have something else to tell you. Can you sit down again for a moment?'

Aden eyed her suspiciously, wondering what in the hell could be worse than what she'd just told him, but he followed her instructions and sat back down on the chair beside the bed, his legs jiggling nervously.

Kirsty sat up in the bed, silently praying for strength. *Fuck me, I'm about to ruin any chance I'll ever have with Aden forever.*

'Aden, um, there's no other way to say this other than

straight-out. *I* was the one driving the car the night of the accident. It was me who killed your sister, not James.'

Aden gasped as he stood up abruptly, sending the chair flying backwards, the confusion and shock on his face clear. He pushed his fingers through his hair as he looked up at the ceiling, his chest heaving. Without thinking, Kirsty reached out and brushed his arm, and he reacted as though burned, leaping back from her touch. His desolate eyes came to rest on hers. She wished he would say something, anything – shout at her for what she'd done, call her every awful name under the sun. But he just stood there, staring at her, devastation contorting his features, his eyes wet with unshed tears. She swallowed down her wretchedness. How did she expect him to act?

Aden squeezed his eyes shut and pinched the ridge of his nose. 'This sucks, Kirsty. I love you so much, but this is just too much for me to take in right now. I honestly don't know how I'm meant to respond. First, you tell me that you want to break up with me in case you die, and then in the next breath you tell me *you* were the driver that night. Fuck!' He rolled his head back and took a deep breath. 'I need some time, alone, to think things over. It's probably best, like you said, that we have some space.' He spun on his heel and walked forcefully from the room.

Kirsty stayed silent as she watched him disappear, her heart disappearing with him. What had she done? She angrily wiped at her tears. She knew exactly what she'd done: fucked up any chance of them ever having a future. And that was even if she survived her cancer. Would Aden ever speak to her again? Would he ever be able to find forgiveness in his heart for what she'd done? Would he expect her to go to the police? Her admission could send her to jail for drink driving, killing three people and concealing the truth. That awareness had weighed heavily on her for six years. She knew she had a good chance of spending the rest of her life behind bars if she was convicted. She'd spent the last six years trying to come to terms with her role in the accident. Yes, she'd been young and stupid, and if she hadn't been driving it would have been someone else with a few too many beers under their belt. But it had been *her* behind the wheel. And she had let everyone believe that it was James who'd been driving. She'd let someone else take the rap, and even though she knew she'd been a terrified young girl, she also knew her own actions had been cowardly in the extreme. Her remorse and guilt had haunted her for six years, causing her suffering every day. But a jury wouldn't care about remorse. 'Fuck it all,' she muttered as she rolled over and buried her face in her pillow, sobbing for all she had lost, including the most amazing man in the world.

The Land Cruiser shook as Aden slid into the driver's seat and slammed the door shut with an almighty crash. Then, cursing loudly, he pulled his shirt from where it had become trapped in the door, only to rip it as he finally yanked it free. Defeated, he threw the keys on the seat beside him and rested his head on the steering wheel, allowing himself a few moments, taking slow deep breaths to try to steady his racing pulse. His heart was aching and his temper was close to boiling point as the reality of what Kirsty had told him settled in the pit of his stomach. His mind was racing with a million questions. The woman he was madly in love with had been the cause of his beloved sister's death. Could he ever look at Kirsty in the same way?

Aden lifted his head and stared absent-mindedly out the windscreen, watching as an old couple walked past him, arm in arm, headed for the front doors of the hospital. He wanted a love like that – deep, lifelong love. If you'd asked him a few hours ago what he wanted most in this life, his answer would have been that he wanted Kirsty to be better so he could marry her, have children with her, share her hopes and dreams, and spend his life with her. But now? Would his answer remain the same?

He slammed his fist hard into the dashboard, wincing as droplets of blood appeared on his knuckles. He couldn't take much more. He needed some space. Yes, *he* needed space. He gruffly wiped the blood from his fingers onto his jeans, shaking his head. He had to take control of himself, control of his fears and emotions, before they took control of him. Losing it right now was not going to do anyone any good. He just needed some time to get his feelings into perspective, and he didn't want to see Kirsty until he did. He knew it was going to take some time – months even – to get his head around this. But one thing was certain: he had to find somewhere of his own to live. He couldn't stay at Flame Tree Hill.

Kirsty sniffed loudly as she stared around the empty hospital room. It was cold and uninviting, nothing like her little cottage back at Flame Tree Hill. Her family and Jo had reluctantly gone home, the doctor telling them there was nothing they could do and sternly reminding them that visiting hours were over. Kirsty had insisted they follow the doctor's instructions. She needed to be alone.

Blowing her nose once again she scrunched up the tissue and tossed it onto the bedside table, which already overflowed with tear-sodden tissues. Then, groaning, she rolled over to stare out the window. She felt like absolute shit, emotionally and physically, like her life was draining away from her.

Darkness was unfolding outside and she imagined loved ones reuniting in their homes after a hard day at work. And here *she* was, the normally free-spirited country girl, stuck in a bloody hospital bed, her life hanging by a thread, and the man of her dreams no longer hers. She wished her life would just end right now, so she didn't have to feel *anything* any more. Somehow, she felt death would be easier.

Her gaze wandering over the room once again, Kirsty spotted her diary in the half-open bedside drawer. She slowly pushed herself up to sitting, grateful her mum had thought to bring it along with her clothes and toiletries, and pulled it out. She ran her fingertip over the wording that Aden had had engraved on the silver pen attached to the diary: *My beautiful Kirsty, I love you, forever and always. Aden.* Kirsty kissed the writing, his words that once filled her with hope and happiness now crushing her.

'I'm so sorry, Aden. I love you too,' she whispered. She took a deep breath, absently clicking the pen, before letting her emotions spill out onto the page.

Chapter 23

POWDER-BLUE skies stretched as far as the eye could see, punctuated by the peaks of lush green mountain tops. Kirsty felt her heart lighten as the four-wheel drive drew closer to Flame Tree Hill. After just over a month stuck in hospital, anything would have looked good in comparison to the four walls of her hospital room, but the scene was breathtakingly beautiful. It felt good to be coming home.

What felt even better was knowing that she was done with chemotherapy – hopefully for good. She'd had her last session while she was still in hospital.

It seemed a lifetime since that day, almost twenty-one weeks ago, when she'd received the cancer diagnosis. And here she was, on the other side: considerably thinner, no hair, exhausted and emotionally wrecked. But despite everything, she couldn't help but feel a little triumphant. She had made it. Even if she now had the next hurdle to cross – the final results – she was a step closer to the end, one way or another.

She gazed dreamily out the window. The entire countryside was awakening, returning to life after the winter months, with pretty blossoms painting the landscape a multitude of colours against a backdrop of vibrant green grass. Her fingers itched to pick up her camera. She might even be able to go for a gentle ride on Cash, now that she was over the flu. It had been way too long. It would be magnificent to feel the sun on her skin once again as Cash clip-clopped beneath her while whinnying in horsy conversation. The freedom to be able to ride her beloved horse whenever she wanted was something she would never take for granted again. And she knew keeping busy would take her mind off Aden, too.

She was both sad and relieved that he wasn't living at Flame Tree Hill any more; he'd found himself a property fifteen minutes down the road. She knew already that she would miss him around the cottage, just as she'd missed his laughter and his love since that fateful day at the hospital. God, how she missed his love! She hadn't seen him since that day and she was doing her best to accept the fact he was most probably never going to speak to her again. She tried not to think about it too much – the pain of losing him was just too excruciating.

She glanced over at Robbie and smiled fondly. He looked the epitome of a lovesick teenager. Things were obviously going very well for him and Jo. Jo had told her bits and pieces about their budding romance on her visits to the hospital but had kept the details to a minimum; she insisted she wanted to focus more on Kirsty's health.

The last five weeks had been harder than anything Kirsty had experienced before. The flu plus the chemo had resulted in unending pain, relieved only by the knowledge that she wouldn't have to go through the chemo again. She couldn't shake the feeling that her body had slowly given in to the cancer, and her hopes of ever recovering were fading away. But all was not lost, yet – she still had her final results to come.

Hank sat between her and Robbie, long strands of slobber hanging from his chops as he panted loudly. In an attempt to cool him down, Kirsty turned the air conditioner up full bore, directing the vents so they were blowing right in his face, making his lips wobble. He looked like he was smiling and Kirsty couldn't help grinning at the sight of him, despite his doggy breath. What had he been eating? She wrinkled her nose as she imagined the endless possibilities. Knowing Hank, he'd probably found a rotting carcass that some fanatical pig hunter had tossed off the back of their ute. Hank would often meander home after rolling in such a ghastly mess, proud of his new doggy cologne. He clearly loved the stench but it resulted in him being briskly washed with the freshest smelling shampoo Kirsty could get her hands on, much to his dismay.

Kirsty gave him a loving scratch on the chin, grateful for his loyal mateship. A huge dollop of slobber fell from Hank's chops, coating her hand. 'Just lovely, buddy,' she muttered as she wiped it onto her shorts. Hank barked his reply and licked her face.

Robbie grinned as he reached over and turned the stereo down, the honky-tonk voice of Alan Jackson fading away as he sat back against the seat and fumbled with the sun visor. 'So, sis, when will we know the final results?'

'Not for another month, give or take a few days. My doctor said I have to give my body a few weeks to recover from all the chemo before undergoing more tests. And then it'll take a week or two for the results to come through.'

Robbie tutted. 'Shit, they like to make you wait, don't they? It'll be hard, not knowing until then.'

'Yeah. But then again, I've been waiting so long to know the outcome, so what's another month, hey?'

Robbie shook his head gently, a frown creasing his features. 'Too true. So, what happens once they find out that the lump's gone?'

Kirsty smiled at his optimism. If ever she needed it, it was now. 'Well, if the lump's gone, I'll have an operation to remove the tissue around where it grew. Just to make sure there's no possibility of it coming back. Then I have check-ups every six months or so to make sure it hasn't, you know, come back.'

'Righto. Does that mean you don't have to have any more chemotherapy?'

'Yep, as long as the cancer stays away. For the next month I can get on with my life like a normal person – well, sort of.' Kirsty patted her bald scalp.

Robbie beamed at her. 'You're just as beautiful without hair as you are with it. And that's brilliant news about the chemo. That means you can come to the Hidden Valley Bush Races with Jo and me next month, to help cheer Aden on. Harry and the race committee have organised a special event in memory of Mary, the Pink Ribbon Race. The riders have to be entirely dressed in pink. And that's the one Aden signed up for. He's going to look hilarious!' Robbie chuckled. 'Anyway, the deal is that the winner of the race gives their prize money to the National Breast Cancer Foundation.'

Kirsty's breath caught in her throat at the mention of Aden, but she smiled to cover her anxiety. 'That's just like Hidden Valley, to pull together for Harry. What a wonderful idea,' she said. 'And sure, count me in for the races. I'll be there with bells on.' She didn't know how she would cope with seeing Aden but she was going to see him sooner or later, no matter what. They were going to have to learn to live around each other – their lives were too closely entwined. She just wished Aden would at least talk to her, tell her how he felt about her, even if it was bad. The not knowing was insufferable. Or perhaps his silence meant the worst. 'Which horse is Aden racing?'

'He's going to borrow my horse. He didn't think it was right to use Cash considering you two have, well, you know . . . broken up. Aden's been training with Star the entire time you've been in hospital.' Robbie sighed loudly and paused for a moment, clearly thinking hard about what he was going to say.

'Aden looks like shit, sis, and I don't reckon I've seen him smile for weeks. I feel really sorry for him. And he asks how you're doing every day. Why did you two break up? He won't shed any light on the situation. I know you're scared of dying and you don't want him to go through that with you, but doesn't love conquer all?'

Kirsty felt a stab in her heart and she turned away to look out the window. 'I don't really want to talk about it right now.'

Reaching the homestead, Robbie pulled up in the shade of a massive old mango tree and turned off the ignition. Grabbing Kirsty's hand, he pulled her back in as she went to step out. Hank pushed past her and made his way straight to Joy, who bleated her delight at his return.

'Kirsty.' The look on Robbie's face spoke a thousand words.

Pulling the door shut again, Kirsty sighed, knowing what was about to come. 'What is it, Robbie?'

'You know I'm not really one for deep and meaningfuls, but I feel like I have to get something off my chest.'

Kirsty turned to face him, already feeling on guard. 'Okay then, shoot, and don't beat around the bush. I've got things I'd like to do before it gets dark.' Her tone came out more snappishly than she'd intended.

'All right, all right. You and Aden clearly love each other, so ask the guy back, for Christ's sake. What were you thinking, breaking up with him in the first place?'

'I can't ask him back, Robbie! What good am I to him if I'm dead soon anyway? Just stay out of it, okay?' Kirsty spat, her frustration getting the better of her as warm tears sprang to her eyes. She let them fall. She had cried so much in the last four months she was surprised she had any tears left.

Robbie reached out and touched her arm gently. 'Please don't talk like that. I can't bear to hear you say that you're going to die. What if you live? Have you stopped to think of what happens then? If you live, you have your whole life ahead of you. A life you could be sharing with Aden. So don't blow it, sis. I'm begging you. Make amends with Aden before it's too late. I'm sure whatever it is can be repaired.'

Kirsty placed her hands over his and slowly exhaled. 'I love you, Robbie. You know that. And I know you mean well, but I really need you to stay out of this, please. It's hard enough as it is. You just have to trust me when I say it's the right thing to have done.'

Robbie dropped his hands in his lap, clearly defeated. 'Okay, you're right – you're old enough to make your own decisions. I don't get it, but I promise I'll stay out of it. Jo warned me not to say anything and I should have listened to her. Sorry, Kirsty. It's just that I care about you.'

Kirsty gave him a quick peck on the cheek. 'I know. Thank you. And yes, you should listen to your lady. Jo knows what she's talking about.'

Robbie smiled shyly, a blush rising on his cheeks. 'I'll definitely pay close attention to everything she says from now on.'

Kirsty slapped him lightly on the arm. 'Look at you! You're so in love. You're blushing just at the mention of her name!'

Robbie nodded as he began to gather his things from the dashboard. 'I *am* in love . . . and it's brilliant.'

'I know how you feel. Love is a wonderful thing. I'll love Aden until I take my very last breath.'

Robbie stepped out of the driver's door. 'Then, if I were you, I'd do something about it. You're not going to be taking that last breath for years and years, and that's a long time to be without someone you love. But don't listen to me – you do what you reckon is best. I promised I'd stay out of it and I will.' He winked.

Kirsty watched Robbie bound up the front steps of the cottage with Hank and Joy in tow. On some level, he was right. Maybe she had to make the first move, try to talk to Aden. He obviously still cared about her if he'd been asking about her every day.

Chapter 24

THE shutter fired rapidly as Kirsty pressed the button. The star-spangled sky was gradually lightening as twilight gave way to dawn and golden rays began to seep above the horizon. She held her breath as she clutched her camera, her skin tingling with anticipation as she captured exquisite imagery of the earth coming to life for another day. She was spellbound. The early-morning dew sparkled like diamonds on the vivid green grass and the rising sun pressed its glow against trees, livestock and buildings, creating lengthening shadows. The land was a living, breathing being, with a depth to it that no human could ever match.

Kirsty stopped for a few seconds, breathing it in. She'd now been back home for a week and was still not over the novelty of being in her own home, free from chemotherapy, and surrounded by the countryside she loved. This was why she had crawled out of bed at four a.m. It was just what the doctor ordered. Daybreak's natural light was ideal for shooting photos, and her whole body pulsed with enthusiasm, her senses on high alert, her photographer's eye scanning every detail of the landscape in search of the perfect shot.

Caught up in the moment, she knelt to follow a large flock of raucous galahs with her lens, leaning at an awkward angle that found her gently falling backwards into the long grass. She focused her concentration on the sea of pink above her as the birds flew off into the distance, squawking as if in excited conversation. The contrast between the birds' pink hues and the lightening sky was striking.

The distant whinny of a horse grabbed her attention and she rolled onto her belly, resting on her elbows for support, her heart skipping a few beats as she spotted where the whinny had come from. Taking a deep, controlled breath and holding the camera firmly in position, she followed the path of Robbie's horse, Star, with Aden on his back. In the privacy of her grass hidey-hole, her heart leapt at the sight of Aden's familiar handsome face. She ached to run to him, to fall to her knees and beg him for his understanding. But she couldn't. She was too afraid of what he might say to her.

She tried to keep still while capturing the moments between man and horse. Aden was speaking firmly to Star, and Star's body language showed he was listening intently to Aden's every command. The respect between the two was clear and it was touching to observe. Aden had a way with horses. It was one of the many reasons she loved him.

Hesitantly, and feeling slightly naughty, she adjusted the zoom on the camera so she could see every inch of his gorgeous features while clicking away. His face was shadowed slightly beneath his wide-brimmed hat but she could still make out his chiselled jaw with a few days' growth, the scar above his full lips, the dimples in his cheeks, which deepened as he smiled at Star. His shaggy dark hair hung about his face in an unruly fashion, and his strongly built body strained against the thin material of his shirt. It was almost too much for Kirsty.

Gasping involuntarily, she clamped her hand over her mouth to quieten herself. Aden briefly glanced in her direction, before directing his concentration back to Star. Kirsty dropped the camera away from her face, breathless. Had he seen her? She hoped not. God, she would look like a right peeping Tom.

She rolled over and lay on her back on the grass again, removing the camera from around her neck. Trying to still her mind, she viewed the images on the screen, her smile broadening with every shot. Aden was very photogenic. There was a charisma about him that brought a deeper element to the photos, and his rough-and-ready look created a certain country charm. Wouldn't it be a dream come true if she could exhibit some of these in her very own gallery one day? But would Aden ever agree to her using the photos in the first place?

Satisfied with her two-hour-long shoot, she lay completely flat and let her body relax into the ground, the soft morning sunlight pleasingly caressing her skin. Star's hoofs sent reverberations through the earth. Lying in the sunlight caused goosebumps to rise over her entire body from the simple pleasure of the activity. It was one of the many things she had been warned not to do by her doctors because her skin was so sensitive to sunlight after the chemotherapy, but to hell with the rules, just for today. She wanted to pretend her life was back to normal.

Her thoughts turned to Kulsoom, who was finally heading back home the following week. Kulsoom had been her rock, her confidante. And Uncle Harry had been so understanding of Kulsoom needing to be here with her. Bless him. It was going to break Kirsty's heart to see her aunty leave. She understood there wasn't a choice – Kulsoom's life was back down south with Uncle Harry, and Kulsoom had already stayed much longer than expected. But it was still going to be hard without her. For now, Kirsty let herself float through an imaginary paradise, in a life where nothing could harm or hurt her. And right here, lying in the middle of a field on her beloved Flame Tree Hill, was the perfect place to do it.

Aden stood before her, a long-stemmed red rose in his strong hands, the sunlight glowing brilliantly behind him. She raised her arm over her eyes, squinting to see his face. What was he doing here? He smiled at her as she lay in the grass, confidence and passion radiating from him, sending anticipatory shivers racing within her. She went to speak but he held his finger to his lips as he eased himself down on the grass beside her.

Lying on his side, propped up on his elbow, he gazed at her, the longing he held for her evident, consuming her, sending waves of heat washing over her body. He slowly leant forward and brushed his lips across hers, lingering for the briefest of moments as he let his warm breath sweep over her parted lips. Kirsty didn't know why he was here, or what he was doing, but she didn't want him to stop. Was this his show of forgiveness? She moaned softly, the desire for him overwhelming. She needed him right now, needed to feel his touch. Forgotten was the fact they were no longer together, that they hadn't spoken in weeks. The ardour of the moment removed any hesitations.

He pulled back and gently smiled at her. 'Are you sure this is what you want?'

She nodded as she reached for him, pulling him into her embrace, her lips urgently searching for his as he moved his hands tenderly over her face. He met her kiss with fervour, teasing her as he ran his tongue over her lips then ever so slowly pushed it into her mouth, circling her own tongue, making her imagine what it would be like to feel him slowly caressing her place of ecstasy, his warm mouth sending her into pulsating pleasure.

Aden let his hands slide away from her as he sat up and unbuttoned his jeans. She joined him in his task, slowly undoing his shirt buttons as he laid soft kisses on her neck, his woody cologne mixed with the scent of leather. Her breath was escaping her in short, sharp gasps and her heart was hammering hard against her chest, making her dizzy with longing. She needed to feel him inside her, now.

Aden, his tanned chest bared and his jeans off, gently began to remove Kirsty's clothes. The shame of her pale and sickly body was not a concern any more – the only thing on her mind was making love to Aden. It was a beautiful freedom. Finally, the intimacy she had longed for was happening; her dreams were coming true.

Both of them now naked, Aden leisurely ran his eyes over her body. 'You're beautiful. I love you so much, Kirsty,' he whispered while gently pressing against her body so she was lying back on the grass. She stared at the blue skies above them, at the feathery white clouds floating casually about, the radiance of it all magnified by the enchantment of the moment.

Aden picked up the red rose, holding her gaze as he ran the soft petals down her neck and over her breasts, continuing on until the rosebud met with the warmth between her legs. Aden tenderly caressed her with it, running the petals seductively over her, the sensation like smooth velvet against her skin, pushing her to the brink as he circled his fingers around her most sensitive spot. She bit her lip, moaning as she arched her back in pleasure, yearning for him to stop teasing her – and yet wanting it to continue. He smiled playfully, leaving her tingling warmth behind and running the rose down each leg, pausing along the way so he could trace the path with his tongue.

Once he reached her feet he gently moved on top of her, kissing her, slowing down to pleasure her in ways she had never been pleasured before. She called out his name, begging him to slide inside her, pleading to him to reach the summit of ecstasy along with her, for she was close, so damn close.

'Wait, beautiful. Not long now. I want to taste every inch of you.' He leant in to caress her erect nipples with his mouth, sending a pleasurable tingle shooting through her as he gradually travelled downwards, his lips sliding sensuously against her skin, circling her belly button with his tongue before slowly bringing his mouth to rest between her legs, sending her spiralling into absolute ecstasy with every mind-blowing stroke of his tongue.

She couldn't take any more. She grabbed for him, her nails digging into his back as she drew his body into her. Aden rubbed his manhood over her wetness, the exquisite sensation making her struggle for breath. She took him into her hand, his firmness showing how much he wanted her.

'I want you, now!'

Fixing his chocolate-brown eyes on hers, he slowly slid himself into her, his breath quickening as he shivered in satisfaction. She swayed her hips in unison with his, riding the wave of ecstasy that was growing within her. And then she could ride it no longer. They clutched at one another, shuddering, calling each other's names as they fell over the edge together.

Kirsty buried her face into Aden's chest. 'I love you,' she mumbled over and over as hot tears stung her eyes. She knew it was over now and she didn't want this to end.

'I love you too, but I have to go.' Aden pulled himself free.

She grabbed for him, trying to pull him back, begging him. 'No, Aden, you can't leave me! Please, stay with me. I know I said that I wanted to break up, but I was lying. And I'm sorry about the accident. I wish I could have swapped places with your sister.'

Aden stood, pulling his jeans on. 'It's too late to go back, Kirsty. The past is the past. We've got to move on or it will just make it harder on both of us.' He picked up the rose and passed it to her. 'Goodbye, Kirsty. I'll always love you.'

Kirsty sobbed as she watched him shrug on his shirt and walk away, his silhouette disappearing into the bright haze of sunshine. He didn't once look back. She rolled onto her side and hugged her knees into her chest, the rose clutched in her shaking hands, sobs racking her body, the excruciating heart-ache choking her as she cried out his name. How could he leave her here like this, all alone? Didn't he care about her? Didn't he love her enough to stay with her, to forgive her?

'Kirsty! Wake up! Kirsty! Come on, wake up. You're having a nightmare.' Aden's worried voice swam into her conscious-ness, stirring her from her sleepy haze.

She sat bolt upright, her mind floating somewhere between reality and fantasy as she fumbled to make sure all her clothes were on. Dazed, she sat staring at Aden, crouched beside her. She was unable to speak, haunted by the awkward feeling that he could read her mind. Star stood beside Aden, nonchalantly chewing on a mouthful of grass, his head slightly tipped to one side, as though wondering why she had been lying on the ground, screaming frantically in her sleep.

Aden reached out and gently wiped Kirsty's face, causing her to jump. The roughness of his thumb brushing at the skin under her eyes created a sensation that was almost electric. They locked eyes, the intensity between them undeniable. But this was no dream. Kirsty cleared her throat, feeling self-conscious. Aden looked terribly concerned, and it melted her heart.

'Are you okay?' he asked. 'You're crying. It must have been a horrible dream. You were screaming out something but I couldn't make out what you were saying.' His brows furrowed. 'And what were you doing asleep out here in the first place?'

Kirsty blushed, wiping at her eyes. How bloody embarrassing. 'Yeah, I'm fine. Sorry if I freaked you out. I was out here before dawn taking photos then I thought I'd just shut my eyes for a few minutes.'

Aden exhaled noisily and then sat down beside her, clutching at his chest. 'Shit, Kirsty! You had me panicking when I heard you. I thought something terrible had happened to you. Thank Christ you're okay.'

'Thanks for coming to my rescue,' Kirsty replied, blushing while removing twigs and grass from her clothes. She was saddened by the fact he no longer called her K. But what did she expect? She should just be thankful that he was finally talking to her.

Aden looked at her, a hesitant smile highlighting his dimples. 'Congrats on finishing your chemo. Any news on the results yet? Robbie's been filling me in on your progress while you've been in hospital.'

'Nah, not yet. I'm having the final round of tests in a few weeks' time, then we'll know the outcome.'

'Geez it's taking a while. How are you feeling?'

'I'm doing all right. I feel better than I've felt for five months.' Kirsty's smile wavered as she contemplated saying what was in her heart. She exhaled slowly, knowing she had to at least try to explain how she felt. 'I miss you, Aden. I'm so sorry about everything. Please, I have to know how you're feeling about what I did, about the accident.'

Aden sat in silence for a few moments, picking at a long piece of grass, and then twirling it around his fingers. 'I miss you too, Kirsty, but it's not as simple as that. What you told me at the hospital isn't something that will blow away with the wind; it was some heavy-duty stuff. Trust me; I've done a lot of soul-searching since then, and there's a heck of a lot we need to talk about.' Aden took his hat off and swished the gathering flies away from their faces. 'So, tell me, when are you going to come and see my new place? I can't wait to show it off to you. You'll love it, I reckon. And it might be a good chance for us both to sit down and talk about things. I'm sorry I haven't come to see you earlier, but I needed time to weigh everything up. What you told me was huge, life-changing. I hope you can understand.'

Kirsty smiled gratefully. 'I understand. I'm just so relieved you're talking to me right now. I thought you'd never speak to me again.'

Aden smiled. 'That would never happen. I care too much for you to cut you out of my life completely. We do have a lot to talk about, though. I think we need to throw everything out in the open, lay all our cards on the table. I have a fair few questions for you. But now's not the time or the place – I only have an hour until I have to be at my first job for the day.'

'I'll call over next weekend, if that's okay? I might bring Cash. How long do you reckon it'll take to get to your place?'

'Follow the back gullies and it would be about a half-hour ride, give or take a few minutes. I've got a shitload of odd jobs to do about the place on the weekend so I'll be around both days. Feel free to pop in any time.'

Kirsty smiled. 'I'll bring some pumpkin scones. You provide the jam and cream and it's a deal.'

'Deal,' Aden replied, smiling.

With the tension easing they sat in companionable silence for a few moments, watching Star as he ripped up clumps of grass to chew on, his tail busily swishing away the flies. What a marvellous morning, Kirsty thought, filled with new hope. They were finally on speaking terms. But how must she have looked rolling around in the grass, shouting, with tears pouring down her face? If only Aden knew what she'd been dreaming about.

Chapter 25

RON lifted the last of Kulsoom's suitcases into the back of Lynette's four-wheel drive, heaving and stumbling a little to the side. 'Holy crap, Kulsoom! What have you got in here, the kitchen sink?' he asked, chuckling, as he regained his footing, dropped the bag in with a thump and shut the boot.

The late afternoon sunlight was fading as the fiery golden orb of the sun gradually inched its way down behind the distant mountains, painting the sky a dusty pink. Kirsty sat on the front verandah of the homestead, slowly moving her legs to and fro in the swing chair, bracing herself for Kulsoom leaving.

'Oh dear, you've caught me out, Ron!' said Kulsoom. 'I tried to fit in your dishwasher and washing machine too, but the suitcase refused to zip up so I had to put them back.' Kulsoom threw her hands up in the air, mock humiliation written all over her mischievous face.

Kirsty joined her mother as she walked down the front steps. Her emotions had been building all day and she was fighting to stay in control of them. If it was possible, she had grown even closer to Kulsoom over the last few months. Their personal battles with breast cancer had united them. Kulsoom's dry humour always made her smile, and this time it momentarily distracted Kirsty from the inevitability of having to say goodbye. She watched as her dad and Robbie said their farewells, giving Kulsoom a quick hug before shoving their hands deep in their jeans pockets and cracking a few little jokes, like don't flush the loo while you're sitting on it on the plane or you might just get sucked right out, making Kulsoom, Lynette and Kirsty roll their eyes.

Lynette gave Kirsty a peck on the cheek. 'See you soon, love. I'll be back from the airport around ten but you make sure you don't wait up for me. You look exhausted and need to get some sleep – mother's orders.'

'I promise I'll be a good girl and be in bed by nine,' Kirsty replied.

Kulsoom put her handbag on the front seat of the Prado then turned to give Kirsty a cuddle, whispering in her ear as she did so. 'Don't give up the fight, my love. You're stronger than this bloody cancer and I know you're going to beat it. The results will prove it to you. You just wait and see.' Kulsoom had gone to Cairns with Lynette and Kirsty the day before for Kirsty's final tests. Now they just had to wait for the results.

Kirsty's face quivered as she fought back the tears that threatened to fall. She squeezed Kulsoom tighter. 'Thank you – for everything. You've given me more than you'll ever know. I love you so much.'

Kulsoom gently pulled back and placed her hands on Kirsty's arms. 'I love you too. But remember, the most important thing right now is that you love yourself. That's what is going to get you through all of this. And when you do find out you've beaten it, make sure you go and get your hunky man back. He loves you, Kirsty. You don't come across men like Aden very often in life. Trust me. My beloved Harry is one of them and I pushed him out of my life, too, when I was going through the worst of the cancer. The poor bugger lived in the shed for two whole months, sleeping on an old camp bed.'

Kirsty stared at Kulsoom through her tear-blurred eyes. 'You – you did the same to Harry? Kicked him out because you were scared of dying?'

'Yep, sure did. And you know what? He never once complained. He just told me to take time out if I felt I needed it. Made me love the old codger even more.'

'But . . . but when I asked your opinion on my breaking up with Aden, how come you didn't tell me this?'

Kulsoom patted Kirsty tenderly on the arm. 'Because it was your decision to make, love, not mine. I didn't want to sway your feelings. You had to do what was right for you. Cancer takes a lot out of you and you need all your focus, all your strength, to fight it. Some people need loved ones to rally around them, and that's okay, but others like me and you, we need to get through things on our own. And that's okay too, even though it drives people nuts.'

Kirsty smiled, sniffling loudly. 'We're similar, me and you, aren't we?'

'Sure are, kiddo. Now, make sure you ring me as soon as you get your results and we'll celebrate the good news by screaming like a pair of maniacs on the phone.' Kulsoom stepped up into the passenger seat.

'You'll be the first one I call!' Kirsty said as Lynette began to reverse out of the drive. She blew a kiss and Kulsoom caught it then clutched it to her heart, just like she'd always done when Kirsty was a little girl.

The sweet birdsong outside her bedroom window woke Kirsty from a deep sleep. She rubbed her eyes and then stretched, a satisfied yawn escaping her lips. She had not slept so soundly in months and it was wonderful to awaken revitalised for a change. She hadn't experienced any nightmares this past week and she was hoping they might have stopped. Maybe her conscience was clearing because she'd finally told Aden the truth?

Allowing herself time to wake up, she rolled onto her side and took a few deep breaths, becoming more aware of her surroundings with each exhalation. Something inside her had shifted. Not physically, but emotionally, like a weight had been lifted from her shoulders. Maybe it was the chemotherapy being finished, or maybe it was the conversation she and Kulsoom had shared last night. Or maybe it was because Aden had invited her over this weekend. It felt like a step in the right direction, a step away from her past.

Poor Harry, having to sleep in the shed for months! Kirsty pondered the notion. Harry and Kulsoom were like two peas in a pod, they were so close. Kirsty found it almost impossible to believe that Kulsoom had kicked him out. Especially when she'd had cancer and needed his support more than she had ever needed it before. Although wasn't that exactly what she had done to Aden? But she and Aden were different to Harry and Kulsoom. They weren't married, hadn't shared years of love, years of unforgettable memories.

Kirsty pushed herself up and out of bed, the morning sunlight flickering through the curtains providing enough light for her to catch her reflection in the dressing table mirror. She didn't like what she saw, but she didn't care. She leant on the bedside table for support, her entire body shaking, her thoughts racing. Everything suddenly made perfect sense. *My God! What have*

I done? Aden and I are exactly like Kulsoom and Harry. She glared at herself in the mirror, determination flooding her, filling her with urgency.

'No more! No more self-doubt, no more fear of the unknown. You hear me? You're going to survive this bloody cancer and that's that! Aden is going to forgive you for the accident – he has to!' She hammered her hand on the dressing table, making her bottles of perfume clatter. 'So, Miss Mitchell, you better damned well do something about Aden before it's too late. And once that's sorted and you get your results back, you're going to fulfil your dream of opening a gallery. Like it or lump it!'

The delicious aroma of freshly baked pumpkin scones wafted around the homestead kitchen. Kirsty pulled a clean tea towel from a drawer and carefully wrapped the little golden goodies in it, slapping Ron's hand as he tried to pinch one. 'I've already put some in the microwave for you, Mum and Robbie for morning tea, so no thieving these ones, Dad.' She tapped the folded bundle gently. 'These little babies are for Aden and me.'

Ron raised his eyebrows. 'Ah . . . for you and Aden, hey? The third musketeer gets all your lovely scones and you leave me just one measly one. Is this a date or just a friendly visit?'

Kirsty's face rapidly flushed red. 'No, Dad, it's not a date, just a friendly visit. I thought I'd better bring him some sort of housewarming gift. What better than homemade pumpkin scones? From memory, they're his favourite.'

Ron threw two heaped teaspoons of sugar into his black tea and stirred vigorously, the teaspoon clanking against the cup as he gazed intently at Kirsty. 'I see. Well, good on you. I know he's been really keen for you to see his new place. I helped him move his things over there and I was very impressed. He's done well for a young lad – a perfect example of how hard work can pay off. A few of the young guys round Hidden Valley could learn a lesson or two from him, especially the ratbag Cooper boys from next door.'

'Yeah, he does work hard.' Kirsty began to walk out of the kitchen. 'He's a good bloke, our Aden. Anyhow, I'm really looking forward to checking out his place so I better get a shift on or I'll be late for smoko time. When you see Mum just let her know I'll be back some time this arvo.'

Ron grinned mischievously at her over the rim of his cup. 'That's fine, love. You take as long as you like.'

'Would you stand still, buddy?' Kirsty grumbled as she attempted to tighten the girth strap for the second time. Cash swivelled his head around, gently nudging her with his muzzle, and then proceeded to try to nibble her earlobe. Kirsty couldn't help giggling as she pushed him away, her balance failing her as she fell on the dusty ground with an almighty thump. She sat in a crumpled heap, laughing in between bouts of coughing, spitting out particles of grit while a cloud of dust circled around her head.

Cash whinnied as if in amusement and softly stomped his foot. She poked her tongue out at him and stood, dusting her jeans off, giving him a quick peck and a scratch on the cheek as she gathered the reins from the hitching post. 'You're a cheeky bugger, Cash! But that's why I love you so much.

I know you're excited to go for a ride. Me too. It's been *way* too long, my dear friend.'

Wrapping one arm over his withers, she ruffled his forelock and gave his neck a sniff, his horsy aroma bringing a satisfied smile to her lips. 'I swear someone should bottle your scent and sell it as men's aftershave. Maybe mix it with a hint of leather and woody spice. I betcha women all over the world would go crazy.'

Cash neighed and nodded his head, as if he completely agreed. She giggled again while she glanced around the stables, making sure she'd packed everything into the saddlebags, a rush of adrenaline filling her as she finally placed her R.M. Williams boot into the stirrup.

Knowing she had to take it easy, she slowly pushed herself up, her body still fragile after the months of chemo. Her excitement bubbled over once she'd settled herself into the seat of her favourite western saddle. It felt so bloody good to be sitting here! She couldn't wait to go for a gallop out in the glorious sunshine. Her days out riding Cash while mustering cattle felt like a lifetime ago.

Placing the reins into position she gave Cash a squeeze with her legs, a smile lighting up her face. 'Come on then, boy, let's head. We've got us some adventures to be had!'

The tranquillity of the bushlands surrounding Flame Tree Hill enveloped Kirsty, the only sounds filling the beautiful silence were the rhythmic clip-clop of Cash's hoofs against the dry riverbed and the rustling of leaves around her as the sultry breeze caressed the thriving native trees. A scrub turkey scampered like a loose hubcap in front of them, darting this way and that, eventually disappearing into a thicket of emu bush. It reminded her of the Roadrunner, that old cartoon character. She smiled to herself, recalling the countless times she, Ron and Robbie used to sit on the couch of a Sunday in absolute hysterics at the antics of the animated characters. Lynette would be in the kitchen, happily tending to the roast dinner. Those days were long gone, but that was just the way life worked. When Kirsty had children of her own one day she could share the same experiences with them, providing them with the love and security that her own parents had blessed her and Robbie with. And she prayed that the father of her children would be Aden.

A trickle of sweat rolled down her cheek and she wiped it away, deciding that it was time to take another swig from her water bottle. She signalled for Cash to stop, resting her weight back in the saddle. He obeyed at once, breathing heavily, his coat slick with sweat. It was still shy of ten in the morning but the humidity was so thick it was stifling, the odds of an afternoon shower high. After drinking steadily from the bottle, she gave Cash's forelock a tussle and shook the bottle at him. 'Do you want some, buddy?'

Cash, accustomed to the request, tilted his head around and tipped his lips up towards Kirsty for a drink. She squeezed the water out of the pump top of the bottle, the stream splashing against Cash's muzzle as he drank, his lips quivering with enjoyment.

Searching for the landmark Robbie had told her to navigate by, Kirsty had a thorough look around, knowing from the distance already travelled that Aden's property had to be close by. She tugged the brim of her hat down, squinting through the dazzling sunlight, elated when the rusty corrugated-iron hut that Robbie had mentioned came into view. What a perfect photo it would make. Leaning over, she grabbed her camera from the bottom of the saddlebag, being careful not to squash her scones. Then she clicked off a number of shots, enthralled by the simple beauty of the old shack among the thick over-growth.

Content, she edged Cash onwards, butterflies fluttering in her belly, the thought of seeing Aden exhilarating her. There could be a myriad of outcomes of this visit and she honestly had no idea how he was feeling about everything or what he was going to say to her, which made her very nervous. Maybe she should have rung him first, to let him know she was com-ing? But he'd said to drop by any time. Exhaling loudly, trying to still her racing thoughts, she motioned for Cash to begin the climb up the gently sloping hill, her heart dancing a fervent fox-trot inside her chest.

As she reached the crest, Kirsty's breath escaped her. Aden's hilltop property was magnificent. Endless pastures rolled out before her, dotted with hundreds of striking purple miniature orchids. A few horses roamed among about thirty head of cat-tle, their ears pricked as they assessed whether she was a threat, before focusing their attention back on the grass at their feet.

Enormous timber stables sat in the centre of fields, and beyond that Kirsty could just make out the gleaming roof of what she knew must be Aden's house. Giving Cash a tight squeeze, she galloped off towards the home, one hand gripping the reins and the other holding her hat. Once the house came into view, Kirsty slowed Cash to a canter, and then to a trot, her mouth hanging open as she took in the stateliness of the Queenslander homestead. It was way too grand to call it a house.

Stopping in the shade of a golden wattle tree, close enough to admire the house, Kirsty pulled the scones from the saddlebags. She allowed herself a few moments to imagine what it would be like living here with Aden as her husband, their children laughing and playing on the manicured front lawn. She felt her belly do a flip-flop as she envisioned the life they could share.

Pristine tropical gardens bordered the sprawling timber verandah that snaked around the entire home, giving it a colonial charm. How in the heck had Aden afforded it? It was unquestionably an old settler's home, and they didn't come cheap these days. No wonder her dad had been impressed. Aden's business must be doing even better than she'd realised. Good on him, she thought. Aden was a diligent worker and he deserved to reap the rewards.

As she gazed dreamily at the house, Kirsty half expected a pioneering woman in an elegant lace blouse and an ankle-length skirt to come swanning out the front door with a tray of iced tea and homemade biscuits. Instead, to Kirsty's great shock, a thoroughly modern-looking woman came waltzing through the screen door with Aden behind her. Kirsty knew it was Tammy. She'd seen enough photos of her in Aden's albums. She watched, her breath held, as they both got comfortable on the verandah, talking and laughing with each other in a way that filled Kirsty with envy. *She* wanted to be the one sitting there with Aden, enjoying his company. What was Tammy doing here? Had the two of them gotten back together? Was *that* what Aden wanted to talk to her about? Fuck. She knew she couldn't hold it against him if that was the case. She suddenly felt stupid for even *thinking* they could get back together after what she'd done. What did she expect after pushing him away, after telling him the awful truth about his sister? There was never going to be any hope for them. They were over, done, dusted.

Wretchedness filled Kirsty's stomach, making her feel sick, and within seconds the heartbreaking emotions she was experiencing became anger – anger at herself for being such a fool. The parcel of scones she was holding slipped from her grasp, the golden mounds scattering at Cash's feet. Kirsty felt a sob rise from deep within her, every one of her nerves feeling like a loose electrical wire dangling in water. She thudded the heels of her boots into Cash's ribs, inviting him into a sudden gallop, and he leapt to attention. They thundered towards the dried-up riverbeds that would lead them back to Flame Tree Hill, back to her safe haven, and away from Aden.

She let her tears fall freely as the rushing wind swept them from her face. Collapsing into Cash's neck, she clung gently to his mane, resting her head against his crest, giving him the freedom to take her home as the reins hung limply in her quivering hands. She had been so stupid to think that life was going to go back to normal. She should have saved herself the heartache. This was her punishment: whether she died of cancer or not, Aden was going to live on, with Tammy by his side, happily ever after in their perfect little world.

Chapter 26

THE pack of scrawny feral dogs scampered in different directions, halting briefly to growl and bare their razor-sharp teeth, warning Aden they would rip him to shreds if he came anywhere near them. Aden thrashed the roo-hide whip against the earth again, the booming crack echoing off the distant hills and ultimately succeeding in scaring off the pack of mutts. He could tell they weren't entirely of dingo blood – probably the offspring of dingoes and dogs that went AWOL. A bunch of wild bitzers. He knew they wouldn't let go if they got the chance to sink their teeth into him. Even if he did survive the attack he would be at risk of catching some kind of ghastly infection.

Waiting until the dogs were out of sight, Aden hurried over to the remains of what they had been feasting on. Concerned it might be one of his neighbour's calves, or even worse, one of his own dogs, relief flooded through him when he spotted the remnants of what appeared to be food. 'Bloody mongrels,' he muttered as he bent down for a closer inspection, crumbling what was left of the feast through his fingers. He sniffed it, wondering how food had got under the golden wattle tree in the first place. His food scraps either went to the chooks or straight into the compost bin. He thought for a few moments, his brow furrowed in contemplation, and then spotting a tea towel a few metres off to the side it came to him. Pumpkin scones! Kirsty had been here, at his place, and had clearly not come up to the house.

He had spent all last night struggling with his feelings of disappointment. She hadn't bothered to visit him over the weekend like she'd promised. He'd had trouble falling asleep, finally drifting off in the early hours of this morning, only to find himself awake at dawn as usual. She'd seemed keen to talk things over. What was she playing at? Close to midnight, after a few glasses of whisky, he had even gone against his better judgement and tried ringing her a few times, but she hadn't picked up her phone. Why? A million different scenarios flashed through his mind, each one taking his unease up a notch.

Aden sat down on the grass as he rubbed his temples, a splitting headache forming behind his eyes. The roller-coaster of emotions and a lack of sleep were getting the better of him. He ran through the entire weekend, studying each snippet of it in detail. Then it dawned on him, the realisation sending a wave of panic rushing through him. *Shit.* Kirsty must have seen him with Tammy. His ex-wife had only been at his place for an hour or so. And Tammy's visit was *not* something he'd wanted Kirsty to find out about until he'd had the chance to explain.

Pulling his mobile from his pocket he swiftly dialled Kirsty's number but once again it went to voicemail. He left a message pleading for her to call him back. Then he tried the cottage phone but it, too, went to the answering machine. He left another brief message and hung up.

What the hell was he going to do? He stood, looking up at the sky, wishing the answer would flash before him. Exhaling angrily, he tried to put everything into perspective. But he was tired, so damned tired. The last year had really taken its toll. He'd separated from Tammy, moved back to Hidden Valley, dealt with Kirsty's cancer, gone through a painful break-up, and processed the bombshell she'd dropped. Kicking at the hard ground with the toe of his boot, wishing he could somehow dig his way out of this mess, Aden swore out loud and jammed his hands into his pockets. He didn't have time to worry about this now. With a full day ahead of him, he had to get to work. He trudged off in the direction of his Land Cruiser. He wasn't going to chase Kirsty this time, she could come to him. If she didn't call him back he knew he'd see her at the bush races in a week anyway, and he would speak to her then, face to face.

The doctor walked out into the hushed waiting room, her long white coat brushing around her shins. Seven pairs of eyes looked in her direction. The women nervously waiting for their appointments were well aware that the folder the doctor held in her hands could either be their pardon from cancer or their death sentence.

Lynette squeezed Kirsty's hand as the doctor pushed her glasses down to the tip of her petite nose, reading the file over the top of them, a hint of a smile curling her painted lips. It passed so quickly Kirsty found herself wondering whether she had imagined it.

'Miss Kirsty Mitchell?'

Kirsty stood, smiling anxiously.

'Hi, Kirsty, nice to meet you. I'm Doctor Portman,' she said, a smile now properly lighting up her elfin features. For the umpteenth time that morning, Kirsty felt her stomach lurch. The smile gave her a small sense of hope that the results, after months of horrific chemo, were going to be good.

Kirsty gathered her handbag from the floor, the vibration within indicating her mobile phone was ringing. She fumbled for it as she and Lynette followed the doctor down the corridor, but put the phone back when she saw the caller ID. It wasn't the first call from Aden she'd ignored. Her fear of what he was going to say was overwhelming. She couldn't speak to him just yet; she didn't want to hear the words that would confirm he and Tammy were back together. She had to find it in her heart to be happy for him before she spoke with him – he deserved happiness, lots of it, and maybe Tammy was the right woman for the job.

Dr Portman ushered them into her room. 'Have a seat, and I'll be with you in a jiffy. I just need to print out a few more reports. I won't be long.'

'Who was that on the phone, love?' Lynette whispered as they got settled.

'Oh, no one important,' Kirsty snapped, instantly feeling guilty. She hadn't told anyone that she'd seen Tammy at Aden's. Kirsty reached out and touched her mother's hand. 'Sorry, I didn't mean to snap at you. I'm just really nervous.'

Lynette smiled as she straightened her dress. 'I understand. How could you not be?'

Dr Portman came back into the room with a sheaf of papers in her hand. 'Let's get you up on the examination table, Kirsty. We'll just have a look at your breast and see how it's all going.'

The ceiling had been a common focal point for Kirsty in the last few months as countless doctors and nurses had felt her breast to assess how the chemo was going. But this time the stakes were much, much higher. Her heart began to gallop as Dr Portman gently probed her chest, touching here and there, a look of concentration on her face. Kirsty tried to breathe slowly as she waited. There was nothing she could do – it was either good news or bad news.

As she watched, a smile spread across the doctor's face. 'It's looking good, Kirsty. I can't feel any lump there at all, which confirms what the recent tests have shown. I believe the chemotherapy has done its job. Have a seat over at the desk, and we'll discuss your results further.'

Kirsty's happiness was too powerful to contain as joyful tears broke their banks and rolled down her cheeks. She covered her mouth, her emotions all over the place, a bout of uncontrollable laughter fighting to explode from her. She cleared her throat, taking a long, deep breath to steady her voice. 'Are you absolutely sure? I'm going to live?'

'Kirsty, your results speak for themselves. You'll have to continue having six-monthly check-ups, but that's routine and nothing to be worried about at the moment.'

As Kirsty pulled her top back on and sat up on the table, Lynette pulled her into a warm embrace, squeezing her tightly, the two of them shedding relieved tears. 'Oh love, that's wonderful! What magnificent news! Your father and Robbie are going to be so happy.'

Kirsty wriggled out from Lynette's grip, squealing as she cupped her mum's face. 'I know! It's the best news I think I've ever had. I can't wait to ring Aunty Kulsoom and tell her. And let Dad and Robbie know – oh, and let Jo know too! I have my life back, Mum . . . the cancer is gone!'

Dr Portman caught their attention by clearing her throat a little too loudly. 'Please remember, ladies, that we aren't completely out of the woods as yet. You still have to have a lumpectomy to remove the surrounding breast tissue. Just to be one hundred per cent sure that we've got it all.'

Kirsty nodded. 'Will I have to have any lymph nodes out?' She'd already been told the lymph nodes in her right armpit might have been affected.

'No. Your cancer was non-invasive, meaning it has stayed contained within the milk ducts of the breast, which is great news considering how aggressive it was. So I am happy to tell you that there is no need to have the lymph nodes removed.'

Kirsty clapped her hands. 'Trust me, Doctor Portman, after what I've been through, one more visit to the hospital to have surgery is going to be a walk in the park.'

The doctor reached across her desk and took Kirsty's hand in hers, their eyes locking. 'You've given the cancer one hell of a fight, Kirsty. You should be proud of yourself and the immense courage it's taken to get through it. So go and live your life to the fullest.'

'Thank you, I will. And believe me – I'm never going to take anything for granted ever again.'

9 September 2012
Dear Diary,

I have beaten the cancer! I'm going to live! I never thought I would be able to write those words, or even say them out loud, but I can. I truly can. I feel on top of the world! I have so many opportunities ahead of me and I know I can survive anything that life throws at me after the past horrendous five months. No more doubting myself or my abilities as a photographer. It's time to follow my dreams, to make them realities. And also, my nightmares have stopped. I haven't had one in almost a month, which I reckon is a great sign. But with this happiness also comes a certain kind of sadness. I wish that Aden could be here to share this great news with me, to hold me in his strong arms and tell me how happy he is. But it was my choice to break up with him; I've made my bed and I'll just have to damn well sleep in it. I have to accept he's not coming back into my life and move on, like he has. I just hope that one day he will forgive me. With all that aside, it's time to live my life – and to celebrate the fact I have been given a second chance to live it!

K xx

Kirsty fondly wrapped the diary in her favourite silk scarf, one that she'd used to conceal her hairless head. Part of her knew it was time to put the diary away for good, now that her journey with cancer was coming to an end. And hopefully she wouldn't need the many scarves that sat on her dressing table for much longer either. Mind you, she was used to wearing a wig around nowadays, preferring that to a scarf when she went out.

By putting the diary away it felt like the beginning of something new, as though her nightmare world of constant pain and fear could be finally laid to rest, left in the past, somewhere at the back of her overstuffed cupboard.

Clutching the diary close to her heart, she recalled the day Aden had brought it home for her, a deep shuddering breath escaping her as she fought to control her emotions. That time seemed so remote to her now. Taking a few moments to silently give thanks for the diary, she opened her cupboard and tucked it away behind old boxes of photos and horse magazines, smiling to herself. It felt so good to be letting go, to finally be moving on in her life.

A cheer erupted from the group in Flame Tree Hill's formal dining room as everyone raised their glasses of bubbly, all eyes on Kirsty.

Kirsty touched glasses with everyone, her happiness illuminating the room. The moment she had prayed for was here. It was really happening, and it felt amazing.

'Thank you, everyone! I couldn't have got through this without you all here to support me.' Kirsty lowered her eyes, emotion welling up once again. 'I feel bad that I've needed so much attention. You've all put your own lives and responsibilities on hold for me in your own ways, never complaining when you've had to carry me to the toilet, bathe me or just simply sit with me and hold my hand. I'm so lucky to have all of you in my life. I feel very blessed.'

Jo wrapped her arm around Kirsty's shoulder, giving her a loving squeeze. 'Aw, mate, we love you. Of course we were going to help you out in your time of need. You'd do exactly the same for us; remember that. No feeling guilty, okay?'

Robbie joined Jo, wrapping his arms around the two women, giving them an embrace that caused him to slosh champagne onto the floor. He quickly rubbed it in with his sock and winked at his mother's disapproving face. 'Yeah, sis. I wouldn't have had it any other way, even though you told me to bugger off on a number of occasions. I'm used to you telling me what to do, though, bossy britches.' He pulled back from the embrace, raising one eyebrow high enough to almost meet his hairline, something Kirsty had always wanted to be able to do. 'Anyway, where's Aden? He should be here with us celebrating your great news – I know it would mean the world to him. Do you want me to give him a quick ring, tell him to come join us for dinner?'

'Oh, that would be lovely, Robbie! I've made plenty, as usual,' Lynette chirped, her eyes twinkling as she glanced at Kirsty for approval.

Ron nodded. 'Why not? The more the merrier.'

'Oh, no, um, I think he's busy.' Kirsty's smile faded. She didn't want to think about Aden right now – she couldn't. She quickly turned her eyes to where Robbie had spilt his champagne. Crouching down, she began vigorously rubbing the spot with her napkin.

Robbie crouched down too, staring at her. He grabbed her hand to stop her rubbing the carpet away. '*Really?* I find it very hard to believe that he'd be too busy. Let me go and call him and I bet he'll be here straightaway.'

Kirsty wriggled her hand free of his firm grip, her happiness threatening to evaporate. Robbie shook his head, disappointment furrowing his brows as he stood. He folded his arms, taking a moment to assess the situation. The room became awkwardly silent.

'I know you told me to stay out of it, Kirsty, but enough is enough. You haven't even told him your results yet, have you? How could you not tell him, after everything he's been through with you, after everything you put the poor bloke through when you broke it off with him? I can't bloody believe you!'

Jo placed her hand gently on his shoulder. 'Now, come on, Robbie, give her a break. She's been through hell and back and doesn't need this right now. Let's talk about this tomorrow, hey?'

'I can sympathise, Jo, I really can, but I *cannot* stand back and let her do this to my mate either. Aden deserves better treatment than this. He's a good bloke. And he's in love with her!'

With Robbie's eyes burning a hole right through her, Kirsty was acutely aware of the blood pulsing beneath her skin, her heart pounding against her chest like a sledgehammer. A deep rage tore at her. How dare Robbie put her in this position, in front of Mum, Dad and Jo! She bit her bottom lip to stop it from quivering as hot tears filled her eyes. She blinked them back fiercely, angry at herself for losing control of her emotions, and angry at everyone for constantly reminding her of what she'd put Aden through. She beat herself up enough over it without them doing it for her as well. Brusquely pushing herself up from the floor, Kirsty shot a fleeting glance around the room. Everyone's disappointment was clear. Her hurt and anger flowed from her as she began to shout, emotions contorting her face.

'I'm the one that crashed the car that night. It wasn't James driving, it was me! That's why I can't invite Aden here. He hates me for killing his sister! *And* it seems he's back with Tammy, too. There, are you all happy now?'

Shocked expressions replaced the looks of disappointment as Kirsty ran from the dining room. She dashed towards the stables, praying no one was following her.

Chapter 27

THE rhythmic rumble of hoofs vibrated through the ground. The stock horses and novice jockeys galloped down the dirt track towards the finishing line, clumps of earth and powdery dust flying out behind them. On the sidelines the spectators – a growing throng of women in feathery fascinators, men in their Sunday best and old timers in weathered Akubras – gathered at the fence line, some with arms held high in the air in an attempt to edge their wagered horse forwards, others hollering their support enthusiastically for their mates.

The Hidden Valley Bush Races were nothing like a typical race day. The jockeys were all local jackeroos and jillaroos, dressed in their best jeans, flash hats, favourite boots and button-up shirts, and the track was made up entirely of dirt. The competing horses were more accustomed to mustering cattle on the surrounding stations than galloping around a slapdash track in one direction. But somehow it all came together and worked brilliantly.

Heightened anticipation filled the air. Groups of frocked-up girls were whispering together, eyeing off the eligible bachelors, while the young men gathered in testosterone-fuelled circles, their deep laughter echoing around the bar area as they occasionally stole glances at the women. The Hidden Valley Bush Races was the event of the year for the small community, and one not to be missed. Kirsty was glad she had come, despite her fears of running into Aden and Tammy. It felt good to be part of the community again.

The announcer's voice boomed over the speakers, his pitch rising as the horses and jockeys pushed onwards, their ultimate goal now only metres away. Kirsty held her breath as she leant against the makeshift railing beside Harry Mallard, squinting as she followed the path of The Mad Hatter, the beautiful bay horse she had gambled on. Her belly performed a backflip as the gelding edged his way up to join the frontrunners, the white snip on his muzzle a breath ahead of the other horses. She was praying for a win – she hadn't had any luck so far.

'Go, you good thing! You can do it! Go!' she cried out as she eagerly smacked the railing, totally swept up in the excitement of the moment as the horses thundered over the finishing line and the crowd roared. She leapt up in the air, clapping her hands with delight. Her horse had bloody well won! She was now officially two hundred bucks up. Woo hoo!

She slapped Harry on the back, a huge grin on her face. 'Thanks for the heads up on the horse.'

Harry smiled wearily, his eyes etched with sadness. 'My pleasure, lass. Anyhow, must run – I still have to tie up a few loose ends before the race that's dedicated to Mary. I'll catch you a bit later on.'

Kirsty reached out and gave him a quick squeeze, waving him off as he limped away. Harry had been thrilled to hear that Kirsty's final results had come back clear, but Kirsty couldn't help feeling guilty. She'd made it, while Mary hadn't been so lucky.

The crowd began to scatter in different directions, the next race was in half an hour. Some betting slips were torn up in dismay and tossed in nearby bins, while others were carefully clutched until the owners could trade them for cold hard cash. Then it was icy-cold beers and head-spinning champagne until the next race began.

Clutching her winning ticket, Kirsty made her way towards Robbie and Jo, chuffed she at last had a win. Things were still a little awkward, and she hoped that the light mood of the day would help ease any residual tension.

Kirsty's bombshell had created massive ripples in her family as her parents, Robbie and Jo struggled to understand why she'd felt the need to lie to them all this time about the accident. She was surprised, and comforted, to learn they were more upset about her inability to open up to them than the fact she had been in control of the car.

After Kirsty had run out of the family dinner, she'd gone straight to Cash and headed out for a ride, trying to deal with the implications of what she'd just admitted. She hadn't ridden far – it was dusk and she was worried about dingoes – and as she'd arrived back she hadn't been sure what to expect. But when she'd walked into the cottage, tear-stained and sweaty, Lynette had been waiting for her, and had taken her into her arms and held her there, explaining through her sobs just how sorry she was that Kirsty had felt the need to go through such emotional torture on her own.

Despite everything, Kirsty's family supported her. She just wished she could gain Aden's forgiveness, too.

'Hey there, babe!' Jo chirped as she threw her free arm around Kirsty, a little unstable in her high heels, her cheeks rosy from the combination of wine and standing in the sweltering hot sun. A stylish burgundy hat was perched on her head but it did little to shade her face, the emphasis being more on the floral embellishments than on actual functionality.

Kirsty wore a hat too, although hers was beige, to complement the sleek coffee-coloured dress that gently accentuated what curves she had left. She felt good, better than she had felt in months, and a little sexy as well, with her stilettos. That morning, after adding the final touches of lip gloss and her long blonde wig, she had been quietly impressed with her reflection. It was a nice change. Now she was slowly beginning to loosen up and enjoy the party mood of the races – no doubt the glasses of strawberry sparkling wine had helped.

Jo downed the last mouthful from her plastic champagne flute and wobbled it in the air, cheekily motioning to Robbie for another. Robbie grinned as he leant down and rummaged through the Esky in search of the strawberry sparkling while Jo turned her attention back to Kirsty. 'So, what've you been up to? You've been gone for ages! Thought you were just ducking to the loo and then the next thing I knew, the race was on and I couldn't find you in the crowd. I was beginning to wonder whether you had run off into the bushes with some handsome bloke.'

'Oh, get real,' said Kirsty, rolling her eyes. 'I've just been catching up on the goss with people I haven't seen for ages – and winning money!' Kirsty slapped Jo playfully on the backside and then waved her betting slip in Robbie's face. 'Harry Mallard was right. The dark bay *was* a dark horse, so to speak.'

Robbie threw his hands up in the air, sloshing beer out of his can. 'Bugger, I should have listened to him. He told me it was a sure thing and to put a hundred bucks on it. I told him he was talking rubbish. Cor! I could have won . . .' Robbie rolled his eyes upwards as he muttered figures under his breath, counting on his fingers as he did so. 'At seven-fifty to one I would have won seven hundred and fifty buckaroos! Bloody hell, that'll teach me.'

Kirsty giggled. 'That it will. Harry's not one to be spinning yarns lightly, especially when it comes to horses.'

Jo leant on Kirsty's shoulder for support. 'Want to go for a walk over to the stables and check out the horses?' she asked, a little too casually.

Kirsty frowned as she crossed her arms. 'No, thanks. You know Aden is over there. And most probably Tammy. What are you up to, Jo?'

Now it was Jo's turn to frown and she, too, crossed her arms defensively, spilling half her wine as she did so. She grabbed Kirsty's arm and gently pulled her off to the side, away from prying ears, lowering her voice to the point where Kirsty had to lean right in to hear Jo over the noise of the crowd. 'Oh come on, Kirsty. Do you *really* think Aden would be back with Tammy? From what he told me, he had no love left for the woman. My God, they hadn't had sex in, like, *six months* before the split. For me that's a huge sign there ain't no love left.'

'He told you that?' Kirsty replied, gobsmacked, but Jo shushed her with a wiggle of her finger as she continued.

'*And* you haven't given him a chance to explain anything, especially how he feels about you being the driver that night. It would have been one hell of a shock for him. Fuck, I know it was for me, so I can only imagine the impact it had on him. You refuse to answer his calls or return any of his messages. No wonder the poor bloke's a mess.'

Kirsty looked down at the ground, suddenly ashamed. 'You're right, Jo. It's been wrong of me to ignore him. But I'm just so scared to know for sure that he's back with Tammy. Crazy as it might sound, I feel that if I don't know, if he doesn't confirm it to me, I can pretend that it isn't happening, and I might still have a chance at getting him back. And on top of that I'm terrified he won't be able to forgive me for Bec's death. God knows I find it hard to forgive myself, so why would he be able to?'

Jo smiled, her voice softening as she did so. 'Well, I reckon he deserves to answer those questions himself. Promise me you'll at least give him a chance to do that, Kirsty. Robbie reckons he looks like death warmed up. You've got the poor bloke stressed out to the max.'

Kirsty nodded softly as she bit her lip. 'I promise.'

Jo wrapped both arms around Kirsty, pulling her into a warm embrace. 'You're my best mate, and I'm only saying all this because I love you. I know you have a tendency to do things your own way, and that's fine, but just this once listen to someone's advice. It'll all work out – you'll see.'

Kirsty smiled as she gently pulled out of Jo's arms, waving her betting slip in the air. 'I did listen to someone's advice. That's why I won!'

The two friends cracked up, the seriousness of the conversation forgotten for now as they wandered back to join their circle of mates and poured themselves another sparkling wine, dropping a strawberry in for good measure, and then clinked glasses.

Kirsty could hardly see the poster tacked to the back of the toilet door. Her vision blurred and unfocused as she sat down on the loo, her weight shifting as she leant forwards to steady herself, her handbag wobbling on her lap.

The wine was beginning to take its toll and she was spending a fair bit of time in the ladies, even though she had only had four glasses. Well, to be fair, they were big glasses . . . and it had been ages since she had drunk alcohol.

Groaning at her own drunken queasiness, feeling as though she was aboard a ship sailing through rough seas, she leant forwards once again and rested her chin in her hands, her elbows wobbling precariously on her kneecaps, her knickers still around her ankles. What a state she was in, after only a few glasses! What happened to the party girl who could drink people under the table and dance all night? Pffft! That girl had disappeared when the cancer arrived. Not that it was such a bad thing. It was time Kirsty grew up and moved on. Only one little operation and the cancer would be a thing of the past, hopefully.

She let her mind wander, enjoying the peace and quiet of the toilets. The final race – Aden's race – wasn't far away. What if Jo was right? What if Aden *had* forgiven her? What if she'd been wrong about him and Tammy getting back together? She exhaled slowly. It was all so bloody hard. But then again, did it have to be hard? All she had to do was to track down Aden to find out the truth. And that was precisely what she was going to do.

The announcer's voice crackled to life over the loudspeakers as Kirsty left the toilets and there was a general rush to the sidelines. This was the race they had all been waiting for: the race for Mary Mallard. The throng of spectators was testimony to Mary's standing in the community. The starting line was ready, all horses and jockeys in the gates. Kirsty held her breath, her eyes glued to Aden, a familiar feeling of exhilaration washing over her as he erupted from the gate on Star. How could he be so sexy when dressed entirely in pink?

'Come on! Ride him like you stole him!' Kirsty shouted, feeling her heart race in time with the thundering of the horses' hoofs. Jo chanted beside her, their voices joining in the tremendous roar of the crowd, the atmosphere alive. The rumble got louder as the horses approached the bend, hundreds of heads following their path, all eyes glued to the track. Aden was in third place, and gaining. Kirsty clenched her fist and punched it into the air. *Come on, come on, come on.* She bit her bottom lip, the tension almost too much to bear as the horses neared the finishing post. The crowd got louder, the riders more determined, and the horses gave it all they had. Star opened his stride, his muscles rippling as Aden leant forward with a fierce look on his face. In seconds, Star had stolen first place, like it was the easiest thing on earth to do. Aden and Star won.

Kirsty couldn't hide her shock as Aden threw his hat up in the air – his head was as bald as the day he was born. He turned in her direction, a triumphant smile on his lips, his eyes searching the crowd before calmly coming to rest on her, the intensity in his look stealing her breath away. He smiled, and something deep and powerful passed between them. And then he mouthed the three words she'd been dying to hear, his lips moving slowly: *I forgive you.*

Kirsty clutched her chest as six years of emotions surfaced. A sob escaped her, followed by another as she fought to control herself among the mass of racegoers. Aden smiled at her again, his eyes telling her everything she needed to know. Hot tears welled and flowed down her cheeks as the realisation hit home. After years of drowning in remorse, desolation and shame, she could finally come to the surface and breathe freely; she finally had permission to forgive herself.

Chapter 28

KIRSTY focused hard on Aden's words. Behind him, the full moon shone brightly, casting his chiselled features in a way that made him look exceptionally dark and mysterious. Aden's colonial homestead was as quiet as the sleeping landscape. Everyone within twenty k's was at the post-race celebrations.

'Then I signed the divorce papers and she left. She *did* try to talk me into giving it a go again but I told her I couldn't, that I was in love with someone else.' Aden looked into Kirsty's eyes. 'And with any luck, that'll be the last time we see each other.'

Kirsty paced the front lawn, gazing down at her feet. She'd been wrong all along, about everything. She wanted to run to Aden, fall into his arms, but not all was cleared up yet. Yes, he'd forgiven her, and Kirsty's heart was light with relief, but she hadn't yet answered his questions about the night of the accident. She owed him that.

Kirsty sat on the grass, nervous and fidgeting with her belt buckle. She could feel his eyes on her, taking her in. Aden had always made her feel so beautiful, especially when she had been at her worst. Throughout her cancer journey, when he had been by her side, he had continued to tell her each and every day just how gorgeous she was. And how did she repay him for his unconditional love? She had left him, told him to forget about ever being together again, and then revealed she was responsible for the death of his beloved sister. She knew now what a fool she'd been. How differently she could have handled things, and how much earlier she should have told Aden. But hindsight was a wonderful thing that never made the present any easier.

Cancer had played some bizarre tricks with her mind, altering the way she saw her life, making her lose her self-belief and perspective. Now that she was out of the deep, dark hole she had fallen into, she could see everything as clear as day. It was time to put things right.

Looking up to face Aden, Kirsty smiled at the sight of his bald head gleaming in the moonlight. When she had asked him about it he had simply replied that it was for her – to make her feel less self-conscious, to show her just how much he was willing to support her. There was already a tiny bit of stubble growing back, and Kirsty had to admit that Aden pulled off a bald head much better than she did. He actually looked sexy. Pulling her thoughts back to the present, she cleared her throat and scrambled for the right words. 'I know that you wanted to talk to me about the night of the accident, Aden.'

Aden's relaxed smile disappeared and the atmosphere shifted. As uncomfortable as it was, Kirsty knew this had to be done. He stood up from the verandah steps and made his way over to sit beside Kirsty on the lawn, exhaling slowly before he spoke. 'Well, there are a few things I'm really struggling with. How come James was named as the driver?'

Kirsty felt her heart begin to race, the horrific images of the night of the crash flooding back. Shit, this was going to be hard. 'Let me start at the beginning. It all happened so fast. One minute we were enjoying ourselves and the next we were screaming and the car had flipped onto its roof . . .' Kirsty wiped her wet eyes, fighting to stay in control of her emotions. Aden placed his hand on her back, silently urging her on.

'I'll never forget the sound when we slammed into the tree. It was deafening, and then there was silence, total silence. I remember frantically trying to undo my seatbelt because I could smell fuel and I was scared the car was going to explode. I was hanging upside down and the steering wheel was pushing into my stomach, and then all of a sudden James was reaching through the driver's window and helping me. He was bleeding so badly, but there he was, helping *me*. I kept asking if everyone else was okay but nobody was answering. It was terrifying. I lost all sense of time, and there are moments that I can't recall at all. I don't know how James eventually got me out of the wreck, but when he did he placed both hands on my face and begged for me to focus. I was tired, so tired, and all I wanted to do was sleep, but he kept shaking me, telling me to stay with him. He told me that he was going to tell the police he'd been driving. Then I remember him dragging me across the road and into the scrub just in time for us to take cover from the explosion.' Kirsty instinctively touched her hip, remembering the searing pain as the piece of shrapnel ripped through her. 'Bits of the Commodore flew everywhere and the heat, it was so fierce, Aden, it felt like I was inside a furnace and I couldn't take a decent breath because of the black smoke.

'To this day I have no idea why James took the rap. If he told me, I don't remember. I tried to argue with him, to tell him not to, but then I must have blacked out. The next thing I knew I was in a hospital bed with tubes hanging out of me. And my parents were beside me, frantic. I tried to speak, to tell them what had happened, but Mum shushed me and told me that

I was the only survivor, and that James had died from massive internal bleeding. Dad was saying over and over that James should have known better than to drive drunk. I've never seen my dad so distraught, it was terrible.'

Kirsty shook her head, shuddering sobs escaping her, the sheer anguish she'd felt returning with full intensity. She clutched Aden's hands as she met his eyes, her body shaking with sorrow. 'I'm so sorry, Aden, so very sorry. I should have known better. I should never have got behind the wheel; I should have spoken up in the hospital and told the truth; I should have told *you* the truth a long time ago.'

Aden brought her hands to his lips and tenderly kissed them before taking her into his arms. 'Oh, K. You were young and in shock, terrified of what people would think about you. I'm so sorry you've suffered silently all these years, I truly am. I can't say it was easy for me to find forgiveness in my heart, but I understand why you did what you did, and I do forgive you. We all do stupid things when we're young and I've been guilty of drink driving more than once. How can I judge you when I've done the same myself? Bec's death was devastating, but I've had years to come to terms with her absence. You're not a bad person, K – far from it. You're one of the most thoughtful and decent women I know.' Aden smiled tenderly 'Other than my mum, of course.'

Holding Kirsty close, he continued, 'I don't think you need to tell my parents. It will only cause more hurt and upset, and it's not going to bring Bec back. This is *our* secret now, okay?'

'Thank you, Aden. What you've just said means more than you'll ever know,' Kirsty whispered as she rested her head on his chest, the beating of his heart against her cheek so comforting. She sighed slowly, finally free to walk away from her past.

A comfortable silence fell over them as they sat on the grass, mesmerised by the stars above, the soft call of cattle in the nearby paddock the only sound for miles. Kirsty turned to face Aden, gazing into his eyes. 'I love you.'

Aden met her gaze with eyes so intense, so full of passion, that they melted Kirsty's heart. 'And I love you. I've never stopped loving you, through all of this.'

A feeling of perfect joy filled Kirsty. She reached out and ran her hand over his prickly head. 'I cannot believe you did this for me. Where did you get the idea?'

Aden chuckled quietly. 'If I tell you I'll have to kill you.'

Kirsty nudged him gently in the ribs. 'Tell me, or else I'll have to tickle you to death.'

Aden flinched jokingly. 'All right, all right. But promise me you won't tell another living soul.'

Kirsty zipped her lips, smiling.

'I was watching telly the other night, off in my own little world and not really taking in what was on the screen, when I noticed I was watching *Sex and the City*.'

Kirsty stifled a giggle. 'Who would have thought?'

'Let me just remind you that I was distracted, thinking about *you* – as usual.'

'Hey! Don't blame me for your closet addiction to girly TV.'

Aden glanced at her, teasing intent in his mischievous eyes. 'Anyway, I was panicking, trying to find the remote, worried the entire town was going to be standing outside the window, taking the piss out of me, when one of the women started talking about her breast cancer. I stopped looking for the remote and sat down to watch, and before I knew it, I'd watched the whole episode. The character's boyfriend, some Hollywood I'm-so-sexy guy, decided he would shave his head to show his girlfriend how much he loved her and wanted to support her. The sheila – well, she just adored him for it. So I thought, maybe that's what I should do to show you my support for what you went through – what you *are* going through.' Aden reached out and gently ran his finger down her cheek. 'God, I've missed you. When do you find out the final results of the chemo? It must be soon.'

A grin lit up Kirsty's face. 'I got the results a few days ago.'

Aden moved away from her, his strained expression conveying his emotional turmoil. Kirsty immediately felt guilty for not telling him sooner. *Shit, why didn't I tell him straightaway?*

'Bloody hell! Why didn't you tell me the minute you found out? Is everything okay? Please tell me you are going to be okay.'

Kirsty wriggled in beside him, close enough to feel his breath on her lips, to smell his woody aftershave, to see the throb of his rapid pulse at the side of his neck. 'I'm so sorry, but I was upset because I thought you were back with Tammy and I didn't want to come around here again and see you with her, or have her answer the phone if I rang to tell you the results.' She took a deep breath, her eyes shining. 'I've beaten it, Aden! The results are exactly what we were hoping for. I'm going to live!'

'Oh, Kirsty! Fan-fucking-tastic! You've just made me a very happy man.' Aden wrapped his arms around her, pulling her into a passionate kiss.

Kirsty melted into his embrace, her tongue caressing his, desire making her tremble, and the love she felt for him filling her with warmth, security and happiness.

Aden gently pulled away, a contented smile lighting up his rugged features. 'I want you in my life, K. No, I *need* you in my life. It breaks my heart not being with you. Let's roll the dice, take a chance, and not worry about the future. I want to wake up with you every morning and go to bed beside you every night. Can we leave the past where it is?'

Kirsty placed her hands on Aden's chest, feeling his firm muscles under her touch. His beautiful eyes held so much love for her that she could barely speak. 'I love you, Aden Maloney. And I want to be with you, for the rest of my life.'

'Well, in that case, why don't we start the rest of our lives together over dinner? I happen to have some fresh prawns, and I can think of nothing I'd like to do more than whip you up some garlic prawns. And then I have a surprise for you. I was waiting to hear your results before I gave it to you. It's sort of a celebratory gift for beating the cancer, which, as I kept telling you, I knew you would.'

Kirsty's face brightened with interest and she placed a lingering kiss on Aden's lips. 'Tell me, what's this surprise? I can't stand not knowing.'

'No way are you going to win me over with seduction, Miss Mitchell. You'll have to come inside to see what it is. It wouldn't be a surprise if I told you, now, would it?'

Kirsty eyed him curiously as he leapt to his feet and held out his hand, grinning like a Cheshire cat. 'Come on then, let's get inside. I can't wait to see your face!'

Epilogue

THE skies were an endless blue and the autumn temperature a glorious nineteen degrees: perfect weather for one of the biggest days of Kirsty's life. And best of all, Aden would be by her side. She couldn't imagine doing it without him. But first she had a few things to do on her own.

She tiptoed across the cemetery, acutely aware she was walking on people's final resting places. Kirsty had already visited Bec's, James's and Peta's graves, and now she finally reached Mary's. She sat down on the grass near the headstone, placing the bright yellow sunflowers she had brought into the vase in the ground.

Wiping the thin layer of dust from the headstone, she shook her head in disbelief as she realised it had been almost a year since Mary had passed away. So much had happened, and yet it still felt like only yesterday that Kirsty herself was battling breast cancer along with Mary. Thank God her own struggle was over. The tissue the doctors removed in her lumpectomy had been perfectly healthy and clear of any cancer, and her first six-monthly check-up had been clear as well. Dear old Mary hadn't been as lucky. Kirsty felt tears come to her eyes as she reflected on the pain Mary had gone through in her final months.

She pulled a tissue from her handbag and wiped her eyes. 'Hi, Mary. Sorry it's been a couple of weeks since I've visited, but I've been flat out organising the grand opening of my gallery. You know that Aden found the perfect spot in town and we've both been working hard getting it all ready. Aden even went to the trouble of making frames for the pieces I'm putting on show tonight. I suspect he's a little self-conscious that he's in a few of the photographs, even though he's assured me he's fine with me exhibiting them. I think I'm still in shock about the gallery – I can't believe that he bought the space for me without even knowing if I was going to live, or if we were ever going to be together again. The night he gave me the official paperwork, with my name on it, will go down as one of the best nights of my life. Aden had more faith in me than I ever did, bless him. He never gave up on me, even when I had given up on him, and myself.'

Kirsty paused and gazed into the distance, the horizon soft against the blue sky. The cemetery was silent but for birdsong and the gentle sound of the breeze in the trees. She felt like Mary was there, in the trees, in the wind, listening to her. And that brought the most incredible sense of peace and happiness to her heart.

The growing crowd wandered around the stylishly designed gallery, champagne glasses in hand, pausing to admire the landscape photography that was showcased beneath the subtle gallery lighting. Kirsty watched her guests from the corner of the room, their reactions filling her with satisfaction and confidence.

The time had come for the unveiling of her *pièce de résistance* and she took a few deep breaths, calming herself before she had to give a speech.

Aden squeezed her hand. 'You'll do great, beautiful, don't worry. Are you ready?'

Kirsty nodded, smiling uneasily.

Aden placed his hand on her cheek. 'Don't fret, K. Look at them all. They love your work. You've sold five pieces already and there's still two hours to go. Mind you, the one of me and Robbie with Joy and Hank prancing about in the background was a doozy. My mum couldn't resist it.'

Kirsty's smile broadened, her confidence beginning to out-weigh her niggling doubts. 'They do seem to be enjoying the exhibition, don't they? Righto, let's do it.'

Kirsty took her position at the microphone while Aden tapped his glass loudly. The crowd hushed and all eyes fell upon Kirsty. She swallowed hard, her heart feeling as though it were beating in her mouth. Lynette, Ron, Kulsoom, Harry, Robbie and Jo, along with Aden's immediate family, all smiled proudly at her from the front of the crowd, their presence boosting her self-confidence.

'Welcome, ladies and gentlemen, to Captivate Gallery. I'm honoured you've all joined me for the opening night. Thank you for making the effort to be here. I hope you are all enjoying the canapés and wine – and, of course, the photographs.' She motioned to her right. 'It is now time to unveil the centrepiece of the evening. This is a photograph that is very close to my heart. I have an admission to make before I reveal it to you all, though; this photo wasn't taken by me. It was taken by my fiancé, Aden Maloney. It's an example of how a photograph can truly capture emotions, which is what inspires me in my work every day.'

She gently pulled the white silk sheet from a massive easel, to reveal the black-and-white image underneath. The woman staring back at her from the photo was a mere shadow of her now radiant and healthy self.

The crowd remained hushed as they gazed at the photo. It showed Kirsty at the lowest point of her breast cancer, and although it was a confronting image, Kirsty wanted people to experience how powerful a photo could be.

Kirsty stood at her bedroom window, the morning sunlight pouring in around her, giving her an almost angelic glow. She was dressed in a white button-up chiffon shirt with a pair of boy leg undies beneath, her wasted limbs evident. Her head was bald, and the toll the disease had taken on her was visible in the frailness of her body. But her face projected an inner strength, her eyes full of passion and determination, a delicate smile on her lips. The contrast between her body and her eyes was startling. The photo seemed to show a woman on the brink of death, but her eyes displayed an inner fire. It was a beautiful, moving, haunting image, and Kirsty finally understood that it was this part of herself – the determination, the will to live – that she had not been able to see. But her beautiful Aden had. By displaying the photo so publicly, she hoped to make her own tribute to the women who had battled, or were still battling, breast cancer. She wanted them to see that no matter how horrible they felt, they were still beautiful, and that they should never underestimate themselves or their will to survive.

Aden took Kirsty by the hand and led her into the bedroom, where the delicate scent of vanilla and musk wafted from the candles he had lit beside the bed. Country love songs floated from the stereo, adding to the romantic atmosphere. The two glasses of red wine Kirsty had enjoyed at the opening had made her slightly light-headed, erasing any self-consciousness she might have felt. Aden hadn't seen her naked before, and she knew that the lumpectomy had left her right breast less than complete. But all that seemed irrelevant now.

She had been waiting for this moment for what seemed like forever, her body finally strong enough to be at one with his. How long had she waited! The soft candlelight intensified his handsome ruggedness, his dimples and the scar on his lip adding to his roguish sexiness.

They remained silent, their eyes saying everything that needed to be said, the energy between them electric. Aden slowly unzipped her black cocktail dress, letting it slip to the floor, leaving Kirsty only in her bra and lace pants. She shivered as he began to lay lingering kisses on her ears, her neck and then down her back, his warm breath igniting her skin, quickening her pulse. She turned to him, her lips searching for his, as he lifted her in one easy movement and carried her to the bed.

Aden moved over her, his kisses hungry, as Kirsty began to remove his clothing. He slid his hands around her pants and pulled them down swiftly as she unhooked her bra for him. Skin on skin, body to body; every inch was now bared for each to kiss, to caress, to discover. Aden brought his lips down to hers, stopping short of kissing her as he lightly ran his tongue over them. Her body responded, quivering with longing. A sigh of pleasure escaped her as his warm mouth travelled down her body and he began to taste her – gently, slowly, irresistibly. She arched her back as she felt herself start to climb towards her peak, every single part of her pulsing, trembling, shivering. It was so tempting to give in to the ecstasy.

Aden stopped, leaving her balancing on the edge of euphoria, kissing her thighs as he made his way back up to her stomach, pausing to tenderly trace his fingers over the scar on her hip, then up towards her lips.

Kirsty took control and pushed Aden onto his back, her entire body tingling with sensation. She ran her lips down his broad chest, biting his nipples, his groans of satisfaction music to her ears. She continued her descent, letting her lips slide teasingly over his groin, and then she blew warmth over the tip of him before slowly moving her tongue downwards, bit by bit. Aden cried out her name, his voice husky with desire as he pulled her upwards and on top of him, his eyes locked on hers.

They paused for a moment, holding each other's gaze, their breathing heavy.

'I love you so much,' Aden said, his voice rough with longing.

'I love you too,' Kirsty whispered. 'Forever and always.'

They wrapped their arms around one another as Kirsty tipped her head back, moving her hips in time with his, their moans of satisfaction filling the room. At first their movements were slow, deliberate, but rapidly the yearning for complete rapture overpowered them. Reaching the summit, they struggled for breath, calling each other's names out in ecstasy.

Kirsty nestled into Aden, his muscular body resting against her own. Aden gently leant across her, blowing the candles out, and the room fell into darkness. He pulled her in closer as he wrapped his arms around her and she shut her eyes, incredibly thankful for everything. For a long time she would never have believed she could be here, lying in Aden Maloney's arms, exhausted after making passionate love to him. Her past was firmly behind her, and her future was bright. It was more than she had ever hoped for, and she was blessed, contented and breathlessly in love.

Acknowledgements

To my darling Chloe Rose. My life wouldn't be the same without you. You make me laugh, fill me with love and inspire me in so many diverse ways. You are my world and I love you with all my heart.

To my brilliant mum, Gaye, you're not *only* my mum, but my best friend too. You've always been there for me, no matter what, and so proudly tell everyone about my books. Thank you, for everything. I love you heaps.

My dad, John, you give quiet compliments that come straight from the heart. Your pride in my achievements means more than words could ever say. Thank you. Love you.

My step-dad, Trevor, you've been there for me my entire life, to talk to, laugh with and love. I adore every minute we get to spend together.

My sisters, Karla, Talia, Mia, Rochelle and Hayley, I am very blessed to have you all in my life.

Aunty Kulsoom, your true strength and beautiful spirit is shown throughout *Flame Tree Hill*. I hope, by reading this novel, you can see just how much you mean to me.

Aunty Debbie, thanks for always being there for me. You're a beautiful soul and always so thoughtful of everyone.

To my fabulous mates, cheers for the unconditional friendship you all give me in your own unique ways. I'm one lucky gal to have friends like you!

To my very special mate, Fiona Stanford, for the many amazing and selfless ways you show your friendship. I am so blessed to have crossed paths with you in this life.

And finally, but most importantly, a big grateful hug goes to you, the reader, for picking up *Flame Tree Hill*. It is you that allows my dream of writing to continue on. I hope my country stories inspire you, make you swoon, make you laugh, *sometimes* cry, and most essentially of all, help you to feel extremely proud of this beautiful land, Australia.

Turn over for a sneak peek.

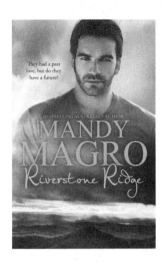

Riverstone Ridge

by

MANDY MAGRO

AVAILABLE NOVEMBER 2019

CHAPTER

1

Riverstone Ridge, Huntingvale

Seething after the horrible events of the day, Nina Jones stripped off her shirt and shorts, shoved her rollerskates out of the way, and quickly checked under her bed one last time before flopping onto it – not that she'd be remaining in it for long. She felt silly, checking for some menacing creature, and deep down knew she'd never find one, but she just couldn't help herself. Two months shy of turning seventeen, and she was still a little afraid of the dark, was wary of anything she couldn't see every nook and cranny of, and that included Riverstone Ridge's top dam. Hell, any dam, to be honest. Why? She hadn't a clue.

Nina found it strange because she could swim in creeks and rivers, and loved to dunk herself in the ocean, but try and drag her into a dam for a swim, and she'd lose her mind. So many times she'd begrudgingly sat on the bank and watched her mates having a blast in the water on their family farms. They'd always have a crack at coaxing her in, but try as she might, going anywhere past dipping her toes into the shallows was unbearable. The irrational fear was just another thing in her unconventional life that she could toss in the 'too hard' basket. How was she meant to know the reasons behind some of her burdens when she didn't know where she'd come from to begin with? Although thankful for Bea taking her in as a baby, gifting her with her last name, being adopted had its challenges …

A sob rose from her chest, but gathering every bit of wilfulness she was known for, she choked it back. She was *not* going to shed any more tears, especially over him, or her. Josh Harper didn't deserve her heartache, nor did Kimberley Lovell. They could have each other as far as she was concerned. It may hurt like hell now, but she'd get through it, she just had to. Thanks to the optimistic nature of her adoptive mum, Beatrice Grace Jones, she believed in a lot of good things. She'd be able to write a list a mile long if asked to, but the male species being virtuous and happily-ever-afters certainly wouldn't get a look-in, not after what she'd been through. Both her parents had given up on her before she'd even been able to string a sentence together, and she'd just lost her boyfriend *and* a girl she'd classed as a friend on the very same day, and none of this was through any fault of her own. Well, that's what Aunty Bea had told her when she'd arrived home in floods of tears from school this afternoon – easy to say, difficult to take on board.

Reliving the sight of Josh and Kimberley groping each other, her aching heart squeezed tighter. Her heart had split in two when she'd busted them behind the sports equipment shed, Kimberley with her blouse unbuttoned and Josh with his hands fondling her breasts and his tongue down her throat. Nina's best mate, Cassie, had warned her not to date Josh, and she should have listened, his reputation of being a player now confirmed – and only days after she'd been stupid enough to lose her virginity to him.

Sighing as though the weight of the world was upon her shoulders, Nina climbed from her tousled bed, dressed only in her bra and undies. Far North Queensland was known for the stifling weather this time of the year, but this was the hottest summer she could remember, the thick heat seeping into her and refusing to give up. Her bedroom feeling like a furnace, she stopped and stood in front of her air-conditioner, groaning in pleasure as the beads of sweat evaporated from her face and belly. Twirling around, she lifted her blonde, shoulder-length hair from her neck – the cool air absolute bliss against her bare skin. The vents rattled despairingly as the ancient appliance competed with the balmy temperature, and then, with a cough and a spit, blew puffs of hot air. She gave it a firm tap, but to no avail – if only they weren't so expensive to replace, but with everything else that needed tending to around here, Bea had enough to keep up with financially.

Exhausted, although determined to get to the paddock party, Nina looked to where silvery light spilled from between her parted curtains. The veil of night having arrived hours ago, it was possibly much cooler outside. She flicked the air-conditioner off at the wall and padded over. With a thrust of her hip she shoved her stubborn bedroom window open and sat on the ledge. The sweet scent of the surrounding mangos and lychee orchids carried upon the breeze, which, to her relief, was a few notches cooler than her bedroom.

Heaving another heavy sigh, she blinked back the next round of gathering tears. She was so sick of crying, was so over feeling like this, and all because of some stupid boy. They sucked. Big time. From now on, she wasn't interested in commitment, her dreams of travelling the world with nothing but a backpack and her love of adventures to guide her much more inviting.

Her gaze went beyond the moonlit backyard with a chook pen in one corner and the dog kennel in the other, and over the many horse agistment paddocks that stretched on and into the distant fence line of Willowbrook. The sweeping landscape that was Riverstone Ridge comforted her. The seventy-acre property was so serene, so very peaceful. Above it all, the velvet-black night was mesmerising, as were the billions of glimmering stars swathing the country night sky. Grateful to call this majestic place home, she breathed all of it in, smiling softly. Bea always said there was a lot to be said for the sensation that came with being thankful. As usual, Bea was right. And although Nina had itchy feet to see beyond the small township of Huntingvale after she finished high school, she would always return here – with its wide open spaces and jaw-dropping views she couldn't imagine living anywhere else. Wild horses wouldn't be able to drag her away for too long. That, she knew, without a doubt.

Biting her already short fingernails, she looked to her dresser, where she'd hidden the cigarette Cassie had given her – apparently it would help. Never having smoked before, and not keen on the smell, she wasn't so sure about that. But, she had to do something to pass the time before she could sneak out to the party, so it was worth a try. Striding over, she grabbed it, along with the box of matches she used to light the candles she so loved to burn. Striking the match, she held it to the end and then dragging way too hard she grimaced and stifled a cough. Her eyes watered as she fought to draw in a breath while ushering the spiralling smoke out her window, terrified Bea would catch a whiff of it. Staring at the glowing end, she shook her head at her stupidity, the vile taste making her gag. Why Cassie thought this would help was beyond her. She stubbed the cigarette out on her windowsill and tossed the butt out the window. She'd pick it up later. Snatching her chewing gum from her backpack, she grabbed two pieces and flung them into her mouth. Mint exploded – ahh, that was better.

Looking back towards where she knew his family's tropical fruit farm was, Logan Steele's handsome face flashed through her mind. He was one of the reasons she'd always want to come back here – their friendship meant the world to her. Although she wasn't interested in starting *anything* with another guy, he was a nice distraction from her current heartache. Two years older than her, the wild boy who had taught her to be a tomboy – and the very first boy she'd ever kissed at fifteen (a stupid spur-of-the-moment slip-up on both their parts) – was home from university for the summer holidays, and she couldn't wait to lay her eyes on his six feet of gloriousness. Now more of a man than the pimply-faced boy she remembered, there was something about him that made her stomach fill with butterflies every single time she was near him. All he had to do was smile in that mischievous way he did, his dimples dancing on his cheeks, and she turned from the tomboy she usually was around him into a gushing girl – but only on the inside. Buddies since they were basically in nappies, there was no way she would ever let him know he could do that to her. How embarrassing would that be?

Allowing herself to float back in time, her toes curled with the memory of Logan pressing her up against the stable wall and kissing her like his life depended on it. Recalling the moment with fierce clarity, she brought her fingertips to her lips. Her surrender to the initial shock of him grabbing her around the waist had given way to a flood of teenage endorphins. Not clumsy, or awkward, it had felt so right, so natural, so intensely addictive. For those few blissful moments, she'd felt suspended within his arms, in a world where there was only her and him. Sweet promise had been there, and they'd both felt it, but hadn't known what to do with it. Then, her horse had stuck his head in and neighed for his bucket of feed, and their bubble had burst. Reality instantly kicked back in, and they'd both pulled away, saying they were idiots as they laughed it off, reminding each other how they were more like brother and sister than boyfriend and girlfriend. Neither of them ever spoke of it again. But, thinking about it now, if she was being completely honest, she wanted another of his yummy kisses. She may not be interested in a relationship, but that didn't mean she couldn't enjoy a kiss or two with the dashing, and very single, Logan Steele at the paddock party tonight, did it?

Her stomach backflipped with the thought.

She really wished she could be there right now, with Cassie and all her mates, dancing beneath the stars to some Cold Chisel tune, but Bea hadn't liked the idea of her being around drunken boys, and had told her she wasn't allowed to go. Nina didn't think it was fair of her overly protective aunt so, in another hour or so, she'd be doing what she shouldn't and sneaking out. But time felt as if it were crawling by. She couldn't tell whether the nerves twirling in her belly were from the excitement of going, or because she was terrified Bea was going to catch her slipping out her bedroom window. She'd be in deep trouble then – Bea was not one to take kindly to disobedience. Either way, Nina wasn't changing her mind – this was going to be the party to end all parties. Wandering over to her bedroom door, she quietly locked it. It was time to get dressed and she didn't want Bea to catch her in the act. How would she explain her way out of that?

Twenty minutes later and with her much-loved Wrangler jeans and paisley top on, she unlocked her door, flicked the aircon back on, jumped back into her bed, and pulled the sheet up to her chin, just in case Bea snuck her head in to say goodnight, like she sometimes did. *The Wonder Years* would be almost over now and, like clockwork, Bea would be making her way upstairs and to bed. Nina made a mental note to put her favourite feather earrings on, brush some blush on her cheeks, and slip a bit of gloss on her lips before she absconded into the night.

Right on cue, footfalls came up the stairs, and then the timber floorboards outside Nina's bedroom creaked. She held her breath as the doorhandle turned and Bea stuck her head in, her short hair in rollers. 'Are you still awake, Nina-Jane?' she whispered.

'Yeah, sort of, it's so hot it's hard to drift off …' Nina said, as softly as she could, as if sleepy. 'You off to bed now?'

Folding her arms, Bea leant against the doorframe. 'Yes, love, I'm absolutely beat after working out in that ruthless sun today – and Frank didn't help none when the cantankerous old brute didn't want to let me shoe him.'

Nina chuckled. 'Yeah, he can be a bit of a turdburger, huh.'

'He most certainly can, but then again he is only four, and we got there in the end.' Bea made her way over to the bed and tenderly brushed a lock of hair from Nina's cheek. 'Are you doing okay now?'

'Yes and no, a good sleep will help me feel a bit better, I hope.' Nina felt awful – lying to Bea didn't sit well with her.

'The gift of tomorrow is a blessing from God, Nina, so use it well, won't you?' Bea smiled with the tender love of a mother. 'I know it's been a tough day, with Josh showing his true colours, but the heartache will pass, just like everything does. You'll see, my love.'

'Yeah, I know it will. It just hurts that it was with Kimberley of all people.'

'Breaking up is hard to do, with boyfriends, and with friends, but it's for the best where Josh and Kimberley are concerned.' Bea rolled her eyes and tutted. 'You deserve much better than the likes of him, Nina-Jane, and you also deserve friends who respect you, like Cassie does.' Bea smiled broadly. 'She's a good girl, Cassie.'

'Yeah, she's tops.' Nina smiled. 'Thanks Aunty Bea, for being here for me.'

'Of course, love, that's my job.' She leant in and gave Nina a kiss on the cheek. 'Night now, and dream sweet.'

'I will. You too. Love you lots.'

'I love you too, Nina-Jane, always and forever, from the bottom of my heart.' Making her way towards the doorway, she paused and sniffed the air. 'Why does it smell like smoke in here?'

Nina's heart skidded to an almighty stop. 'I have no idea.'

Oh crap, oh crap, oh crap …

'Hmmm, you aren't silly enough to start such a disgusting habit, are you?'

'Noooooo way.' Nina's held breath came out in a whoosh.

'Good.' Bea sniffed again, and shrugged. 'Okay, I'll catch you in the morning, bright and early – we have to muck out the horses and fix the fence down at the bottom paddock before it gets too hot.'

'Yup, no worries.' Nina groaned inwardly as she watched Bea disappear, followed by the click of the door closing.

She was going to be absolutely knackered after staying out half the night, but she wasn't about to try and get out of helping Bea. It was the least she could do, lending a hand in her spare time, after everything Bea so selflessly did for her. Bea was such a good motherly figure, Nina often wondered why Bea didn't ever have children of her own. She'd asked once, and Bea had told her, quite sternly, that life just turned out that way, and she didn't want to talk about it. Grateful for having Bea in her life, Nina had never pushed the subject again. It was very possible that Bea was never able to have children of her own, which was why she chose to adopt her in the first place.

Slipper-clad footsteps faded off down the hallway, followed by the click of Bea's bedroom door. After waiting another ten agonising minutes, Nina slipped from her bed, being as quiet as she possibly could, grabbed her torch, eased her window up, and, one leg after the other, climbed out and onto the roof. She took one last look over her shoulder, feeling awfully guilty for defying Bea, before sliding the window shut. Desperate to go and dance so she could let her hair down and forget about the day, she did her very best to swallow the shame.

Scooting her butt over the wooden shingles, she eased her legs over the side, grabbed onto the branch of the big old Bowen mango tree that always scraped against the house in storms, stirring flying foxes from their upside-down perches, and scaled down it just like the skilled climber she was – Logan had taught her well. As soon as her thong-clad feet hit the sodden earth, Bea's bedroom light went on, and a surge of panic and urgency gripped Nina. Being grounded would be a walk in the park compared to what Bea would dish out as punishment for defying her – horse-poo pick-up duties for a month straight, cleaning the attic out, no friends over. She half thought of climbing back up and staying put – but it was a fleeting thought when the light went out and she felt as if she could breathe again.

As she bent to pick up the cigarette butt she'd tossed out the window, Roo, her crazy six-year-old Kelpie, scooted over to meet her. *Crap*, she'd forgotten to lock the kennel door again. The clever bugger knew how to open it with his paw when she hadn't. Tongue hanging out to the side, his tail eagerly slapped her leg. He was panting as if he'd just bolted across the paddock. Knowing him like she did, and the mischief he got up to on a regular basis, that was probably what happened. She just prayed to god he hadn't been chasing Logan's mum's cat again. It might just be a bit of harmless fun for Roo, but the poor moggie didn't feel the same.

'What are you doing out of your kennel, mister.' Squatting down, she put her nose to his muzzle, now red with mud, and, catching a whiff of something very unsavoury, screwed hers up in disgust. 'Cor, buddy, you've been rolling in something again, haven't you?'

Roo gave her a slobbery lick up the cheek. She didn't dare think about the fact he might have had a bit of a chew of whatever he'd rolled in before he kissed her face.

'I love you, Rooster, but seriously, that's just plain gross.' Grimacing, she wiped the slobber off with the back of her hand and onto her jeans. 'Now come on, you, back to your bed before you and I both get busted sneaking about by Aunty Bea, and then we're in a world of bloody trouble.'

Light on his feet, Roo stuck to Nina's side and obediently slipped into his kennel. Flopping down on his hammock bed, he eyed Nina beneath sleepy brows. Nina made sure to firmly lock it this time. Smiling lovingly towards her loyal mate, she bid him farewell before making a break for it. Creeping across the backyard, she shushed the two horses Bea had left in the round yard before slinking into the shadows of the bushlands surrounding Riverstone Ridge, and hurriedly turned on her torch – you could never know what the shadows might be hiding. Then, following the timeworn path through the scrub that hummed with insects, she headed straight for the long dirt road that would lead her into the moonlight, to her friends, and hopefully, to him.

*　*　*

A few hundred metres along the main road, the crunch of tyres dragged Nina's gaze over her shoulder. It must be one of her mates, she thought, heading to the party. Pausing, she raised a hand to help shield her eyes as she squinted into bright headlights. Keen for a lift, she stuck her thumb out, along with her leg, and playfully wriggled both. But, to her surprise and embarrassment, when the grubby car pulled to a stop beside her and the driver rolled his window down, it was a face she wasn't familiar with. She didn't bat an eyelid, though – it wasn't an uncommon thing around these parts at this time of the year, when people would blow in from all corners of Australia, and sometimes overseas, for the fruit harvesting season – annually Huntingvale would almost double with inhabitants.

As she dipped her head to try and peer inside the rattly old Commodore, the unmistakable melody of Led Zeppelin's 'Stairway to Heaven' greeted her. 'Hey, there, great tune,' she said with a friendly smile. 'Sorry for making you stop, but I thought you were someone else.'

'Hey, no worries at all.' The middle-aged bloke ran stubby fingers through thinning salt-and-pepper hair as he flashed her a gappy smile. 'And yes, the Zep rocks, don't they?'

'They sure do,' she replied as he turned the music down. A short silence settled, and she felt the air around her shift a little, but she shrugged it off. 'Are you working around here?' She rested both hands on the windowsill.

'Oh, yeah, I'm picking fruit down yonder.' He thumbed over his shoulder, in the general direction of Logan's family's fruit farm, Willowbrook.

'At the Steeles' place?'

'Yeah.' He took a swig from a beer, and then jammed it back between his legs.

Something told Nina he was lying through his yellowing teeth – there was no way Logan's dad would hire such an unsavoury-looking bloke.

'So what are you up to, out roaming the dusty trails this time of the night, girly?'

The air around her went icy cold. She stepped back and shoved her hands in her jeans pockets, wishing to god that she'd let Roo come with her on her trek. 'I'm heading to a mate's place for a paddock party. Just over there,' she stammered, pointing to where light faintly glowed above the towering treetops.

He laughed and then wriggled his brows suggestively. 'You meeting your boyfriend there?'

Hope shot through Nina. This was her out. Maybe this strange bloke would leave her alone if she lied. 'Yes, yes I am. He's waiting for me.'

With beady eyes, he looked her up and down. 'A gal's gotta get it too, so good for you.' He took another swig of beer, his weathered lips smirking ever so slightly. 'When I was your age, I made the best of it, with the girls.' He nodded deliberately and chuckled. 'Not that you might believe it, but I was a stud back then, and they all chased after me.' He momentarily closed his eyes and smiled grossly, as if travelling back to those times, and when he came to look at her again, there was a wildness in his gaze that wasn't there before. 'But there was this one girl, she won me over good and proper. She told me I was her everything, but then went and broke my heart. The nasty bitch.'

'I'm so sorry to hear that.' The stale stench of alcohol coming from inside the car was making Nina want to cover her nose.

'Oh, don't you worry, girly, I had my day, and made her feel the heartache like I did.' He glanced around. 'Come to think of it, why isn't your boyfriend walking with you to make sure you get there safe and sound?'

Nina's gut shouted a dark, twisted warning as panic quickly set in. 'Ahh, he's just ducked off into the bushes to take a leak.' She prayed to god she sounded convincing.

'I thought you just said you were meeting him there.' He pointed at her with his beer. 'Gotcha, didn't I?

'Oh, yeah, nah, sorry … he's just …' Nina scrambled to come up with another lie to cover up her last one. Things were going from bad to worse, very quickly.

The bloke held his hands up, gesturing for her to stop. 'No need to explain.' He chuckled and shook his head. 'Don't worry,

I'm no serial killer, or axe murderer.' He laughed again, rolling his eyes. 'You want a lift to your paddock party?'

'Oh, thanks but no thanks.' She gestured up the road with a tilt of her head, assessing if she could safely make a run for it. 'It's not that far.' Wrapping her arms around herself, she took another step back as the icy fingers of a chill skated up her spine and beads of cold sweat inched across her neck.

The bloke smiled from ear to ear, but it was far from friendly. 'Oh, come on, get in, it's not like I bite.' He swigged the last of his beer, tossed the empty bottle to the floor and then belched. 'I can get you to your friend's way faster than two feet and a heartbeat.' He was still smiling, but his tone of voice and the glint in his eye was by no means lighthearted.

Nina took a few more measured steps back until a puddle of water replaced the gravel that had been underfoot. She felt the mud squish between her toes as a million scenarios raced through her mind, none of them pleasant. 'I'm all good, but cheers, hey.' Offering him a wobbly smile, she wondered if he could hear the frenzied beat of her heart. 'I better be off, so I'll catch you later.'

With her heart trying to bash its way out of her chest, Nina turned to walk away, as fast as she could without looking as though she was fleeing. The monster she'd been looking for beneath her bed all these years *was* real – and she'd walked right to him. This. Was. Terrifying. She felt so alone, so vulnerable – Bea's satellite phone would be great right about now. To her horror, there was a heavy sigh, and a door creaked open behind her. Nina dared not look over her shoulder, but instead picked up the pace. But before she could make a decent run for it, the bloke raced up beside her and grabbed her by wrist.

'Hey, where's the damn fire, girly?' His grip tightened.

Fear lodged in her throat, so much so Nina found it impossible to answer him.

'Like I said, I'm not here to hurt you.' He belched again, the stench nauseating. 'I just don't want to have it on my conscience if I drive off and something happens to you.' He swayed a little, his eyes intent, yet eerily vacant. 'That's all, easy as.'

'Please let go of me.' She tried to jerk free of his grip, but he tightened it even more until it was vicelike.

'I will, if you stop being so stupid and get in the bloody car.'

'Please, you're hurting me.' Her voice was choked with fear and hot tears stung her eyes.

'Don't do this, Nina.' He huffed impatiently and shook his head. 'Because I really don't want to have to drag you kicking and screaming.'

Her heart pounding like galloping horses' hooves, Nina swallowed down hard. 'How do you know my name?'

The greasy-looking bloke was momentarily blindsided, but recovered quickly. 'It's a small town, everyone knows everyone's name.'

'I don't know yours, and I would if you were from here,' she said, hoping he'd tell her what it was so she could ask around, see if any of the locals knew him, if she lived to do so.

'Oh, I've been away for a while, working overseas, only just got back into town a few days ago, for the, um, fruit picking.' He turned and his attention locked onto the sound of an oncoming four-wheel drive.

Nina felt a rush of relief as headlights bounced off the row of mango trees behind her and flittered over barbwire fencing. The drone of music had him wide-eyed as he glanced towards the approaching rumble of a diesel engine. His grip loosened and she freed herself from him. Her held breath released in a whoosh when she spotted Logan Steele at the wheel, driving straight for them – her knight in his dusty old LandCruiser, coming to her rescue, and not a second too late. Thank god.

She felt a rush of courage and folded her arms defensively. 'Here's my boyfriend now, looking for me. I told you he was waiting for me.'

Teeth bared in a snarl, the man pointed at her. 'You mention a word of this to anyone and I'll come after you, and Bea, and you don't want that, you understand?'

A new wave of fear overwhelming her, Nina nodded.

'Good.' He spun and walked away from her, and was back in his Commodore as Logan pulled into a skid beside her.

Shivering to her very core, despite the balmy temperature, she watched as the creepy bloke took off down the road, gravel flying out from his tyres.

'You okay, Neens?' Looking out the driver's window, Logan's voice was thick with worry.

Nina used every bit of strength she could to turn and offer Logan a smile. 'Yeah, thanks, he just needed directions.' She bit her bottom lip to stop from crying.

'Really? Then why do you look as white as a ghost?' Concern written all over his handsome face, Logan jumped out and wrapped a protective arm around her shoulder. 'You sure he wasn't hassling you?' He looked to where taillights disappeared around the corner. 'Because if he was …'

Nina cut him off. 'Yeah, I'm sure.' She sucked in a deep breath and met his eyes. She couldn't help but be touched by way he was regarding her, so anxiously, so protectively. She needed to change the direction of the conversation, fast. 'It's so good to see you, Logan.' And by god, it was, in so many ways.

'Ditto, three months is a long time between visits from uni.' Logan's concern lightened somewhat as his tight lips gave way to a charming smile. 'You look real pretty tonight, Nina-Jane.'

CHAPTER

2

Brisbane
Twenty Years Later

Nina woke to the local tomcat she'd befriended and aptly named Tom gently pawing at her face while meowing for his breakfast. Gone were the days of him having to sift through the apartment block's rubbish bins for food. Smiling softly, while trying to resurface from a dream she couldn't quite remember, she cuddled him to her. Purring loudly, Tom rubbed his face against hers.

'Aww, love you too, buddy.' She said, scratching the spot behind his ears he loved.

'Lucky cat … you don't ever say that to me, Nina,' a croaky voice mumbled playfully from beside her.

As she blinked her eyes to life, and her bedroom came into blurry focus, Nina was quickly overcome by a pounding headache, the fact her bed was so tousled, and that it was actually her bra hanging from the fan spinning lazily above and not a shadow cast by the light peeking through the curtains.

'Oh, hey, you,' she muttered, as she glanced at the muscle-clad arm flung over her. Then, catching a glimpse at her bedside clock, panic fired through her. 'Shoot, Nate.' With Tom leaping to the floor, she clambered from the bed, taking the sheet with her. Being naked within the cover of night along with the Dutch courage of quite a few bevvies after work was fine, but in broad daylight, and stone-cold sober, there was no bloody way.

'What is it?' Nate's voice was husky with sleep.

'I forgot to set the damn alarm,' she shrieked.

'That's pretty standard, isn't it?' He chuckled, his head half buried into a pillow.

She slapped him on the butt. 'Come on, rise and shine sleepyhead.' Scooting towards the hint of daylight, she flung the curtains open, momentarily blinded by the flood of golden sunshine. 'It's time to get up and get out. I've got to be at work in …' She did the maths. 'Less than an hour.'

'Far out, talk about making a bloke feel welcome.' Nate rolled over to face her, as naked as the day he was born, his hand shielding his sleepy gaze from the sunlight streaming through.

'You know me, I'm not the kind of gal to make a bloke feel welcome.' She offered him a cheeky smile as she went in search of a can of sardines, Tom hot on her heels.

'True that,' Nate called after her.

After grabbing a can of John West – only the best for her moggy mate – from the pile in the half bare pantry, she cracked it open and plopped the contents into the bowl she'd designated to Tom, gagging at the smell of the stinky fish. Tom did a figure eight around her ankles while he waited for her to plonk it down on the floor.

After washing her hands, Nina then headed back towards the bed, the sheet still clutched around her and dragging around her feet. She was fighting not to trip over it. 'Some of us aren't lucky enough to have a day off ... and it's looking to be a beautiful one out there.' She waved towards the view of endless blue skies, masked a little by city smog, out of her rented Newmarket studio apartment's window. 'Haven't you got things to do and people to see?'

'Maybe, possibly, dunno yet.' Nate shrugged. 'I haven't really thought that far ahead.'

Grasping the doona from the foot of the bed, she yanked it off his feet in a whoosh. 'Come on, chop chop, times a wasting and I want to make this damn thing so I can go for a shower.'

Nate groaned as he sat up. 'My god, you're so bloody bossy in the morning.'

'I'm bossy all the time ... you should know that by now, too.' Folding her arms with the sheet firmly pressed against her chest, she grinned as she watched her friend with benefits climb from her bed.

'I reserve my right to remain silent, it's safer that way.' He offered her his charming smile before grabbing his clothes from where she'd tossed them to the floor at some ungodly hour this morning.

Dropping the sheet while he wasn't looking, she quickly plucked her robe from the bedhead and tugged it on before he had time to turn back around and catch a glimpse of her. Then, shaking the sheet out, she let it fall to the bed with a flutter.

Jocks now on, Nate stopped getting dressed to help her.

A perfectionist when it came to cleanliness – and she knew full well it was a way she could at least control some of her environment, and in turn, some of her life – Nina had to bite her tongue as she watched him leave the sheet crinkled up beneath the doona before tossing the pillows back onto the bed in a cluttered heap. She fought not to fix it up – she'd do it once he'd left.

'Sooooo, what are you up to tonight, after your shift, sexy lady?' Nate said, a little too casually.

'Ummm, I'm not sure.' Nina swallowed down hard – after five months of uncommitted bliss, was Nate about to go and ruin a good thing? Fluffing her pillow, she placed it neatly on top of another, and buying time, padded towards the bathroom. 'I haven't thought that far ahead,' she called back lightheartedly.

'Smart-arse,' Nate called after her.

'Sure am, and you love it,' she called back. Turning the taps, she slipped her robe off, tugged the shower curtain closed, and then dove beneath the water before it had even had enough time to warm up. Goosebumps covered her entirely as she jiggled on the spot, switching from foot to foot.

Nate joined her in the bathroom, and the unmistakable trickle of a man peeing soon followed. Nina's panic rose a few more notches – were they now at the stage of doing such a thing?

Noooooo!

'I asked what you were up to because I was going to offer to cook you dinner.' Still peeing, he stuck his head past the shower curtain. 'You know, real home-cooked food, not like those protein bars and pre-made salads you eat like they're going out of fashion.'

'You were, hey?' Fighting to ignore the fact he was not only peeing where she could see him, but was doing so while regarding her with hungry eyes, Nina lathered her body up with her favourite sandalwood soap. 'And just for the record, protein bars and salad are very healthy.'

'Not when you eat them for breakfast, lunch and dinner.'

'I firmly disagree,' she said, challengingly.

Nate grinned and then to her absolute horror, without even washing his hands, grabbed her toothbrush, plonked some toothpaste on it, and then proceeded to brush his teeth.

Gobsmacked, she tugged the curtain open and stared at him incredulously before finding her voice. 'You right there, using *my* toothbrush.'

He shrugged. 'Well, you won't let me bring mine,' he garbled, right before spitting white foam into the sink.

'Uh-huh.' She slunk back behind the shower curtain, so he couldn't see the combination of shock, irritation and dread that was surely written all over her face.

She liked Nate. He was funny, charming, he actually cared about her, and he was safe – a commitment-phobe like her, or so he'd led her to believe. She'd taken great comfort in the fact *this* wasn't going to go anywhere. They hung out occasionally, were there for one another if something went belly up – without all the pressures of pledges and promises that would inevitably be broken, if not by him, then by her. But now he'd gone and ruined it, by offering to cook her dinner, and peeing while she was in the same room, and using her toothbrush – which she was now going to have to replace because that was just plain gross. Not all his fault – she had issues, she was well aware of that, but she wasn't about to work on those issues for Nate. As gorgeous as he was, the spark she'd only ever felt once in her lifetime just wasn't there with him.

The curtain flew open again and this time Nate stepped in with her. There was a first time for everything, but her privacy felt invaded, and she abruptly began to feel like she couldn't breathe, as if he were suffocating her with the damn pillows he'd so haphazardly placed on her bed. A spark of annoyance rushed through her. He was getting a little bit too comfortable, and too close for her comfort. And she didn't like it. Not one little bit.

'So you keen?' He looked hopeful.

She knew exactly what he meant, but played ignorant as she shampooed her hair into a foamy frenzy. 'For what?'

'Dinner?'

Alarm exploded inside her and she mentally tried to shake the sensation off. 'Oh, I can't tonight. I'm busy.'

'I thought you hadn't thought that far ahead, so how could you have something else on?' His tone was laced with something she couldn't quite pinpoint.

'I forgot I was busy.'

'Right, well, how about tomorrow night then?'

'I think I've got a thing on.' She squeezed past him and stood beneath the spray of warm water, staying busy by rinsing her hair before grabbing her bottle of conditioner.

'Oh, do you? And what *thing* might that be?' His questioning gaze was searching hers.

She rubbed her conditioner in, and then shook her head. 'Nate, please stop. I can't, we can't … I …' Damn it, where were her usual nerves of steel when she damn well needed them?

'Okay, I get it … you're just not that into me.' He laughed it off but she could see the flash of hurt in his coffee-coloured eyes.

Feeling awful, she reached out and gave his arm a squeeze. 'It's not you, Nate, it's me.'

'Oh for god's sake, I reckon that that's even worse, the whole it's-not-you-it's-me spiel.'

'I'm sorry, but it's the truth.' Eyes closed now, more to stop from seeing the hurt she was causing than keeping the conditioner she was rinsing out of her eyes. 'Besides, you knew that from the get-go, and you agreed that's how you felt about this too, so what's changed now?'

'You.'

'Me?' She wiped the water from her face.

'Yeah, I can't help it, you're addictive, Nina Jones, and I want more of you, more of the time.'

'I'm sorry, but I can't give that to you.' She wasn't interested in getting into a relationship, especially with an accountant who was allergic to a day spent in jeans and a t-shirt.

'All good, hey … forget I even mentioned it.' He shook his head and turned his back to her. 'Just consider this a moment of delirium caused by a bit of a hangover,' he added, while facing the wall.

'I'm sorry, Nate. I really am.' And she genuinely was.

Rinsing the last of the soap off, Nina left him to shower. She quickly dried off, got dressed in her usual black skirt and t-shirt in the blink of an eye, and then made a beeline for her coffee maker. Flicking the radio on, she welcomed the distraction of Pink's latest hit as she made them both a coffee to-go. His belly now full, Tom curled himself around her ankles, purring.

The soft scent of soap followed Nate into the kitchen nook. 'Feel better after a shower?' Nina avoided his eyes for fear of giving in to his dinner offer.

'Muchly, thanks.' He leant against the bench beside her. 'I'm sorry I put you in that awkward position. I know what this is, and I shouldn't be pushing the boundaries just because I want more.' He sighed. 'You've been upfront and honest the entire way, Nina, and I appreciate it.'

'All good in the hood.' With a smile, she passed him his coffee. 'We don't need to speak of it again.'

'Good. Great.' He brushed a kiss on her cheek. 'Catch you sometime this week, at the bar?' he turned and walked away from her.

'Sounds like a very good non-plan, plan,' she called after him, as he headed for the front door, grabbed his keys and jacket from the entrance table, and then with one last look over his shoulder, vanished.

'Oh thank goodness that's over with,' she breathed. Hooking her handbag over her shoulder, she grabbed the keys to her beloved Jeep Wrangler, slipped on her trusty super-soft black work shoes, and then raced out the front door. 'I'll see you back here later, matey, okay?' she called to Tom.

Tom meowed a reply, and then with a swish of his tail, jumped up on the couch to get comfy for the day. Nina smiled as she shut the door and rushed to the lift. Tom was her perfect male companion … easygoing, uncomplicated, and certainly not needy. She felt bad turning Nate's offer of dinner down, but she also had to be honest with herself, and Nate. Yes, maybe Aunty Bea was right in saying she might end up a lonely old spinster with only a cat for company, but there was only one thing to do when confronted with such a painful reality: deny, deny and then deny some more.

Driving out of her quiet suburban street, and towards to the pub she'd worked at in Fortitude Valley for twelve years – after eight years spent travelling the globe as a backpacker – she hit the highway and drove into the absolute nightmare of rush hour. With cars bumper to bumper, she almost pulled to a standstill. Shoving the last bite of her brunch on the run – a chocolate and orange protein bar – into her mouth, she propelled the wrapper into the little rubbish bag she always had hanging from her gearstick. Hopeful she'd make up for lost time by exceeding the speed limit just a little, she smacked the steering wheel and huffed for what felt like the hundredth time in a matter of minutes. If she got out and walked to work, it would be faster.

Surrendering to the traffic jam, she put her Jeep into park, quickly texted her boss to say she was going to be late, before settling in for the wait. Grabbing her water bottle, she took a swig, grimacing because it had gone hot overnight, while at the same time pondering her life. She constantly lived on borrowed time, in a borrowed apartment, and was driving a car bought with borrowed money. Since leaving Riverstone Ridge almost twenty years ago, at first she'd tried to run away from her problems by jumping on a plane, her entire life in a backpack and only enough money in her pocket to get her from one job to the next. She hopped from country to country, but when that got old, she'd dedicated her life to trying to get ahead, but had never seemed to be able to. There was always another bill, another unbudgeted dilemma. It was frustrating to say the very least – but it was the life of many, especially in the big cities.

Hearing Bea's voice of reason in her head, Nina knew she had to try and remain grateful for what she *did* have, instead of focusing on what she didn't. Recalling leaving a voicemail message for her aunt yesterday morning, asking her to call her back, Nina wondered why Bea hadn't. It was very unlike her not to respond. Grabbing her mobile from the centre console, she asked Siri to dial Riverstone Ridge's number. On hands-free mode, it rang through her speakers – five rings – before it went to the message bank.

'Hey, Aunty Bea, it's me again, your favourite daughter in the whole wide world. I left a voicemail yesterday too, but you must have gotten sidetracked. I hope everything's okay? Ring me back as soon as you can, so I don't worry myself stupid. Love you to the moon and back.' Sighing, she hung up.

Something unnerving settled in Nina's gut. If she hadn't heard back by tonight, she'd make a point to ask one of her aunt's CWA friends to go and check in on her. With the horse agistment farm being a twenty-minute drive from town, a neighbour would be an easier bet, but there was no way, after all these years of no contact, she was going to call Logan Steele and ask a favour. Uh-uh. Nope. Definitely not.

LET'S TALK ABOUT BOOKS!

JOIN THE CONVERSATION

**HARLEQUIN
AUSTRALIA**

@HARLEQUINAUS

@HARLEQUINAUS

HQSTORIES

@HQSTORIES